TEST DRIVE

A Crossroads Novel

RILEY HART

Copyright © 2016 by Riley Hart
Print Edition

All rights reserved.

No part of this book may be used, reproduced or transmitted in any form or by any means, electronic or mechanical, including photocopying, recording, or by any information storage and retrieval systems, without prior written permission of the author, except where permitted by law.

Published by:
Riley Hart

This book is a work of fiction. Names, characters, places and incidents are products of the author's imagination or are used fictitiously. Any similarity to actual persons, living or dead is coincidental and not intended by the author.

Printed in the United States of America.

All products/brand names mentioned are registered trademarks of their respective holders/companies.

Cover Design by X-Potion Designs
Cover Image by Jean-Baptiste HUONG (www.jeanbaptistehuong.com)
Edited by Prema Editing and Flat Earth Editing

Special thanks to Riley's Rebels member Robyn for letting me use your name. Also, to Carly Rose and Amanda Souliotis for all your help with the details about chemo, hospice and cancer. Any mistakes are my own.

Dedication

To Ryan Burdett. Thank you for the support, conversations, and for helping me choose Drew's career. You are a joy to talk to.

PROLOGUE

JUSTIN EVANSON SAT in the busy club and eyed the guy seated down the bar from him. He hadn't kept his eyes off Justin all night, and Justin hadn't been inclined to take his eyes off him either.

His dad, who had been the picture-perfect father from the moment he'd come into Justin's life at eight years old was dying—and his vision of that man was shattered. He'd discovered that his dad wasn't who he thought he was. When he'd finally made his way into Justin's life, he'd done so on the heels of abandoning a son and daughter, and until he realized he didn't have much time left, had pretended they didn't exist.

Now, Justin was in a new town, in a new fucking state, waiting for his father to find a way back into the lives of the kids he'd abandoned, and he had no idea how he really fit into that equation. How would he fit in with his father's new family, which was really his original family?

His older sister, Shanen, had gotten married today. His older brother, Landon, had walked her down the aisle to give her away. Justin had spent the day playing cards and watching television at a piece of crap, yellow table with his depressed father, who was upset he couldn't be there. They didn't know their father was back.

They didn't know Justin existed at all.

Talk about a shitty fucking hand to be dealt. He figured he deserved an anonymous hookup with a sexy guy he met in a club, and the blond with the strong jawline and hooded eyes just might be exactly what he was looking for.

Sex was a whole lot more fun than dealing with the other shit.

Justin couldn't imagine how Shanen and Landon would feel when they found out about him—and more importantly, when they found out about their father. His chest felt hollowed out just thinking about the situation, thinking about the family he didn't know. The things they'd missed—holidays and summer vacations. Fights and laughs and all the things that came with family. Basically, he was feeling really fucking sorry for himself. Hence the reason he sat in a club hoping to fuck the night away. It was the least he deserved.

After finishing his drink, Justin stood up and walked toward the sexy blond. For a brief second, he thought the guy was going to bolt, but he didn't move, just continued to follow Justin with his eyes as he made his way to him.

"Hey." Justin looked down at the guy as he swished whatever he was drinking around in his glass. His blond hair was short, buzzed closer around the edges and slightly longer on top. Every now and then his face would change colors—blue, red, green, as the strobe light shined around the room.

"Hey."

"I'm Justin."

The blond nodded. "Drew." He had a deep, sexy voice. All gravelly and…almost commanding, but somehow a little unsure at the same time. It got his dick hard, but then again, he hadn't had sex in a while, so he wasn't sure that was a difficult feat.

"You looking?" Justin asked. There was no reason to beat around the bush. Drew would say yes or no. They'd fuck or not. He wouldn't pretend this was anything other than what it was.

He watched as Drew's steel-blue eyes darted around the club—toward the door and then back at Justin again. Had he read the guy wrong and he wasn't interested? Or hell, maybe he just wasn't into hooking up with someone he didn't know. Some people were and some weren't. He didn't judge one way or the other.

After bringing his glass to his lips, Drew downed the rest of his drink in three long swallows. He set the glass down a little hard on the counter and then flinched. "Let's dance," he finally said, a slight quiver to his voice.

Fuck. Was he in the closet? The thought made Justin's gut cramp. He hated it when people had to live like that. Luckily, it had never been a problem for him but he knew it was for too many people.

Whether Drew was in the closet or not, there was one thing he had to confirm. "You married? Man or woman, it doesn't matter. Are you in any kind of relationship at all?" He didn't fuck around with a man who was with someone else. That's how he'd been born. His dad had cheated on Landon and Shanen's mom, and then gone back to her. Justin's mom didn't know how to get a hold of him, so she raised Justin alone until he was eight and she found out where his dad was. He'd gained a father around the same time Landon and Shanen had lost theirs. It didn't matter to him that pregnancy obviously wasn't an issue here, he didn't touch someone who was cheating. He made damn sure he asked any time he hooked up.

"Nope. Are we going to dance or not?" Drew replied.

Jesus, he was sexy. He had narrow eyes like he hid secrets inside of them, and yeah, that mouth. It was pretty as fuck. He had nice, full lips that Justin wouldn't mind seeing wrapped around his dick. None of that had anything on his jawline, though. It was defined, square and strong, with some sexy stubble Justin wanted to feel against his skin. Drew had a good body, too. Justin could tell he kept in shape. "Yeah, we're dancing."

Justin stepped back, while Drew stood and immediately started walking. Justin followed him through the packed club. They weaved their way around men kissing, dancing and talking.

Drew didn't stop moving until he found what was probably the loneliest, darkest corner of the club. It was Justin who grabbed hold of Drew and pulled him close. If they were going to dance, he wanted to feel the other man. He'd always been like that—he liked touch. Loved the feel of a man against him, inside him, around him. He wasn't picky on the how of it.

They both began moving together, slower than the music that pumped from the speakers, and vibrated through Justin. He ran his hands down Drew's muscular back. His T-shirt was slightly wet with sweat, but that just made Justin pull him closer, inhale deeper.

He felt Drew's muscles move under his hand. Drew gripped Justin's sides, his fingers digging into Justin's flesh.

Drew felt good, smelled like soap and alcohol and clean sweat. He let his hands travel down Drew's back until they landed on his ass. Drew groaned as he palmed the globes. Oh yeah. He definitely worked out. He wasn't a muscle-head, but there was no doubt that Drew was physical. He could feel it in every twist and turn and the tight constriction of his body movements.

He slid one of his legs between Drew's, pulled their bodies flush against each other, felt Drew's erection rub against his dick. That was all it took for blood to travel to Justin's crotch as his own cock grew and hardened even more than it had already. Why were they wasting time? He wanted to fuck, to come, to forget about all the other shit he was dealing with.

"Let's get out of here, and I'll take care of that hard-on for you. It feels like a nice fucking dick." The second Justin's final word left his mouth, Drew's lips took his. It was a hungry kiss, an urgent kiss. His tongue demanded entrance and Justin opened up and invited him inside.

Their tongues dueled, both of them obviously ravenous for each other. Justin wanted to devour him. It wasn't Drew specifically, even though the man was fucking gorgeous. He just wanted someone, something to take his mind off of everything else. Off his father dying and his fear over how his siblings would react to finding out about him. Their father had left them and ended up raising Justin. How could they not hate him?

He groaned into Drew's mouth when he pressed the palm of his hand against Justin's erection. They kept moving, Drew slowly backing him farther into the corner.

The pressure against Justin's dick got stronger and stronger. He squeezed Drew's ass tighter, and this time, he was the one who got to eat Drew's groan.

They kept kissing, kept rubbing against each other, and then both of Drew's hands were on him. He stood in front of Justin, who had his back against the corner. His fingers fumbled with Justin's button, then his zipper.

He almost stopped him, almost told him they could go somewhere else, but hell, why couldn't they do this first and then fuck later? Coming twice was always better than coming once, right?

As Drew opened Justin's pants and shoved a hand inside, Justin went for the button and zipper on Drew's jeans. He opened them much quicker than Drew had his, and then they were rubbing each other's cocks and eating at each other's mouths. It didn't matter that they were in a busy club. They'd hidden themselves and what they were doing as best as they could. The end result was all Justin could concentrate on.

Drew's hand was sweating when he squeezed Justin's cock. He had callouses on his palms, right beneath his fingers. The rough skin felt good against his aching erection.

Justin had never done this before. He'd fucked men he didn't know, but jerking off in the corner of a club was new for him…and exciting. His heart beat against his chest, as his dick got harder by the second.

Drew was thick in his hand, thick and long and hot. His skin seared Justin and he couldn't wait to taste him. This was exactly what he needed. The more he thought about it, the fuller his balls got. They pulled up tight as Drew jacked him faster.

Justin squeezed with more pressure, picked up the pace and it didn't matter that they were going at this dry. It was fucking working.

Drew came first. His body went rigid. He pulled his mouth away and whispered, "Oh fuck," as he shot into Justin's hand. The raspy pleasure in Drew's voice went straight to Justin's balls and he let go, spurting two long ribbons of come into Drew's hand. The pressure was still there, though. He wanted more, even as his body wanted to slump against Drew's.

"Jesus, that was hot," Justin said, breathing heavily.

"Yeah…yeah, it was." And then Drew was shoving himself back into his pants before he began buttoning and zipping them.

He grabbed napkins from a table beside them that Justin hadn't even realized was there, shoved one at Justin and then wiped his own hand. Justin stood there, feeling dumbstruck. He pushed himself back into his pants just as Drew said, "Thanks. That was…that was amazing. I'm sorry. I have to go. I'm sorry."

He didn't turn back around as he weaved his way through all the bodies. Didn't slow down until he disappeared from sight, leaving Justin horny and half-hard with dry come on him.

Well, shit. That wasn't how he expected that to go.

CHAPTER ONE

"JUSTIN, YOUR BROTHER is on the phone. He wants to talk to you." He tried not to flinch at the excitement in his dad's voice. There was a part of Justin that was thrilled. The majority of him was thrilled, actually. He had siblings, something he'd always wanted, but things were still awkward, and that was putting it lightly.

There had been a week or so that he'd worried about how everything would go. Joy and his dad finally came clean about Larry being back; Shanen had been immediately accepting when she discovered she had a brother and that their dad had returned. Landon...well, things hadn't gone quite as smoothly with him.

Justin understood it. Landon's whole world had changed, but Justin's had too. Everyone's reality was altered and they all had to figure out how to deal with it.

He and Landon were okay now. Landon accepted him, but the family dynamics were a work in progress for all of them. They were all fumbling their way through this as best as they could, but their father wanted it all, right now. Justin understood his reasoning but that didn't mean he was always comfortable. But Larry didn't know exactly how much longer he had left, so, yeah, he was ready for the *one big happy family* thing, but for Justin, sometimes just hearing the words *your brother* was strange for him.

He walked over to his dad and took the cell phone from his bony hand, the familiar hum of his oxygen tank in the background. He'd lost so much fucking weight. He wasn't the same man Justin grew up admiring. They'd just finished a round of chemo, which meant they would have a short break before the next one started. The goal right now was to give him time, to slow the growth of his lung cancer. It hadn't responded to previous sessions. They'd caught it late, Larry's own stubbornness having kept him from ignoring signs that something was wrong. Now slowing it was their only option. "Thanks, old man." He winked and got a smile, one that Justin couldn't bring himself to return. His father had more wrinkles now than he used to. He looked as though he'd aged twenty years since the initial diagnosis.

It hurt to look at him, so Justin let his eyes dart away, put the phone to his ear, and said, "Hello?" He was talking to his brother. He had a brother. It still took some getting used to. He knew Landon felt the same. It was only a week ago that Landon and his partner, Rod had come over to the small house that Justin and his dad rented so Landon could have his first real conversation with their father. That one week had felt like a hundred weeks, yet just an hour at the same time.

"How's he doing today?" Landon asked as Justin made his way outside to sit on the wood porch that was so small, he wasn't sure it could be considered a porch at all.

"He's okay. Spent most of the morning vomiting. He's watching a ridiculous reality show now."

"Reality TV? You didn't tell me he had bad taste," Landon joked and it helped loosen some of the tightness in Justin's chest. He wanted a relationship with this side of his family. Wanted it so much he felt guilt over it sometimes. He was stuck between wondering if he had a place with them, and determination to demand one. It didn't help that it sometimes made him feel like he was leaving his mother out in the cold.

"Eh. We all have our flaws. His is shitty television. When we know each other a little better, I'll share some of mine. I'm not sure if we have enough time today."

Landon laughed and damned if it didn't sound a whole hell of a lot like their dad. "You and me both," he said. "I only have a minute. It's my first day back at work after getting my cast off, but I just wanted to give you a heads-up. Shanen wants to have a big party for Dad's birthday next week. I know it's last minute, but..."

She's making up for lost time. He's dying. There were so many ways that Landon could end his sentence and they were all shitty as hell. "Yeah, I get it. As long as he's physically up for it, we'll be there. My question is, who else will be?"

He didn't mean to sound like a dickhead, but who did their dad know? Fortunately, Landon laughed. "No shit. That's what I told her. Basically people who don't know him except for you, me, her and Mom...my mom," he corrected and the awkwardness found its way into the conversation again. Justin's mom was still in North Carolina where he'd grown up.

"I'm inviting Nick and Bryce. They're friends of ours. Bryce is the guy I work with at the shop."

"Yeah, okay." Justin knew that. Their dad talked a lot about Landon's work at the shop. The two men shared their love of motorcycles. Justin enjoyed them too, but not with the same passion that Landon and their dad felt.

"Shanen is inviting friends of hers, and I think Jacob's parents will be there. That's Shanen's husband. It's going to be weird as fuck."

It would be, but what in his life wasn't weird anymore? "Okay. Sounds good. Thanks for letting me know. We'll be there."

They were silent for a moment because really, what did they have to say? They still didn't know one another all that well. The weather was a ridiculous thing to bring up. The man inside the house was too painful. Justin was at a loss.

"Okay, well I better get back to work. I'll talk to you later," Landon said, and he could have sworn they both let out sighs of relief. It wasn't supposed to be this way and he hated the fact that it was. Brothers should know each other, feel comfortable talking to one another.

"You too. Thanks for calling."

Justin hung up the phone, and it wasn't five seconds later when he heard his father retching inside. His stomach dropped, and he couldn't keep himself from closing his eyes, shaking his head and giving himself just a second. Sometimes the anti-nausea meds worked, but they usually didn't. Fucking chemo. Yeah, it was the only way to fight cancer, but so many times it felt like it killed the person too. Or at least it made them feel like they were dying.

"Shit," he whispered when he heard the vomiting again. He hated this. Christ, he really fucking hated it.

He didn't know how to do this—how to watch his dad suffer. How to try to find his place in a family who didn't know him, and honestly, couldn't be real happy about the fact that he existed.

He'd left his mom, his home, his job, his schooling, and he wasn't sure how he fit into this new position. This new Justin that he had to try and figure out.

Still, he pushed those thoughts out of his head and stood. He had to go inside and take care of his father.

CHAPTER TWO

JUSTIN AND HIS dad pulled up at the address Shanen had given him. He'd known the second they pulled into the neighborhood that her home wouldn't be like anything he was used to, and he'd been right. The Colonial-style house was massive looking, like something out of a movie. Sure, it was nothing new for him to see, but it wasn't the type of place he'd been raised in. Shanen either, but from what he learned from their dad, her husband was from money.

"Wow...it looks like your sister has done real well for herself," his dad said softly from the passenger seat.

For some reason, the statement made his stomach sour. "Why?" Justin looked at him. "Because she lives in a big house?" In his mind, the four walls around a person didn't say anything about how well someone had done. "And please, don't call her that. She has a name." It was strange because sometimes he wanted nothing more than to build a meaningful relationship with his siblings, but other times, he couldn't hide the twinge of jealousy he felt. Jealousy he had no right feeling. Jealousy he hated, but it was there all the same.

Landon and Shanen were his siblings, but he didn't really know them. They'd always had each other, but Justin hadn't. On the flip side, he'd had their father, and they hadn't. It was all such a clusterfuck that made him feel the need to pump the brakes. He understood his dad's urgency, but it was overwhelming at times.

"What's wrong, Justin? Are you okay?" There was nothing but concern in his gaunt face. It was etched in the wrinkles that hadn't been there before his diagnosis. Cancer and chemo were both taking its toll on his now frail body.

"Nothing." He shook his head. He needed to get his shit together. They were dealing with things that were much more important than him pouting over his past. "I'm just not feeling too hot today. Let's get in there and celebrate your birthday, old man." Justin winked at him and his father smiled. He got out of the car and walked around to the passenger seat to help his dad out. Christ, he had to help his father out of the fucking car. His dad had never been the kind of man who asked for help with anything.

Justin handed him his cane, which he'd been determined to use rather than his wheelchair. He didn't always have to use the chair, but Justin had figured it would be a good idea today, since they'd have a big day. His dad hadn't agreed—not that Justin could blame him. He would likely be the same in that situation.

With one arm wrapped around his dad, they made their way toward the house. He had his portable oxygen tank with him. It was small enough to be strapped to his back.

They passed two motorcycles in the driveway, telling him that Landon and Rod were already there. Justin was thankful for that. Despite the anger Landon had when he found out about Justin, Landon was the sibling he felt more comfortable around. Hell, maybe it was because of the anger, because he could relate to him. If Shanen felt any of that, she didn't show it. No matter how much Justin tried to hide or deny his anger, it was always there, eating through Justin's bones and he thought Landon felt the same.

The door opened as soon as they hit the steps of the front porch. Shanen rushed out. Justin tried not to go rigid when she wrapped her arms around him. "Hi. Thanks for coming."

"No problem," he told her before she turned to his—no, *their* dad.

"Hi, Daddy." She pulled him into a hug. Justin almost felt like someone kicked him in the gut, and right behind it the guilt came in. She had every right to their father that he did. She'd lost him, and now had years to make up for. None of this was as easy as he wanted to pretend it was.

Justin followed behind them as Shanen helped their father inside. They walked into a large foyer with a chandelier over it. About twenty people, mostly faces he didn't know, filled the room to the left.

"Bob? Wow. Look at you. It's been a long time, buddy!" his dad said to a man who looked about his same age. Justin didn't know who he was. His dad had never spoken about anyone from his past.

They embraced, and Justin stood in the background. The second he saw Landon in the corner with Rod, some of the weight eased from him. "Hey, Dad. You okay here?"

"I'll help him," Shanen told him. "You're fine."

He tried to thank her with a look and Shanen smiled, showing him she got it. He made his way toward his... brother and Landon gave him a quick nod.

"Is this as weird for you as it is for me?" Landon asked.

Justin exhaled. "Yes. Christ. I didn't expect it to be." Which didn't make sense. Of course it would be strange. They were a mismatched family, celebrating his father's birthday when the man looked like he would pass out at any second.

"What? How could you not expect this to be uncomfortable? Hell, I'm just Landon's boyfriend and it's even awkward for me," Rod said, and Justin glanced up to see Landon lovingly roll his eyes, before he wrapped an arm around Rod's shoulders and pulled him close. Rod was smaller than Landon. He wore black eyeliner that made his eyes stand out.

"Please, don't hold back for us," Landon replied.

"I wouldn't think of it," was Rod's response, but Justin thought he knew what Rod was doing. He wanted to make Landon laugh, wanted to take the edge off, and he found himself grateful that Landon hadn't let the fact that Rod found out about Justin and his dad before Landon did come between them. They were a strong couple. You could see the love between them.

The three of them chatted for a few minutes before Rod excused himself for the restroom.

"I should probably go talk to him." Landon crossed his arms and leaned against the wall. There was no doubt in Justin's mind whom he was speaking about.

"I know he'd like that. I get that it's hard, though."

Landon turned his way. "What do I say? Jesus, it's really shitty that I don't know how to talk to my own dad."

Anger burned through Justin's insides. He was angry at their dad for putting them all in this situation. How hard would it have been to tell Justin and his mom about Shanen and Landon? To be a father to them, too? He bit back the anger and said, "Hi. Happy Birthday. Anything will do."

Landon didn't move, though. He eyed their father on the other side of the room. Justin followed his stare, which is how he saw the man walk in. But not just any man. Drew. The guy he met in a club the night Shanen got married. His brows pulled together. What in the hell was he doing here? Because this wasn't awkward enough without the guy he wanted to fuck obviously knowing Shanen. "Ah, hell. I think I jerked off in a club with the guy who just walked in."

"What?" Landon's voice actually cracked on the word. He looked from Justin, to Drew, and back to Justin again. His gut sank, and he was pretty sure he should have kept his mouth shut because this was about to get a whole lot worse. "That's Shanen's brother-in-law. He's Jacob's brother, and I'm pretty sure Shanen would have told me if he wasn't straight. I know he's not close with Jacob, but she would have thought it was coincidence enough if she married a man with a gay or bisexual brother."

Oh fuck. Damn it all to hell.

Justin tried to hide his shock. He looked at Drew again, studied him—the scruff on his face, that jaw and those fucking lips—of course it was really who he thought it was. Still, he said the first lie that popped into his head. "Shit. That's not him. Hair's not right and I'd remember that mouth anywhere." Which was true. It was the first thing he'd noticed.

Wasn't this just perfect? He'd come here to get to know his family, and out of all the men in Virginia, he'd somehow ended up jacking off with his sister's husband's brother, who was obviously in the closet.

The brother of the year award definitely wasn't going to him.

Landon eyed him, skepticism in his eyes. Before he could say anything, Rod stepped back up and wrapped his arms around Landon.

"What did I miss?"

DREW FELT UNCOMFORTABLE, just stepping through the door. He knew the invitation only came from Shanen and not Jacob. His brother had never been interested in spending time with him. They'd never been close, even when they were younger. They were too different, and Jacob had never hesitated to point out the fact that Drew never did what was expected of him, and Drew didn't get why that was a bad thing.

And then there was Iris. Their parents were friends and she'd been around most of their lives. At some point, she and Jacob had started dating. It had been a surprise to Drew. With their families being so close, it seemed awkward. Plus, Iris and Jacob couldn't have been more different. She was a lot wilder than his brother. Shit went downhill from there. She'd just made a rocky relationship a fucking landmine, though he couldn't completely blame her.

But hey, Shanen tried, and she was a nice lady. She'd recently had a big upheaval in her family and the least he could do was try and be supportive.

"Thanks so much for coming, Andrew!" Shanen wrapped her arms around him, and Drew immediately tensed up, while cursing himself for it at the same time. He patted her on the back and then pulled away, trying to be friendly but also not upset his crazy brother, either.

"Thanks for having me."

"I'm not sure if you should be thanking me for that. I'm kind of a mess here." She chuckled humorlessly, just as his brother walked up.

Drew nodded at him. "Hey."

"Hello." Jacob wrapped an arm around Shanen and kissed her head. Jesus, the guy was an idiot, trying to mark his territory the way he did. He might as well raise his leg and piss on her, though Shanen would kick his ass for that one. She was a strong woman. He liked that about her. She'd probably lose her mind if she knew some of the things that had gone down between him and Jacob.

"How are things going at the gym?" Shanen asked just as Drew let his eyes roam around the room. He didn't know anyone here other than Shanen and Jacob. He'd met Shanen's brother, his partner Rod, and her mom, but he couldn't say he knew them well. His own parents would be here any second and that would just make things worse.

That's when Drew saw him. The dark-haired guy from the club stood in the corner, his eyes firmly trained on him, and he sure as hell didn't look happy. "Oh shit," escaped his mouth.

"What?" Shanen asked.

He looked at her then back at the guy again—Justin, he thought his name had been.

Justin stood next to Shanen's brother, Landon. Looking a whole lot like…

No…it couldn't be.

"What are you looking at?" Jacob asked, with an edge to his voice that he always had when speaking to Drew.

"Nothing." He shook his head, hoping he didn't look as spooked as he felt. He had to be imagining the resemblance he thought he saw. If not, he was fucked. "I thought I saw someone I know, but it's not him."

Shanen nodded. "That's Justin standing with Rod and Landon. He's the brother we just found out about."

Fuck. *Fuck.* This couldn't be happening. He'd jerked off with his brother's wife's brother, who she just found out existed. Even thinking about the relation was a confusing mess. Oh, and his own brother already hated him. All he needed was to give Jacob another reason to be pissed.

"How's that going, by the way?" His voice cracked, and he hoped no one noticed. Shanen had asked him about the gym he owned. He should have answered that question. Why had he chosen to ask about Justin? Justin the sexy man he'd wanted to fuck—or at least blow, before he lost his shit and bailed.

Jesus. What were the fucking odds? Courtesy of Jacob, he'd felt pretty shitty the day of the wedding. His own brother had warned him to keep his distance from Shanen, as though he thought Drew would go after his brother's wife. That part of Jacob's issue with him was because of Iris but the situation with Iris hadn't been what Jacob thought it was. Iris had kissed him, not the other way around.

On the wedding day, he'd needed to get his mind off their argument so that's what he'd done. Go from one touchy subject to another, even though the second subject wasn't something his family knew existed.

Apparently he did that with his long lost brother-in-law.

He was so fucking dead.

"It's going as well as it can go, I guess. It's hard—finding out I have a twenty-six-year-old brother I didn't know about. And with Dad being sick, too…"

Jacob kissed her forehead and looked at her with a sincerity Drew didn't often see from his brother. Jacob loved her. There wasn't any doubt in his mind about that, which partially excused his asshole behavior toward Drew at the wedding. Would be a bigger pass if he wasn't always an asshole to Drew.

"Anyway." Shanen straightened her posture. "Come on. I'll introduce you to the rest of my family."

Drew's pulse sped up, wondering how Justin would react. Would he admit that he knew—okay, maybe *knew* was a strong word—but would he admit that he'd met Drew before? He was pretty sure the guy wouldn't say *how* because coming in someone's hand on a dance floor wasn't real PC, but he might say *where*.

"No. That's okay. He looks busy."

"He's not too busy! We're family after all. My mom will be here soon, too." She grabbed on to Drew's wrist and he simultaneously wanted to scrub the word *family* out of his brain when it came to Justin, and also fight not to dig his heels into the carpet and make her drag him over like a five-year-old kid who knew he was about to get into trouble.

They weren't family. Not really. Justin was the half-brother of his brother's wife, but it definitely put an uncomfortable spin on things.

Drew followed Shanen to the other side of the room. Justin's dark eyes zeroed in on him, narrowed and...he was pretty sure the guy had a vein pulsing in his forehead that was dangerously close to popping. He was going to make Shanen's brother have a stroke. This day kept getting better and better.

The vein bulged again and he crossed his arms. Oh yeah. He was pissed. Not that Drew could blame him. He'd walked away, practically leaving the guy in the middle of a club with his dick hanging out. It hadn't been his best moment.

He was sexy, though. Jesus, he was fucking sexy. He was about an inch taller than Drew's six-foot frame. He had a nice body—long, lean muscles, short, dark hair, and a dimple under the left side of his mouth that definitely wasn't there at the moment.

They stopped when they reached the trio in the corner. Or he thought there were three people standing there. Drew couldn't take his eyes off of Justin.

"Andrew, you remember Landon and Rod." Shanen was all happiness and sunshine while Justin looked like a fucking storm cloud.

"Hey, man. How's it going?" Landon asked. They shook hands and then he shook Rod's next, when Rod said, "Hi. Good to see you again."

"Good to see you guys too." Jesus. Did his voice just crack again? It was like he was going through puberty for the second time—though in a way, that almost made sense.

"This is my other brother, Justin," Shanen continued. "Justin, this is Jacob's brother, Andrew."

"Hi. Nice to *meet* you," Drew rushed out first, hoping that Justin got the hint and kept his mouth shut.

Justin stalled, and Drew really thought the motherfucker was going to rat him out. But then he offered a tight smile. "Hey. You too, An*drew*."

Oh yeah. Justin wanted to kill him. He had a feeling none of them would be forgetting this party any time soon.

CHAPTER THREE

JUSTIN COULDN'T KEEP himself from looking at Drew—or Andrew. At the club, he'd introduced himself as Drew, but he noticed everyone here called him Andrew. Maybe the Drew was part of his persona when he went looking to jerk guys off in clubs before running away.

"The food is delicious, Nick. We appreciate you catering for us," Shanen said.

"Thank you. It was no problem." Nick smiled at her, and his partner Bryce grinned at him like Nick created the whole goddamned world with his hands, instead of making tasty finger-foods. He looked at him like he could do anything, like maybe he was everything.

Landon and Rod looked at each other the same way. It was odd to Justin, not really because he didn't believe in love, he'd just never experienced it. Even when his parents were together, they didn't look at each other the way the four men did.

Nick and Bryce wandered off, followed by Rod and Landon. Shanen was next, making a trip around the room.

People mingled and ate, some standing, some sitting. The sitting was happening for his dad because as the day went on, it was becoming obvious to Justin that he was getting weaker and weaker.

Drew stood with his parents, his brother, Shanen, and her mom in one of the corners of the room. He was outside of the circle of people, but every once in a while, someone—mostly his mother—would say something to him and he'd reply.

He didn't have a plate in his hand, and his arms were crossed as he leaned against the wall. There was something about the way he stood, about not only the stiffness it looked like he tried to hide, but also the distance he was from his family that made it pretty obvious that Drew felt like an outsider, in a way. Like he wasn't quite part of the group, or didn't know how to be.

Likely, Justin was making that up because it was the way he felt—like an outsider, an interloper in his father's family—but then, he was pretty sure he was right. Something was different in the way Drew interacted with his family compared to the way Jacob did. Jacob rarely spoke to Drew at all.

He saw Drew reach up—at first looking like he grabbed for something, maybe a hat—before he settled on running a hand through his blond hair. His hair was styled today, the longer hair on top, spiked.

Their eyes met. Justin felt the annoyance rise up in him again, but not with the same fervor he felt earlier. He wasn't sure if he had the right to be frustrated or not. He was annoyed because he spent quite a bit of his time irritated now, but there was something in the way Drew looked at him, in seeing him slightly distanced from his family, that made Justin see himself in the other man.

Which bordered on insane. Pretty soon he'd feel electricity from across the room. He'd go hard looking at Drew, the way people talked about in movies and books, which never happened in reality.

He did want to know Drew's story, though, if for no other reason than to not have to think about his own. The last thing he would do was draw attention to the fact that he had met Drew before. He wouldn't risk outing the man if he was in the closet, and he also had a feeling Shanen and Landon wouldn't be too happy with him.

The ground they were on was too unsteady to let a near-hookup screw with their relationship.

DREW HEARD MUFFLED voices beside him. They were speaking about a case Jacob worked on and how proud their dad was of him. Joy, Shanen's mom, added how wonderful it felt to see your kids succeed and do what they loved.

Jacob loved the courtroom. Their father had too. There had never been a time in Drew's life when he thought that was the life for him. He'd tried for a while, but it hadn't fit. He was one hundred percent okay with that.

His parents had been slightly miffed at first, because that's just what Sinclairs did. It's what his family had always done, but they'd gotten over it. Mostly.

His family was incredibly different from Drew. He wasn't extremely close to them because he'd rather hike, or go for a bike ride, than ever wear a suit, but he knew his parents loved him. He knew they wanted him to be happy, and that they probably struggled the same way he did with the fact that they didn't have much to talk to Drew about. Not the way they did with Jacob. They just didn't know how to relate to each other.

He didn't know why his choice not to go into law irked Jacob so much, but then he figured no matter what he did, his brother wouldn't like it. Maybe that was a typical brother thing; he didn't know.

His eyes followed Justin as he said something softly to his father. The other man shook his head. Justin spoke again but got the same response. He could practically feel the heavy breath that pushed from Justin's lungs at whatever he'd been denied. He shook his head and walked away, moving toward Landon, Rod, Nick, and Bryce, who stood about ten feet away from Justin's dad.

Every once in a while, Justin's eyes would dart his way. Drew knew he had to be wondering what in the hell was going on. He wanted to find a way to talk to him, but he was also a little too chickenshit to do so. He'd run out on the guy like a fucking idiot. It was embarrassing.

He probably should do some explaining, though, so he waited to try and find the right time to get him alone.

When he saw Justin dismiss himself and head for the hallway, Drew pushed off the wall. "I'll be right back," he said, interrupting a conversation that had been going on without him, and made his way through the room.

He grabbed a piece of paper and pen from the table by the door, and scribbled his phone number on it, cursing himself for not having business cards with him.

By the time he made it to the hallway, he heard water running as though Justin was washing his hands.

The second Justin opened the door, Drew said, "You're Shanen's brother," as though Justin didn't know it.

Justin froze in his retreat from the bathroom. "As of a few months ago, yeah."

There was pain in Justin's voice and Drew winced. What they were going through had to be difficult on all of them.

"Listen...I'm..." sorry I jerked you off and ran? Jesus, he didn't know what to say. "Maybe we can talk. Here's my number." He held out the paper.

Justin stalled, took it, and then a clatter came from the other room. There was a gasp, an obvious shuffle, and movement of people and that was all it took for Justin to move. He pushed his way around Drew and went back for the other room.

Without making it to the room, Drew knew it had something to do with Justin's father.

"I'm fine. I'm fine. I just slipped. It's not a big deal." Drew rounded the corner, just as Justin's dad, Larry, finished speaking.

Joy, Shanen, and Landon all kneeled beside him as he sat on the floor next to the chair he'd been in. Rod stood behind Landon with his hands on Landon's shoulders. It was obvious Larry was embarrassed. He covered his face with his hands, and the closer Drew got, he noticed his thin fingers were shaking.

"I got him." Justin kneeled beside him. "Come on, Dad. Let's get you up." He wrapped an arm around him. Landon reached out to help, but Justin shook him off. "I said I got it," he snapped. Jesus, was that statement laced with pain.

"Hey," Landon put a hand on his shoulder. "Let me help you. That's...that's what I'm here for."

Drew wanted to offer his assistance as well, but it didn't feel right. This was a moment for Justin and Landon—two sons, bonding over helping the father they both loved, despite the fact that Drew knew they had to be angry at him.

Justin nodded and the two men held their dad up. He put an arm around each of them.

"Thanks for the party, but I think we should head out," he heard Justin say to Shanen.

"He can rest here. We have the spare room. Maybe—"

"No," Larry cut her off sharply then winced. "I just...I want to go home."

She had tears in her eyes as she nodded and hugged him, then Landon and Justin began to help him walk.

The room was heavy. Thick. Drew felt it in his bones.

He forced himself to snap out of it, before walking over and opening the front door for them. Words teased his tongue, but he didn't know what to say. If he should say anything. Was it his place?

"I should have made him use the wheelchair. I don't know what in the fuck I was thinking," Justin mumbled to Landon as they approached the door. And then his eyes caught Drew's again.

Drew wanted to tell him to call. Wanted to tell him he was sorry for the club and for what he was dealing with, but Justin turned away. As he walked past, Drew reached his fingers out, brushing them against the warm skin of Justin's arm, trying to silently offer his support.

Justin didn't respond, didn't look back as he and Landon helped Larry to the car, and didn't take a backward glance before he and his dad drove away.

CHAPTER FOUR

"IF IT ISN'T Cinderella," Justin said as Drew approached his booth in the sports bar. He wore a black baseball cap, turned around backward and Justin swallowed a gulp. He'd always had a thing for guys with backward hats. "I looked for your glass slipper when you ran off, but I think you forgot the part of the story where you lose it. Also, there's the plot twist that you're my brother-in-law."

He was partially trying to keep the tone light. He'd seen the pity in Drew's eyes when he'd left with his dad. Justin didn't do pity. Because of that, he hadn't been sure he would call Drew, but damned if he wasn't curious about the man.

Drew sat down across from him. He leaned back, dropping his head against the bench seat. The position looked awkward because of the hat. "Sorry. I thought you were looking to get off, not to find your prince charming."

Well hell. He had Justin there. "Good point. I still would've liked some kind of warning that you only planned to jack me off on the dance floor before you split." He might have chosen someone different to hook up with that night—though probably not. Drew was fucking gorgeous. He'd caught Justin's eye the second he'd seen him, and he'd be lying if he didn't admit that doing what they'd done around all those people didn't turn him on. Apparently he had a kink for public displays. Who knew?

Drew glanced away, almost sheepishly. His eyes darted down and Justin could have sworn his cheeks were slightly pink.

Damned if Justin's gut didn't churn. He was right about Drew.

He was in the closet. Fuck. Leave it to him to rub one out with his new sister's husband's closeted brother. Even just saying their relation was a tongue twister. Still, as awkward as this whole situation was, he wanted to make sure Drew knew he wouldn't out him. Even though Justin had come out when he was young, he understood that not everyone was able to do that. It was important that people came out in their own time.

"Listen, no hard feelings, okay? We both got what we were eventually looking for. No harm, no foul. No one needs to know." *Especially not Landon or Shanen.* The last thing he wanted was to risk his relationship with his siblings before they had a chance to really build one. "Your secret is safe," Justin added. "They won't find out you're gay from me."

Drew's wide, steely eyes somehow went even wider. Then a slow, easy smile spread across his face. "Aren't you chivalrous? But I'm not gay and in the closet. I'm…trying to figure shit out?" Drew's eyes darted away again.

Before Justin could reply, the waitress approached their table and asked if they were ready to order. He hadn't even looked at the menu.

"Just a Coors for me, thanks," Justin said without looking at her. He was trying to figure shit out? What in the hell did that mean?

"I'll take the same." Drew handed the waitress his menu and then Justin's as well. His hands rested on the dark, wood table. They were nice hands. Strong and full of veins.

"What does that mean?" Justin asked. Not that it was any of his business.

"It means exactly what I said. I'm figuring shit out." He looked around and then lowered his voice. "I've always been…curious? I guess you could say. I just assumed I'm bisexual. I've always found men attractive, but I've never explored it much. The first time was a fucking disaster. Don't ever kiss one of your friends unless you know they're interested." He cocked a brow and Justin found himself wanting to know the story.

"There were a few rub and tugs in college, but nothing major. I'm attracted to women as well, and it just seemed easier than dealing with the rest of it. Been thinking about it more recently. Decided to give it a go. End of story." Drew winked. "See? No Cinderella here. Just a bi-guy exploring his bi-side. Not really looking for the happily ever after."

Anger spiked through him. He had no right to be upset. He knew that. What did it matter to him *why* Drew had gone looking? But it still rubbed Justin the wrong way. "So what? I was your test drive? Wanted to see if fucking around with a man could get you off?" He was offended, but he wasn't sure if he should be.

"You were my hookup." Drew's brows pulled together. "Kind of. I hadn't meant for it to go down the way it did. My dick definitely wanted to go further, but I freaked. I've had more practice since then." The motherfucker winked at Justin and he suddenly had the urge to punch him.

Maybe it was jealousy because he hadn't had an orgasm with anyone other than himself since that night. But *that* night of all nights, he'd needed more than Drew had given him. Maybe that was what had him feeling so irritated.

That didn't explain why he wanted to know what kind of practice Drew had…

The waitress approached and gave them their beers. Justin gripped the cold bottle, taking long pulls until it was almost gone. As he drank, he realized he needed this—a night away from home. His dad had been worn out since the party a few days ago. It was getting more and more like that. One day out could wear him down. For one night, Justin wanted to pretend his father wasn't sick. Wanted to pretend his life was the way it used to be. "So, I was the first guy you've touched in years, and now you've had more? I must have done a good job."

Damned if Drew didn't look a little shy again, which for some reason, Justin thought was sexy as hell.

He recovered quickly though, shrugged and said, "It was all right," before he picked up his beer and took a drink. It took Justin a second to realize he was smiling too.

"IT COULD HAVE been better if you hadn't run out." Justin eyed him from the other side of the table. He had his arms crossed, corded muscles in his lower arms showing. Drew had a thing about muscles. Not that body-building, overzealous, *look-at-me* kind, but yeah, he loved fitness and definitely noticed firm, toned bodies.

"So you're not going to cut me a little slack?" He'd jerked a guy off in the middle of a club. Although it hadn't been the first time he'd touched a man, and though he'd always known he was attracted to men, it was still a defining moment for him. It was the beginning of Drew deciding it was time to explore the piece of him he'd only teased himself with before. Maybe he hadn't dealt with it in the best way, but there were no *how-to* manuals about this kind of thing. Everyone lived their lives their own way.

"Where's the fun in that?" Justin cocked a dark brow at him. There was something about him Drew liked. Sure, the situation was a little awkward, but he could tell that Justin was someone he would get along with. "Why now?" Justin added after a moment.

The truth was, he couldn't say for sure why he'd waited so long to really explore his bisexuality. Not that he'd spent the last couple months fucking everyone in sight. Hell, he hadn't even gotten to the fucking yet, but Justin wasn't the only man he'd met in a club recently. "I don't know. I guess I just got tired of pretending it doesn't exist? Or hell, maybe I'm just a horny bastard. Who knows?" All he knew was he'd been upset that day. He'd wanted to drink and fuck and he'd found his way to a gay club.

But then...there was probably a little more to it than that, wasn't there? It had always been important to Drew to be who he was, to do what he wanted. If he felt something, if he wanted something, he wanted to actually live it. It was vital to him, being true to himself and leaving himself open to live his own life. This was just another part of who he was.

"Fair enough." Justin picked at one of his blunt nails before grabbing his beer and finishing it. On the outside, everything about him looked relaxed—the way he leaned back in the bench seat, the softness in his face, the smiles and jokes, but his eyes told a different story. They were stormy, dark, and sad. How could they not be? It wasn't as if Justin didn't have a lot on his plate.

"I'm sorry about your dad." He was sorry about the whole situation, but he didn't think it was appropriate to bring Justin's family circumstances into it. Drew knew enough from Shanen, though. Knew that Justin had just met his siblings. That his father had walked away from half of his family and started a new one with Justin.

The second Justin's eyes met his again, Drew wished he hadn't mentioned his father. His dark eyes went even darker. His posture went from relaxed to rigid. The right side of his jaw ticked—one beat, two beats, and then three before Justin nodded and gave a stiff, "Thank you."

They both looked at each other for a moment, and he wondered what they were even doing here. Why they'd met just to discuss a hand job at a club. It happened; they couldn't change it. They wouldn't let it cause problems in their personal lives. The end.

But he also realized he wasn't quite ready to go home yet. He wondered if Justin knew anyone here other than the father he was losing, and the siblings he'd gained, but didn't really know. Drew couldn't imagine being in a situation like that, despite the fact that he and Jacob weren't, and had never been close. He knew who his family was. "I'm hungry. I think I'm going to go ahead and grab some food. Do you want something?" Drew tossed out the rope, and now Justin had to decide if he wanted to grab on, or if he wasn't interested.

"I could eat," Justin replied, so Drew flagged their waitress over. She gave them each menus again, and they browsed for just a minute before Justin ordered a burger and fries, and Drew grilled salmon and rice.

"That stuff will kill ya, you know?" he teased Justin when their waitress left.

"Ah, hell. Don't tell me you're one of those. Food is meant to be enjoyed."

Drew chuckled. He was half-teasing and half-serious. "Salmon is enjoyable, and it doesn't clog your arteries the way a burger will."

"Just when I was thinking I might start to like you. I guess I'll go back to hanging out for the view." Justin gave him a cocky grin.

Heat coiled low in Drew's gut at the compliment. Justin was a sexy man. He enjoyed the view too. "Are you flirting with me?"

Justin shrugged. "Maybe. You have me intrigued, Cinderella. What can I say?"

The name had to go. "You call me that, and I'm going to start thinking you want to be my prince charming. Family drama, remember?"

Justin winced, but Drew could tell it was playfully. "Shit. I forgot. You ever think life would be a whole hell of a lot easier if we didn't have families? I mean, they're supposed to be there for you, right? They're your tribe. Your people. But most of the time, it's family that makes shit even harder than it should be. I mean, without them, we might be fucking by now."

Justin winked at him, but even if he hadn't, it would have been obvious that he was giving Drew shit—about the fucking at least. The other stuff? He had a feeling they were on the same page when it came to family dynamics. "You can say that again."

Just then the waitress returned with their second round of drinks. Justin picked up his bottle of beer first and held it up. "To family…even when they do fuck up our lives and keep us from getting laid."

Drew clanked his bottle against Justin's. "To family."

CHAPTER FIVE

"YOU REALLY OWN a fucking gym?" Justin picked up his bottle of beer and put it to his lips before he realized it was empty. He'd definitely had too many of them this evening. He and Drew had finished eating over an hour ago, but neither of them had made a move to leave yet. He enjoyed their conversation when he hadn't enjoyed much in a long time. He figured he deserved to enjoy something.

Drew's eyebrows knitted together. Justin noticed a couple sat in the brown leather booth behind Drew, glancing their way before turning. "Yeah. Is there a problem with that?" Drew asked.

"Nope." Justin laughed, though he wasn't sure why. Something just felt funny all of a sudden. He should have expected something like being a personal trainer. It wasn't that Justin didn't keep in shape, because he did, but he'd actually never had a gym membership before. It wasn't really his thing. It just... "I don't know. It almost feels pretentious sometimes."

Drew nearly choked on his water. He began coughing and sputtering. "What? How do you mean? Why does wanting to be healthy make me self-important?"

Justin laughed again. He really needed to stop laughing, but thinking that just made him do it even more. It was as though a switch had been turned in him and now he couldn't flip it off. "No, it's not. It just feels so...*look at me. I'm fucking sexy, and I want to show it off.*" Was he making sense? He wasn't sure if he was.

The blonde waitress stopped by and asked if they wanted another beer. Justin told her yes, and then she looked at Drew. "No, thanks. I'll stick with water from here on out."

Speaking of water, why in the hell was Drew drinking that? They had beer. Justin liked beer. He wanted more of it. "Too many calories in alcohol?"

Drew rolled his eyes. "No, I just figure it's a good idea to stay sober. Also, not that I don't enjoy being called sexy, because I do, but—"

"Did I call you sexy?" Justin asked.

"You did."

"Okay." He shrugged. "It's true."

Drew adjusted the cap on his head and gave Justin a half-smile. "As I was saying, that's not what it's about. I couldn't give a shit what everyone else thinks. I exercise because it makes me feel good. I own a gym and train others because I want to make them feel good as well. You'd be surprised at how working out regularly can make you feel. It's a great stress reliever and a good way to work out pent up energy."

"So is sex."

Damned if Drew's cheeks didn't slightly redden. He liked that...Drew's blush. The woman at the booth turned and looked at them before shaking her head. Apparently sex wasn't an acceptable topic of conversation. It was acceptable as hell to Justin.

Leaning back, Drew crossed his arms. He smirked at Justin, who grabbed his beer when the waitress returned with it and drank almost all of it down. Drew's brows pulled together again. "Do you need to be home with your dad tonight?"

The question doused his good mood. Felt like it somehow poured cement into his gut again. He just wanted to forget everything right now. Wanted to forget all of it. "Nope. Landon and Shanen's mom, Joy, is going to start helping more. She used to do caregiving, but stopped. I don't know why because—well, hell, because I don't really know her. I don't know any of them. Anyway, he's okay for now, but we don't really like to leave him alone.

Depending on how things go, and how long he continues treatment, he might start to stay with her for a while. She can help better than I can." And from there it would be hospice care. Goddamn, the cement flooded through his body from his gut, up to his chest, and down his arm.

Justin picked up his beer and finished drinking the rest of the bitter liquid. They were both quiet for a moment, and he knew his reply had thickened the air around them. He waited for Drew to ask more about his family, his father's cancer, or what they were going to do, but he didn't. Instead he just asked, "What about you? What do you do?" And Justin exhaled a heavy breath, so fucking thankful he didn't have to talk about the things that made him feel like he would fall apart.

He didn't want to do this right now. He didn't want to do it ever, but especially not right now. Right now, he just wanted to *be*.

DREW WISHED LIKE hell he hadn't had to bring up Larry, but looking at the guy, he could tell he was already sloshed. He'd considered saying that maybe the last beer wasn't such a good idea, but then, who was he to tell Justin what to do? Not only that, but Justin had a lot going on. More than Drew could understand. He figured Justin might need an evening to just let go and forget everything. That's why he'd needed to make sure Justin didn't have somewhere to be. Now that he knew, he'd hang out with him, make sure he didn't drink too much, and make sure he got home okay.

"I used to work construction. It's not what I want to do, though. I've been going to school to be a paramedic. Needed a change, but I had to put my schooling on hold to come here. Landon and Rod's friend Nick is giving me a job at his restaurant until I head out. I'm going fucking crazy not doing anything."

The sadness was back in his voice again. It ripped Drew apart. He couldn't imagine how all of this felt to Justin, so when the waitress came back and she glanced at Drew when Justin ordered another beer, he nodded and held up his finger, as if to say one more.

"You should come by the gym. It might help you at least burn off some energy." Drew winked at him. "I'll even waive your registration fee."

"Oh, you'll wave my registration fee, will you? How generous. How much is it?"

"We have a special going on now. It's a whole twenty bucks." Drew smirked at Justin, who laughed.

He wasn't sure how smart it was to get close to Justin. Not with him being related to Shanen, and Drew's relationship with Jacob being so rocky. But hell, Justin knew something about Drew that not many people did. He'd had the guy's come on his hand, for Christ's sake. Even more importantly, he enjoyed Justin's company.

The waitress returned with Justin's final beer, which he went straight for. Drew watched his throat move as he swallowed, his Adam's apple bobbing. Watched his jaw work as Justin drank until the bottle was completely empty, setting it down on the table a little too hard before saying, "Oops," and then giggling. He had a feeling Justin wasn't a giggler. The guy was definitely cut off, no matter how cute his giggle happened to be.

"So…this gym offer. That out of the kindness of your heart? Feel bad for the guy who broke up a family and is now an interloper with his own father? Or you just looking for an excuse to spend more time with me?"

Drew's chest squeezed, and he felt the corners of his lips turn down into a frown. Justin had said it like a joke but the pain in his sad eyes was very real. The hurt played clearly on his face, in the tightness of his jaw, and in his frown.

"Oh no. Fuck no. Don't do that. Don't feel sorry for me. I gotta take a piss. I'll be right back."

Justin stood, wobbled slightly. When Drew moved to grab for

him, he shook his head before stomping off toward the bathroom. "Fuck," he groaned, before adjusting his hat and rubbing a hand over his face.

This was a mess. It had the potential to be a fucking disaster, but how could he not want to be friends with the guy? How could he not want to support him if Justin was interested at all in that? He had no one, nothing. His whole life had been ransacked, and Drew wondered if anyone paid attention to that fact.

He flagged the waitress over and she gave him their bill. By the time he paid, Justin wasn't out of the bathroom yet. He made his way down the hallway. "Justin?" he called as he pushed the restroom door open. When he walked in, he saw Justin leaning with his forehead against the wall. His hands were fisted against it, on both sides of him. He breathed heavy—in, out, in, out, and Drew could feel the anger radiating off of him. Could feel the fear and confusion and sadness.

The veins in his arms tightened, and Drew knew it took everything in him not to punch something. Oh yeah. They definitely needed to get him into the gym.

"Christ, I don't know what in the hell is wrong with me." His right hand started to shake as though the need to hit something grew.

"You're human. We can only take so much before we crack." What *wasn't* Justin going through right now? He'd left his schooling and had moved to another state. Discovered his father lied to him, that he had family he didn't know about, and not only that, Justin was losing his dad. It was a wonder he hadn't cracked apart before this.

Or maybe he had, and no one knew it.

Justin turned his head and looked over his shoulder at Drew. Gone was the drunken silliness from earlier. He was stripped bare in a way that sometimes only alcohol could provide.

"Come on." Drew jerked his head toward the door. "Let's get

out of here."

The edges around Justin's eyes narrowed, his hazel irises softened. He pushed away from the wall, and Drew backed out of the restroom, Justin right behind him.

Drew didn't know which car was Justin's, and thankfully Justin didn't try to go for it. He followed Drew out to his truck, and after Drew hit the unlock button, he climbed right into the passenger seat.

Not sure where else to go, Drew headed for home. They were silent, their flirtation a thing of the past as they made their way out of town and toward his place. He lived on two acres, away from any neighbors, because as much as he enjoyed being around people, he also liked having his space. His own place for peace and quiet.

They pulled down the long, gravel driveway, Drew's headlights shining right on his house.

"Christ. All this just from owning a gym?" Justin asked, his voice rough and tired.

He knew how it must look from the outside—the large wrap-around porch. The oversized windows. The wood beams. Justin couldn't even see the deck out back yet. His house was impressive, and he knew that. "I'll be paying it off for the rest of my life." Because he wouldn't take money from his family. It wasn't his style. "I designed it myself, though. I wanted to see if I could do it, and I did. This place will always be my baby." Because it was his. His vision and paid for with his own money.

He'd had no choice but to use part of the money set aside for him and his brother when he'd started up the gym, but this? This was all Drew.

"It's incredible," Justin said as Drew killed the engine. Warmth spread through his chest. He was proud of his house and it made him feel good when someone appreciated it.

"Thank you." They climbed out of the truck. Justin wobbled slightly and Drew realized he still felt the effects of all the beers he'd had to drink.

The motion-sensor light clicked on as they got close to the house. He smelled beer and man on Justin's skin as Justin stood so close, their arms touched. His dick twitched, perked up with interest, but Drew tried to ignore it.

He fumbled the keys, and they hit his porch.

Justin chuckled.

Fucker. He bent to pick them up and when he stood, Justin was even closer. They were body against body, Justin's front against his back. "You're doing this on purpose."

"I know," Justin replied.

"We can't fuck around." At least not tonight with Justin's emotions so raw and the half a keg of beer in his gut. No. What was he thinking? They needed to keep their hands off each other altogether. Fucking around would be too messy.

"I know that too. It's still fun to tease you. When you're turned on, your breathing picks up, and you tremble slightly. I noticed that when we were dancing."

It was a distraction for Justin—plain and simple. Drew understood that. Flirting with Drew was a lot easier than dealing with the shit he had to deal with. Justin had been all over the place tonight, but that didn't mean Drew's cock didn't take notice of every move Justin made. Of his muscles as they tightened, and his hands as he reached for something. Drew wanted to tremble against Justin, wanted to feel Justin tremble against him. Still, he said, "You're an asshole," and unlocked the door before they stepped inside.

"Third thing in a row I know! We're on a roll. What all have you done?" Justin closed the door.

Hell, were they really going to do this? "I told you earlier. I've gotten as far as blowjobs." Drew quite enjoyed them too. There hadn't been a lot of them, and he wasn't sure how good he was at them, but he liked dick in his mouth.

"Oh yeah. I forgot. I'm drunk."

Drew rolled his eyes as Justin walked over and fell onto the couch. He kicked out of his shoes, put his feet up, his shirt showing the dark trail of hair on his taut stomach. "No shit." Drew turned around before he decided it was time to do a little more exploring, and buried his face against Justin's abs so he could see what the hair felt like against his skin.

"How many?" Justin put his hands behind his head.

Apparently they really were going to do this. "Given one, gotten two. You thirsty?"

Justin chuckled. "I thought you said we couldn't fuck around?"

Ah hell. There went Drew's dick again. It pulsed, strained behind his fly. They were not going to talk about swallowing each other's come. "You know what I mean. Jesus, you're frustrating when you're drunk. I'll be right back. I'm going to get you some water." And find a way to calm himself down before he forgot why he was trying so damn hard to be a gentleman.

When Drew got into his kitchen, the first thing he did was lean against the dark, marble island in the middle. Justin was off limits. If he wanted to do some experimenting, he needed to do it with someone else. Not with his brother's wife's long, lost brother.

He took a few deep breaths, took off his cap, tossed it to the counter, and then picked it up and put it on again. It was only for something to do, so he could ignore the erection Justin gave him with one simple joke.

The thing was, Justin was just his type. He was the exact kind of man that turned Drew on—funny, sexy, confident.

But it was a disaster waiting to happen.

And Justin was drunk.

He filled two glasses of water before draining one of them himself. When he thought he was calmed down enough, Drew took the water in for Justin…and found him passed out on the couch.

A soft snore came out of him, and he turned, tucking his legs up as he lay on his side, completely asleep. For the first time today, he looked at peace. Not trying to be funny, not hurting...just free.

Jesus, he couldn't imagine the fucked-up thoughts going through Justin's head. What his heart felt like. He obviously needed to unplug. To turn everything else off. Drew hoped he was able to give him that tonight. He walked over to Justin, and touched his shoulder. "Hey. I have a spare room. Do you want to go in there?"

Justin groaned, shook his head, and buried his face into the couch cushion. It was cute watching him cuddle into the couch, but it couldn't be very comfortable.

When Drew got the same reaction the second time, he sighed, set the water on the coffee table, and then got a blanket for Justin. He covered the other man up, looked at him for a second, and then made it all the way to the bottom of the stairs before he heard a soft, "I'm sorry."

His heart ached for the sleepy man on his couch. "You have no reason to be," Drew replied, unsure if Justin was talking to him, or about his situation with his family. "You have no reason to be," he said softly again, before turning off the lights, and heading upstairs.

CHAPTER SIX

JUSTIN WOKE UP to two conflicting things—a pounding headache, which sucked. And the smell of bacon, which didn't suck.

He rolled over, thankful that Drew had a large, comfortable couch, and saw a glass of water and a bottle of pain killers beside it.

Thank God.

He sat up, feeling a little lucky that his head didn't spin too much, opened the bottle, and took two pills. With his elbows resting on his knees, he rubbed a hand over his face and bit back a groan. He couldn't believe he'd gotten so drunk last night. The last time he'd done that had been his twenty-first birthday, except for then, there had been vomit. He was really fucking thankful there hadn't been vomit last night.

He felt like a fool, though. It wasn't as if he'd done anything major last night, but he and Drew both knew he'd drank to forget, and he felt a little embarrassed about that. He was too old for that shit, and it had never been his style anyway.

Still, when he heard Drew whistling in the kitchen as he cooked, Justin couldn't help but smile.

He glanced at his phone to see it was eleven, before he pushed to his feet. He hadn't slept this late in years. There was a nagging voice inside him that said he needed to call Joy and check on his dad, but he didn't. Maybe that made him a bastard, but he wanted a little more time away. To pretend this all wasn't happening. He was just a guy who passed out before a hookup, and now they would have the awkward morning after.

Justin carried the glass through the living room and into the kitchen. It was a large space with an island in the middle of it. The counters were all marble, and all the appliances stainless steel. Drew stood in front of the stove, with his back to Justin, wearing sweatpants, no shirt, and an apron. He chuckled. "Mornin', Cinderella."

Drew looked over his shoulder and gave Justin a half-smile. "Mornin', Sleeping Beauty."

"Ooh. We have pet names for each other. Aren't we fucking cute?"

"Well, I am." Drew shrugged and Justin laughed. It made his brain rattle a little, but not too badly.

"Last night you said I'm sexy," Justin reminded him.

"I believe you're the one who said that about me."

Obviously. He'd have to be blind not to see how attractive Drew was. "Well no shit, but I'm pretty sure you returned the sentiment." Justin set the glass of water on the island and walked over to Drew. He leaned against the counter, far enough away that he didn't get popped with grease, and crossed his arms.

"Why do we always end up having this conversation?" Drew didn't make eye contact with Justin as he flipped the bacon. It was obvious he kept his eyes diverted on purpose, not because he was frustrated, but because he was smiling.

"Because I'm a cocky motherfucker who likes getting my ego stroked."

That got a laugh to jump out of Drew's mouth, and it somehow made Justin's head hurt slightly less. It felt good just to laugh with someone.

"Shut up and get the egg whites out of the fridge."

Justin dropped his head back and looked at the ceiling. Drew was going to kill him. "Egg whites? You're fuckin' killing me with this shit. People deserve yolk."

There was another laugh, a throaty, deep laugh that Justin liked the sound of. "People deserve yolk? Is that what you'll have on your sign when you march? And yes, you deserve yolk sometimes, but not all the time. We're making up for the bacon, and I'm telling you, I make an incredible egg white omelet. You won't know the difference."

"Yeah, I'm pretty sure I will, but since you're cooking, I won't complain." Justin pushed off the counter and walked over to Drew's stainless steel fridge. Plastic containers were stacked inside labeled with days and lunch or dinner and suddenly Justin's head started to hurt again.

He wasn't sure why seeing this surprised him. It didn't feel like Drew for some reason, but it wasn't as though he really knew the guy. So instead of commenting about it, he grabbed a carton of egg whites and set them beside Drew. For the first time, he noticed a plate with chopped onions, peppers and grated cheese, making his stomach growl.

"Oh my God, you are my fucking hero. I'm starving but next time, I cook, and I can promise you it'll be fried."

Drew cocked a dark-blond brow at him. "What kind of oil?"

"I don't know. Tell me what the worst kind is and that's what I'm getting."

"I'm not sure I can hang out with you anymore." Drew winked, and as Justin stood there watching him make the omelets, he realized he felt good. Not okay. Not alone or angry or sad or like he didn't belong. But good. He wished like hell it could last.

THEY ATE MOSTLY in silence. Drew's eyes darted up numerous times to watch Justin as he ate. He didn't say much but he seemed to be enjoying the food. So far, in some ways the day felt very much like the morning after a random hookup, but not in others. There was a comfort between the two of them, or at least Drew felt it on his side. This didn't feel like it was one of the first meals they shared. They were friends who could laugh together and talk together, but who weren't uncomfortable with silence either. There was just something welcoming and comfortable about Justin that Drew enjoyed.

"You have onion on your lip." Justin shifted his way, and Drew tapped his own mouth to show Justin where it was. Justin didn't turn away as he grinned, let his tongue slip out of his mouth, and ran it across his bottom lip.

Drew did his best to ignore the sexual innuendo of the movement and said, "You like my egg white omelets," as Justin sat his fork down on the empty plate.

"Do not."

"Do too."

"Maybe a little."

"Maybe a lot," Drew added.

"Fine! You win. They were delicious and healthy and I'm not very happy about it. Do you have any cookies to make up for it?"

"Cookies with breakfast?" Granted, it was closer to lunch, but still.

"Is there a better time to have cookies? Well, other than in bed, I guess."

Drew shook his head and smiled, not sure if Justin was serious or not. He thought most of the whole healthy food versus junk food thing was a joke—not that it mattered either way—but it just made him more curious about Justin for some reason. He was interesting, and Drew found that the more time he spent with him, the more he wanted to know about him. "I don't know what to think about you."

"Eh. I don't either most of the time. I'm just your everyday guy who's going through a tough time. What about you? What's the deal with you and your family?" Justin leaned back, let his legs stretch out, and crossed his arms.

He didn't ask how Justin knew there was one. Perhaps he'd mentioned some of his history with his brother. He couldn't remember. But he also knew that Justin had seen it at Shanen's house. Hell, maybe everyone saw the quiet tension all the time, and Drew just didn't know it.

He leaned forward, resting his elbows on the table and shrugged. "Like you said, family can be hard. My brother and I have always been complete opposites. We've never gotten along well. I mean, it's normal, I guess—sibling jealousy, yet we're grown *up* but haven't outgrown *it* yet."

"You were really never close?" Justin asked.

It was a sad question, because it shouldn't be that way. Sure families had hard times, but there should always be a sort of togetherness there. A bond that Jacob and Drew had never felt. "It's not that we hated each other. I just don't think we knew how to relate to one another. Jacob is very…smart. He's locked down tight in a lot of ways. He's not very emotional. He goes by rules, and responsibility, and has a hard time just letting go and really living." He shook his head. "No, I can't really say that. To him he *is* living. We just choose to live in different ways. I played sports and went to dances and got drunk when I was too young. Jacob has always been older than his years. He couldn't understand that kind of thing. To him, I was just an irresponsible kid who didn't take anything seriously. To me, he needed to chill the fuck out once in a while."

Both men laughed. "So yeah, the animosity and hell, the fact that we just couldn't understand each other was always there. People say their sibling is their best friend, but I've never known that. It got a whole hell of a lot worse when I only finished part of law school and decided that there was no fucking way I could ever do that with my life. Dad's a lawyer. His dad was a lawyer. The firm has been passed through our family. Everyone except for me, I guess. I was skirting my family responsibility to play in the gym. That's what Jacob thinks, at least."

There was more to it than that, obviously, but Drew didn't feel like getting into the whole situation with Iris. Didn't want to share that yes, in a way, he'd fucked up. He hadn't initially pushed her away when she kissed him, but also, it hurt like hell that Jacob would think that of him. That he'd think Drew would try to take a woman away from him.

Justin didn't reply for a moment; he didn't look at Drew either. His eyes were lost, his brain a hundred miles away. Drew could see it in the way he spaced off. Drew immediately felt like shit for complaining about his relationship with Jacob. At least they had one.

"Maybe I should be grateful I never knew I had siblings then?" He tried to smile, but his eyes didn't light up when he did. Sure, they hadn't known each other for long, but he'd seen Justin's smile. It was electric, when he meant it, but the spark wasn't there this time.

Drew waited. Maybe he should say something. Maybe it wasn't his business. Just when he thought he couldn't hold back, Justin spoke. "I wonder sometimes, how our lives would have been different if we'd grown up knowing about each other. If Shanen and Landon would have come and spent summers with us, or if we would have sent Christmas cards every year. Would we be close? Hell, maybe we'd hate each other if we'd grown up together. It's really fucking shitty to have had that taken away from us. Not to have had a say in the whole damn thing."

The pain in Justin's voice was a punch to Drew's gut. Jesus, he felt bad for the man. "I'm sorry." He wished there was more he could say.

"Yeah, me too." Justin shook his head and then pushed to his feet. "You cooked so I'll do the dishes. After that, I should probably head out. I hate to ask you this, but can you take me back to my car?"

Drew waved him off. "Of course. It's no problem at all, and I'll help with the dishes." Somehow he knew if he told Justin not to do them at all, he would insist.

So that's what they did. Justin rinsed and Drew loaded the dishwasher. He gave Justin the spare toothbrush he hadn't opened yet, and while Justin brushed his teeth, Drew threw on a shirt, shoes, and socks.

It was only a few minutes later when they were out the door and heading back to Justin's car. When they pulled up, Drew let the engine idle, and Justin didn't get out. He felt it, the need to say something, but what, he didn't know. That he respected Justin? To repeat how sorry he was for what he was going through? That he enjoyed Justin's company and wanted to hang out again? All of those things were true. What he settled on was, "I'm serious about the gym. I'd love for you to come down and exercise with me. Or by yourself. Whatever."

"You just want to ogle my ass while I work out."

Ah, so they were back to the flirting. He liked the flirting…but he liked the other stuff too. "So? It's a nice ass."

"You don't know the half of it." Justin winked at him, and then said, "We'll see. I'm not sure how things are going to go with my dad. I have your number. I'll call you."

Drew nodded. He understood but also felt a knot in his gut at the same time. "You can call for more than that, too. I think I might like hanging out with you, Sleeping Beauty."

Justin nodded, nudged him with his elbow and replied, "Right back at you, Cinderella."

Drew watched as Justin opened the door, got out, and then slammed it. He made it a few steps away before he stopped, turned around, came back and opened the door again. "Thank you. For letting me drink, and taking me home with you. For the talks, breakfast. Just…thank you."

Before Drew could tell him no problem, Justin closed the door. This time, he didn't turn back, and Drew didn't look away. Not until Justin climbed into his car and disappeared from sight.

CHAPTER SEVEN

"THANKS FOR COMING out here with me." Justin glanced at Landon in the passenger seat. They were almost to Nick's, the restaurant Bryce's partner owned where Justin would be working as a waiter. It wasn't his dream job, but hey, it would work. It would get him out of the house, which was something he desperately needed.

"No problem. Figured it would give us some time to hang out." Landon's voice was similar to their father's. Justin wondered if he realized that. If he knew that when Justin closed his eyes, he could swear it was their father speaking. Not their dad now, but the way he'd been when he was growing up.

He'd been told that about himself as well. Justin didn't hear it. Did Landon hear it in himself? Did he hear their father's voice in Justin? Did he think they sounded like each other? "Check us out. We're doing the brotherly bonding thing." Justin played it off like it wasn't a big deal. As though he didn't feel conflicting emotions and fears where his family was concerned.

"Better than punching walls," Landon added and they both chuckled. When Landon first discovered his dad was back and his sibling status had changed, he hadn't been happy. They'd spoken, just the two of them, and the day ended with Landon breaking his hand on a wall, and Justin taking him to get it checked out.

"That it is." Justin exited the freeway and then asked, "How's Shanen?" Because he didn't know what else to talk about. It had been two weeks since the party at her house. They talked a few days ago on the phone, and she stopped by to see their dad often, but

Justin tried to give her space when she did. Both Shanen and Landon had missed so many years with their dad, it didn't feel right to encroach on that time.

"She's good. Keeping busy with work, her husband, and everything else she does. We have a strong sister. She'll always be okay."

The words stabbed at his heart. They weren't meant to be taken negatively but they were. Landon and Shanen would always know each other better than Justin would know them. They would always have stories that Justin would never be a part of. "That's good to hear."

"She's always been mentally tough. I'm not sure I'd be with Rod right now if it weren't for her. If she hadn't helped me to get past my fears, I might have let myself walk away from the love of my life before I even had the chance to realize that's who he was."

He was surprised at Landon's admission. They didn't talk about things that really mattered much. He figured there were too many to choose from, or they were both just tired of the heavy, so when they spoke, it was usually about superficial topics instead of the elephant that was always in the room.

"I'm glad you guys had each other." And he was, but that didn't mean there wasn't a very real part of him that was jealous too.

"Shit. I'm sorry. I didn't mean..."

"No. It's okay. It is what it is," Justin added as he made another turn. There was no reason for Landon to feel guilty about anything that had happened to them. He'd done nothing wrong. That had all been their father.

"So...Dad and your mom...they never tried to have any other kids or anything?" He heard the slight quiver in Landon's voice. The pain in the question. Justin had been an accident. Did their dad *try* to have other kids after leaving Landon and Shanen behind?

"She got pregnant once. I don't know if it was intentional or not. She lost the baby. It was hard on her. Dad had a vasectomy not long afterward."

Landon nodded, and Justin didn't know what to say after that. Fuck, this was hard.

"When we were kids, Shanen wanted a little sister. Mom was single, of course. She never dated anyone seriously after Dad left, so Shanen did all this research on adoption. This will give you a little insight into our sister. She wrote a ten-page paper about the benefits of adoption. How many kids were looking for homes, what feeling unwanted could do to someone's mental health, and basically ragged on having a brother and how much happier she would be with a sister."

He laughed and Justin found himself smiling too.

"Well hell. I've already disappointed her since I'm a man."

"You and me both, brother," Landon added and the word brother settled into Justin's chest. It was a figure of speech like *bro*, or *man*, but it still sent warmth through him.

"What'd she do with the paper?" Justin asked.

"She sat Mom and me down and presented the whole damn thing to us like a speech. I just wanted to go outside and play. Mom tried not to laugh because Shanen put so much work into it. Obviously, there was no sister, but Shanen was proud of herself regardless. She's always been that way. She's a good person. She goes for what she wants."

Justin realized then that he wanted to hear more. Wanted to know those stories. To be a part of them. He had stories of their dad, but he couldn't tell those. How could he? How could he say, *Hey, this is what I did with our dad after he left you?* It wouldn't be right. So he asked, "Have you always been close?"

"Yeah," Landon replied. "Always. I think that's why it bothers her so much that Jacob isn't close to his brother. I could see the tension between them at the party. Could you?"

Yes...yes he could. He also knew about it from Drew. There was a small twinge of guilt at that, like Landon was opening up to him and Justin was keeping something from him. "Yeah. And what do you mean it bothers her?"

"She just wants them to be close. I think this—what's happening with us has to do with it as well. She called me angry the other day because she got in an argument with Jacob about his brother. I guess she wants to involve him more in their lives, bring them closer, but Jacob isn't having it."

First, Jacob sounded like a dickhead to him. What the fuck was his problem with Drew? It all sounded pretty superficial to Justin. Second, he realized Landon and Shanen really were close. They leaned on each other and spoke to each other. He envied them that. And third, he wasn't sure if it was a good idea to bring up the fact that he and Drew had spoken, flirted, spent the night together—even if Justin had been passed out on the couch—and that he thought he wanted to hang out with the man again. He didn't want to cause any problems within his new family.

Which probably meant he shouldn't spend time with Drew at all.

Justin didn't respond because they'd pulled into the parking lot of Nick's. It was a nice restaurant. The sign boasted about their unique comfort food.

A fucking restaurant.

It wasn't that he had a problem with working in one, but it just added to the already massive mountain of changes in his life. He'd finally decided to pursue a career he would love, and now, even though it was temporary, it felt like going backward instead of forward.

They made their way inside to see Nick standing at the hostess counter waiting for them. The dark-haired man held out his hand for Justin and he shook it. "Hey, Justin. It's good to see you again."

"Good to see you as well. I appreciate you giving me this job under the circumstances." The truth was, he'd likely only work a day or two a week. This wasn't permanent. When his father passed, he'd go back to North Carolina. That couldn't be the kind of employee Nick was looking for.

"It's no problem. Seriously. I wouldn't do it if I didn't want to. It works out perfectly, actually. One of my waitresses took a semester off college so she's looking to pick up hours, but not permanently. She can take the hours you don't, and then when you leave and she's back in school, I can hire someone else on. It helps her out, and she's a good kid, so that's important to me."

That was nice of him. Justin respected him for it. Not a lot of employers would look at it that way.

Nick gave him a tour of the restaurant, a uniform, and a few other things. He'd already filled out all of the information he needed to online.

If he was being honest, he hated it. Hated this whole situation. He didn't want to wait tables a day or two per week. He wanted his life back, but he also knew that he couldn't continue doing nothing. Some days he felt like he would burst at the seams from all the pent-up energy.

It wasn't long before they were on their way out again. Just as he turned for the driver's side, Landon grabbed a hold of his arm. "Listen…I was thinking I'd like to take Dad out on my motorcycle before the weather changes and…before he's not able. Not right now, but soon. Shan said I should talk to you about it first." Landon let go of him and ran a hand of over his face. "And hell, part of me is nervous to do it at all. It feels like…like too much. Because I'm still pissed at him. So fucking pissed it hurts to look at him. I don't know how you do it, man. How you let go of that, but I know it's important to try."

Justin's gut rolled and his muscles went rigid. He hadn't let go of anything. He'd told Landon that, and the more time that passed, he realized he was more and more angry too because he didn't know his own fucking place in his family.

He didn't answer with any of that, though. He just smiled and said, "Yeah, I think he'd like that." Justin knew his dad would love it because, more than anything, he knew that man wanted to fix his relationship with his first son.

CHAPTER EIGHT

"**G**OOD WORKOUT TODAY, Martha. You should be proud of yourself." Drew wrapped his arm around the older woman and gave her a quick hug.

"I am. Thank you. I...I feel a little invincible." She smiled, having used the gym's name, and Drew's chest filled with warmth. She'd never exercised at a gym a day in her life before she came to see him six months ago. Her husband of thirty-five years had passed away of a heart attack at the age of sixty-five, and Martha made the decision that she wanted to start taking care of herself in different ways. To make sure she was around to torture her grandkids the same way she'd done her children, she'd joked with Drew.

"You are," he told her. He loved this part of his job. Loved making people fall in love with physical activity and hard work.

"You better watch out." Martha winked and squeezed his bicep. "I'll be just as strong as you before you know it." He chuckled and watched as she made her way to the women's locker room. He didn't have another client today, but did have a mountain of paperwork in his office that he needed to get done. He'd put it off too long, and set today up specifically so he could take a couple hours for it.

Drew turned to head for the desk so he could let his front desk manager know that she was in charge while Drew went to his office. That's when he saw him—Justin standing at the circular counter in a black, sleeveless T-shirt. He was leaning over the counter, speaking to Robyn, and damned if Drew didn't realize he was smiling.

Drew crossed his arms and walked, slipping behind the counter to stand beside Robyn. "Well, look who it is," he said to Justin.

"I heard you're running a special. No registration fee."

Robyn started, "Oh no. We're not—"

"It's okay, Robyn. Thanks. I'll take care of him."

She looked back and forth between Drew and Justin for a moment, before heading to the computer and sitting down.

"You're here," Drew said and then immediately realized he was a fucking idiot. Obviously, Justin was here since he stood right in front of him. He felt slightly off balance, a little surprised to see him, though he wasn't sure why it mattered so much.

"That I am. There's no contract, right? I feel like you have to hand over your life to cancel your gym membership."

"How very Chandler of you," Drew replied. "I'm pretty sure we can work something out. Follow me." He led Justin to one of the three tables to the left of the front desk where they signed up new members. He sat on one side of the large, dark pine while Justin sat on the other side.

"It's nice," Justin told him, as he leaned forward with his elbows on the desk. "I like it."

He looked around, tried to see it through Justin's eyes—the inspiring quotes on the walls. The two sections, some with mirrors and some without. Some people fed off seeing themselves as they worked out, others didn't. He wanted the environment comfortable for everyone.

On the other side of the desks where they sat was a juice bar for smoothies. He had bright couches in the area for people to relax after changing if they wanted.

"Thanks. We have a room for cycle classes. They kick your ass. There are saunas in the locker rooms and obviously weights, resistance, and cardio." He felt odd, as though he was trying to sell himself to Justin, which in a way he was. That was part of the gig.

Justin shrugged. "I love a good cardio workout."

Drew grinned. "Are we talking sex here?"

Playfully, Justin gasped. "Someone has their mind in the gutter...but now that you mention it, it does burn a whole hell of a lot of calories in a fun way."

It wasn't as if he could argue about that. It had been a while since Drew had sex, and if he was being honest, the idea was quite appealing. But he'd be lying if he didn't admit there were nerves as well since he'd never fucked a man before. "True. Unfortunately, it doesn't go over real well in a public gym."

"Sometimes they make the shittiest laws. People are offended by everything."

He couldn't help but laugh and Justin did too. He had a million things to do that afternoon, but still he found himself pulling out the forms to be signed. There was no reason he couldn't have Robyn do this, but he knew he wouldn't. Paperwork could wait. He'd come back in tonight to do it if he had to.

Drew handed the forms to Justin. They spoke about fees and he entered Justin's information into the computer. He was silent as Drew did so, looking down and picking at the brand name on his basketball shorts.

There was something heavy in the set of his shoulders, which really wasn't a fucking epiphany or anything. The guy was going through hell, but Drew had a feeling today had been an especially bad day. The urge was there, teasing at his tongue to ask him, but Drew didn't know if he should. If it was his place. If he were in Justin's situation, he doubted he would want to talk about it.

"Come on." Drew stood after finishing the paperwork. "I'll give you a tour. I was going to work out anyway, if you want some company."

Justin paused, studied Drew in a way he didn't understand and then said, "Yeah, I think I'd like that. Just don't try to show me up. I'd hate to have to embarrass you."

Drew playfully rolled his eyes. "I wouldn't think of

it…but…what did you call it? Pretentious?"

"What? I would never say a thing like that!"

They moved around the desk and toward the main section of the gym. "Oh, my bad. I don't know what I was thinking."

"Maybe that's some internalized shit going on there. It's okay to admit that you like to look sexy. That you want people's eyes on you."

Drew nudged him in the side with his elbow. "You keep calling me that."

"It's true. Should I not, though? Fuck. I'm sorry. I don't think anyone heard me. I didn't think about that."

"No, no," Drew told him. No, it wasn't really a known fact that he was bisexual, but Drew also didn't worry about keeping it a secret. If people found out, they did. He wasn't ashamed of who he was attracted to. "It's fine. Call me sexy all you want."

"Oh, so you like it when I flirt with you?"

"Who doesn't like to be flirted with? Now quit stalling and come on. Don't expect me to go easy on you just because you think I'm hot."

Justin laughed a deep, throaty laugh that Drew liked the sound of.

"I wouldn't think of it," he said, and then they got to work.

THEY STARTED OUT doing twenty minutes of cardio on the treadmill. Justin jogged at a nice, steady pace but it didn't take long for him to realize that he sucked at running. Drew had hardly broken a sweat and yet salty liquid burned his eyes.

But the slight burn in Justin's muscles was welcoming. It made him feel strangely alive. It wasn't that Justin wasn't physical, because he was. He played basketball and liked to hike. He didn't keep himself locked up in the house, but it was a different kind of exercise than this.

When the twenty minutes was over, he stepped off the treadmill. "Well, looks like I have better stamina than you," Drew joked.

"Oh, no, no, no no. We aren't going there. I promise you. My stamina is just fine."

"Just making an observation," Drew added and then, "Come on. I'm not done with you yet."

He let Drew set up a workout routine for him. He grabbed a clipboard and wrote everything down for Justin as they went. Every once in a while, he'd stop to talk to a club member—to spot someone, or to show them the right way to perform an exercise.

It was obvious the people here loved Drew. He stopped and spoke to most people or they'd stop him, even if it was just to say hi. Justin could see how much Drew loved what he did and how much the people here thought of him. He wasn't surprised about that, not in the least, because regardless of the fact that he didn't know Drew well, he thought a lot of him too.

If he was being honest with himself, he'd admit it was why he came here in the first place. He was acting like a child after his afternoon with Landon, spending way too much time being angry, and he wanted something to distract him from that.

Another dose of honesty? Despite the fact that their workout was ending and he needed to get back to his dad, he wasn't ready for it to be over yet.

"Can I let you in on a secret?" Drew asked as he wiped his face with a towel. Justin did the same.

"Yep."

"Pizza is my downfall. I might have some in the fridge in my office."

Justin cocked a brow at him. "You're a fake. Talking shit to me about healthy eating and you hide pizza in your office. I don't know if I can believe a word of what you say anymore."

Drew crossed his arms and frowned. "When someone lets you in on a secret, you're not supposed to make them feel like shit about it. Now come on before I regret telling you I practically get off on cheese and pepperoni goodness."

Christ, he liked Drew's sense of humor. "Lead the way."

He followed Drew to an office that he unlocked before leading Justin in. It was… "Ever thought about cleaning this place? I heard you should do that at least once a year." There were papers everywhere. Stacked on the desk, on the shelves—folders and papers and sticky notes and anything else you could think of.

"Hey. Fuck you. I know where everything is." Drew closed the door and Justin couldn't help but think about how different this was from Drew's home. It had been incredibly clean there, everything put together, yet this place looked like a goddamn tornado had run through it.

"I think it's impossible to know where everything is in this place."

"Sit down before I regret bringing you into my inner sanctum."

As he moved toward one of the chairs, he realized how sweaty he was. "I should probably just go. Some asshole just ran me ragged out there."

"Sounds like a smart asshole," Drew replied. "And sit down. I own a gym. Like I give a shit about sweat."

So he did.

Drew grabbed a small pizza box out of the fridge and put two pieces on two paper plates. He popped the first one in the microwave, then grabbed a bottle of water from the fridge and tossed it to Justin. "Eat pizza but drink water. I'll hook you up with some good protein drinks as well."

Fucking protein drinks. What in the hell was this guy trying to do to him?

When the microwave dinged, he gave Justin the plate and then popped his own in. A minute later, they were sitting across the desk and mountain of papers from each other, eating pizza and drinking water.

"How was your day?" Drew asked him.

He shrugged. "It was okay. Landon and I went out to the restaurant his buddy owns. I'll work there a day or two a week. Joy will help with Dad. Got my paperwork filled out and looks like I'm ready to go."

He felt a pang in his chest. *It's temporary,* he told himself, but the shorter the time he had to spend at Nick's meant the shorter time his father was around. He had no reason to stick around here once he was gone.

Gone.

Christ, that word made his gut ache.

Drew finished chewing and then swallowed some water. "You've temporarily changed your whole life. You left your home. I hope people see that. The sacrifices you're making."

His head snapped up and his eyes locked with Drew's blue ones. *Thank you* was there because he really fucking appreciated Drew saying that, Drew feeling it, but he just shook his head. "It's not a big deal. You do that shit for family."

"It *is* a big deal, though. Maybe some people do those things for family but others wouldn't. That doesn't change the fact that you're here and you've sacrificed things. You should know that it's important, and I respect you for it."

He'd needed to hear that. Fuck, he really had. Part of Justin hated the fact that he did but it soothed some of the pain inside of him. "Thank you. I appreciate you saying that."

They looked at each other again and Drew nodded. "It's true. And family is a funny thing. I think we both know that. Some of the most complicated relationships are with those we're supposed to love the most. Those who are supposed to be there for us through thick and thin."

Justin got that. He could see that Drew did as well. They both felt it because of different circumstances in their own lives. It connected them. Made Justin feel like he had someone here who had his best interests at heart. Or maybe he was being dramatic and he should just think of it as actually having a friend here.

Yes, he had his father. He had his siblings, but they had each other in a way Justin wasn't a part of. Justin had more time with their dad, but as much as he hated feeling that way, he thought he owed Shanen and Landon this time because of it. This time to fix their relationships, which left Justin on the sidelines.

Much like Drew seemed to feel in his own family. Drew got that part of him that probably no one else could.

"I should probably go." Why the fuck did he just say that? Still, he tossed his plate in the trash and finished his water. "Thanks for the workout and the food."

Drew finished his drink and then stood as well. They both walked to the door together, Drew behind him. Justin reached out…grabbed the knob…and stopped. "Fuck," he whispered before leaning forward and letting his forehead rest against the door. "I had a shitty day. Not the whole thing. It was nice to be around Landon. To get to know him some more, but then—Christ this is hard. There are no rules for this. I'm jealous when I shouldn't be and angry when I shouldn't be. I just…" he shook his head. His brain told him to shut the fuck up but he didn't. His mouth just kept moving.

"I came here because I somehow knew you'd get it. Nothing in Virginia feels like it's mine—the house, the job, my family. My dad doesn't even feel like he's mine anymore. This friendship is the only thing that feels like it belongs to me." What the fuck was wrong with him? Justin didn't do shit like this. Didn't get emotional like this. Hell, this was only the fourth time he'd seen Drew and here he was making a declaration like that? Especially when the truth was, even this friendship wasn't really his. Not when you looked at it. Drew was Shanen's brother-in-law. That was more important.

"My head is all fucked up. Can we pretend I didn't say that?" He pulled away from the door and stood straight up. When he turned around, Drew was there, closer than he had been before.

Drew reached his hand up and cupped Justin's cheek. Then his other hand was on the other side of his face. Drew was holding him and then leaning forward, his tongue swiping at Justin's lip.

It was a different kiss than those they shared at the club. Slow and exploratory. Still fucking hungry as his tongue probed Justin's mouth. As Drew moaned into him, ground his body against Justin's, pushing him against the door.

But it wasn't a *fuck-me* kiss. Not that the erection against him didn't say that. Still, it was passionate, and honest, in a way Justin wasn't sure he'd ever kissed anyone.

He wanted to drop to his knees. Wanted Drew's dick in his mouth. Drew's come on his tongue…but this was nice too, really fucking nice. Drew's hard body against his and the slight scent of sweat teasing his nose.

Drew's lips slid from his mouth, down his throat, and then he licked Justin's collarbone. Shoved his face in Justin's neck and nipped at the skin there before pulling away completely.

"I want to see you again. Outside of here, I mean. I know you have things going on that are much more important than hanging out with me, but if you have time, I want to see you."

"Yeah," Justin told him. "I think I'd like that too."

CHAPTER NINE

"IT WAS YOUR closing argument that sealed the deal, Jacob. That was incredibly powerful stuff." Drew glanced at his father, who sat at the head of the table. It wasn't often they had family dinners like this. His parents traveled a lot, but they'd been home more recently. He thought it might be because of Shanen's family, and what she was going through.

Pride gleamed in his father's eyes as he looked at Jacob. He had to admit, it had hurt a bit when he was younger—the fact that whatever he did would never be as good as what Jacob did—but he'd come to terms with it now. They were different people and wanted different things. Drew was damn proud of what he'd accomplished.

"Thank you," Jacob replied before taking a drink of his wine. Shanen sat beside him, gleaming at her husband, and it made him think of Justin. He'd been doing that too often since Justin left his office the week before. They'd exchanged texts a few times since then, and he'd seen Justin one other time at the gym, but they had yet to spend more time together.

Maybe he shouldn't have asked Justin when he had. Maybe spending time with Drew would just be something else to add to his list, but he hoped not.

Jacob added, "Raymond never would have been charged if he hadn't been black. You and I both know that. It was important to me. You know how I feel about that kind of injustice."

And it was true. Despite their rocky relationship, Drew highly respected Jacob. He fought for what he believed in. He was fair.

He'd taken the case he'd just won, pro bono because it was the right thing to do. Jacob believed in the law. In following the rules. In right and wrong and justice prevailing when it was the *right* thing, and not just to win.

In that moment, when the burn hit his chest, he realized how much it really did bother him that they weren't closer. That they didn't know how to speak to each other. "Congratulations, Jake. I'm proud of you," Drew said, and he really was proud of his brother.

Jacob looked his way and gave him a quick nod. "Thank you, Andrew."

Jesus, he wished his family would call him Drew. He'd always preferred it to Andrew, but with his family, the name had never stuck.

"What about you, Andrew?" his mom asked. "Are you keeping a steady number of memberships at Invincible?"

Drew almost laughed at the question. Again, not that he wasn't proud of what he did, but the glaring differences between him and Jacob were a bright, fucking beacon that you couldn't really miss.

"It's good, Ma. Thanks for asking."

She rolled her eyes, but had a playful smile on her lips. "*Ma.* I almost expect you to give me a high five when you talk to me like that. It sounds like you're speaking to one of your friends."

He winked at her. "Sorry, Mom. But things are good. I'm implementing this new—"

"Oh, Jacob, I've been meaning to ask you, about the Charleston case," his dad interrupted and the conversation was officially off of Drew and back to Jacob. He didn't mind. Not really. They weren't passionate about the same things, and that's just the way it was.

Drew took a bite of his salad, and when he glanced up, Shanen looked at him, a sad smile curling the edge of her lips down. She tried to smile at him, but she felt bad for him. Drew could see it in the way she looked at him. It was a surprise but he wasn't sure why.

He gave her a quick nod, trying to say it didn't matter.

He wanted to ask her about Justin. Wanted to tell her he was hurting, because he wasn't sure Justin let any of them know he was. Obviously, they had to know his father's illness pained him, but did they see that his life had been turned upside down as well? Did they know the sacrifices he'd made?

He wondered how they would feel if they knew he and Justin were becoming friends. Shanen wouldn't mind. There was no doubt in his mind about that. Jacob would feel Drew was encroaching in his territory, in his life, there was no doubt about that either. Landon, he wasn't sure about. He assumed the man wouldn't have a problem with it, but he didn't know much about Landon other than the fact that he was Shanen's brother, and that he loved motorcycles and his boyfriend.

He let his eyes drift to his family. Watched as they spoke about Jacob and another case. How would they feel if they knew Drew was bisexual? His family was fairly liberal. They really were good people, but they also sometimes judged without realizing they were judging. They also likely wouldn't understand that Drew was attracted to men *and* women. They were very black and white, left or right, right or wrong. They sometimes struggled with things that weren't one or another.

"How's your father doing, Shanen?" his mom's soft voice asked when there was a lull in the conversation.

That caught Drew's attention immediately. His pulse quickened and his stomach rolled.

Shanen didn't answer right away. Jacob wrapped an arm around her shoulders. The air in the dining room changed, got heavier. They were eating on expensive China and the room was decorated in expensive things. The table sat ten, the other half empty. Everything in this room was perfect looking at it, but in the grand scheme of things, none of it mattered. What mattered was family and friends.

"The chemo and cancer have definitely taken its toll on his body. I don't…he doesn't look good. There's an appointment coming up, so I guess we'll know more then, but I don't anticipate it being good news." Jacob wiped the tears from her eyes as he pulled her closer and kissed her forehead.

The rolling in Drew's stomach turned to a heaviness in his chest.

"Is he still living with…I'm sorry. I can't remember his name, but your other brother?"

"Justin," Drew answered his mom's question before Shanen had the chance to. "His name is Justin." Four sets of eyes turned his way. "I remember from the party." Drew shrugged.

"He is," Shanen replied. "I've considered talking to him about it, though. I feel like we should be helping more. He stays with Mom sometimes, but Jacob and I have a lot more space. Justin is sleeping on the couch in the house they're sharing. I've been considering asking him if maybe Dad should stay with us. We could also get a part-time nurse to help out, but I'm not sure if that's the right thing to do. I don't want Justin to feel as though I'm trying to take over. It's just—" she shook her head, a few more tears rolling down her face—"it's a touchy situation that I don't know how to navigate. None of us do."

Touchy was putting it lightly. He had a feeling Justin would be crushed if they wanted Larry to stay with Shanen. Justin would take it personally, as though he wasn't included. His heart hurt at the thought.

Drew leaned away from the table, suddenly having lost his appetite.

JUSTIN WALKED TO the kitchen table and sat across from his dad. He was doing a puzzle, his wheelchair locked tight as he worked on it.

It was so strange seeing him like this. It was his father. He'd always been larger than life. Before Justin met him, he used to imagine all of the different things he could be—a SWAT team member, the president. Maybe he'd been undercover and was traveling the world protecting people, which had been why he couldn't be with Justin.

When his dad came back into his life, it hadn't mattered that he was none of those things. It hadn't mattered that he hadn't been around. The only thing he'd cared about was the fact that he was his father, and was there.

The older he'd gotten, things changed, of course, but he'd never had anything except respect for his father. Had never seen him as anything other than strength, and love, until he found out about Shanen and Landon.

Then his dad had become a liar, the kind of man who left his kids.

And Justin struggled to see anything other than his illness when he looked at him, especially since they were in the middle of another round of treatment and each one was harder on him.

Every time he saw his father, he noticed more differences. Joy had stepped up to the plate a lot lately. During training at the restaurant, he'd agreed to work extra days. They were short shifts, but in the last two weeks, he'd worked six days. "Maybe this job thing wasn't a good idea. I feel bad that Joy has to keep coming over to take care of you."

His dad scoffed. "No one has to take care of me. I told you both I'd be fine on my own."

"Can we not do this again?" Justin sighed. "You could do a whole hell of a lot worse than having people who care about you and want to make sure you're okay."

His father flinched and then leaned back in his chair. "You're right. I know you're right, and I know I probably don't deserve any of it. I'm just feeling extra tired today. Not really feeling so hot."

Worry bounced around inside Justin like a pinball in a pinball machine. "Why? What's wrong?" Did they need to go to the doctor? Hell, maybe he should tell Nick he was sorry but the job hadn't been a good idea. He already felt like he was skirting responsibility but the money he had put away wouldn't last forever either…

"Has the diarrhea gotten any better?"

"Please don't. I know you want to help but," his dad groaned, "speaking with my son about how often I have to take a shit, having you help me to the bathroom in a hurry it's…hard. It makes me feel helpless." He shook his head. "I have cancer, Justin. I'm always going to be tired and I'm always going to feel bad. I didn't mean to worry you. I'll be okay." His hands trembled and he squeezed his eyes tightly for a second.

His dad had never been good at accepting help. He'd never been good at vulnerability, and now he didn't have a choice. Justin knew how much the man hated that. He couldn't imagine dealing with the things his father did. It was hard enough on his side, hard enough to see. How would he handle it if he was the one who couldn't do these things on his own? Justin wouldn't want to talk about it either.

"You have cancer? Holy shit. I didn't know. That explains a lot." It wasn't something to joke about. He wanted to tell his dad it would be okay. That he would beat his disease, but they both knew that wasn't likely. But like Justin hoped he would, his father laughed.

Before he had the chance to say anything else, there was a knock at the door. Justin stood to get it, but as he began walking away, his dad reached for him and grabbed his hand. "Thank you, son. I don't know that I've thanked you for all that you've done for me."

Justin opened his mouth, but the words were lodged in his throat. His dad's thanks played through his head. As much as he hated it, he'd needed to hear those words. Needed to know he still held his place in the man's life. "It's—"

Knock, knock, knock.

"Come in!" His dad's rough, sickly voice called, taking away Justin's chance to say anything back.

Joy came in and he saw his dad's eyes light up at the sight of her. He let go of Justin's hand, as she kneeled on the other side of the wheelchair. "How are you doing today, Larry?" she asked.

"Good," he told her. "Thank you for coming."

And for no damn reason, Justin knew he had to get the fuck out of the house before he lost his mind.

CHAPTER TEN

JUSTIN'S HEAD WASN'T in the game all night at work. He had no real reason to be a mess. Well, no reason besides the same ones he had every day, but the longer he spent taking orders and carrying trays of food back and forth, the more on edge he felt. He'd spilled two drinks and gotten an order wrong.

There was a strong possibility he'd also bitten a few heads off with snappish replies.

But he'd made it. It was the end of the night, and he was getting ready to leave when Nick approached him. He nodded toward a table next to them and asked, "Got a minute?"

He tried not to curse out loud. For all he knew, someone had complained about him and they probably had every right to. Justin knew he'd been a bear all night, and not the sexy, leather kind. It was more of the *I'm-a-dickhead-so-stay-out-of-my-way* variety. He owed Nick better than this. The man had given him a job, and Justin took that seriously. He prided himself on good work.

He pulled out a chair and sat. The second Nick sat across from him, Justin said, "Listen, I'm sorry about tonight. My head's a mess right now, but that's no excuse. I apologize if anyone complained and I promise you, it won't happen again."

Nick frowned, little wrinkles forming beside his mouth. "I was just going to ask you if everything is okay. No one said a word, but I could tell you're having a rough night. Is there anything I can do?"

Jesus, he appreciated that. Nick was a good man. Justin didn't know him well, but that was obvious. It made him feel even shittier about doing a bad job tonight. "No, thank you. You've already been incredibly kind. I appreciate you giving me a shot. I'll make sure my moods don't show while I'm here."

Nick leaned back in the chair, and looked at him. There was understanding in his eyes, mixed with what looked like sadness. "Make sure you take care of yourself. That's the most important thing. I know it's easy to abandon what you need for others, but taking care of yourself has to be a priority and…" Nick cleared his throat, before he continued. "I lost my father some years back. We don't know one another well, but if you need someone to talk to, I'm around. If you need anything, don't hesitate to ask. Bryce and I will both do whatever we can to help." Nick's face lit up at the mention of his partner's name. Justin could see how much they meant to each other. He'd seen it the night of his dad's party and he saw it again now.

"Thanks, man. The two of you…I can see how happy you are together, and by the sound of it, you're both good guys." It was partially said to change the subject, but also because his words were true. He was glad Landon had friends like them. It was important to him to know that his brother was surrounded by kind people.

"Thank you. He's a crazy son of a bitch. You'll see when you get to know him better. Sometimes I think I want to strangle him but I don't know what I'd do without him. He makes me look at the world differently. Makes me smile when I don't feel like smiling. Takes a special person to do that."

Briefly, he wondered if his dad had ever felt that way about his mom. Hell, if she felt that way about him. He didn't think so, and that hurt. There was something between Joy and his father that he'd never seen in his own parents. "I have a feeling he'd say the same thing about you," Justin told Nick. There wasn't a doubt in his mind that Bryce felt just as strongly about Nick as Nick felt about Bryce. It was the same way between Landon and Rod.

Nick chuckled. "Probably. He'd likely say a whole lot of things, half of which would embarrass the hell out of me. I was going through a pretty big life change when I met him. We started out as friends, just spending time together and talking to each other. The more I was with him, the more time I *wanted* to spend with him. Before I knew it, I realized I looked forward to talking to him more than I ever had anyone else. And the rest is, as they say, history."

He knew the only reason Nick was likely saying all of this to him was to distract him. To try and take his mind off of things and Justin appreciated it. But as much as he appreciated the effort, he still couldn't shut his brain down. He couldn't stop himself from seeing his dad in his wheelchair or overthinking Joy and Landon and Shanen—his father's family. "Sounds like fate did some intervening there." He wasn't sure he believed in fate, but it sounded nice.

DREW SAT IN his office taking care of paperwork. It was late. The gym had closed a while ago. Everyone long gone except him and too much shit to do.

He was beat.

Drew pushed back from the desk, dropped his head back and groaned. He wanted to go home. Go to bed. Wave a fucking magic wand and make all this stuff he had to do go away.

He startled when his cell vibrated against his desk. Okay, so that didn't typically startle him. He definitely needed some rest. Drew fumbled to pick the phone up, because people didn't usually text him this late.

He was surprised to see Justin's name on the screen. He punched the button so Justin's text popped up.

> **I didn't pay close enough attention to the hours of operation. Guess it's a good thing for me you're a workaholic? Standing outside. I probably look like I'm casing the place to break in. Come save me. Getting arrested is the last thing I need.**

A laugh tumbled out of his mouth as Drew pushed to his feet. He grabbed the keys off his desk and then made his way to the front door. Sure enough, Justin stood on the other side of the glass. He had a gym bag in his right hand and looked to be wearing his uniform from the restaurant.

He ran his left hand through his short, brown hair and the second their eyes made contact, Justin shrugged as if to say sorry...or maybe that he didn't know what he was doing here, which made Drew a little sad. He wanted Justin to know he could come to Drew. They were friends, but he also wanted Justin to have more than just him. To feel comfortable in his own family. Drew knew what it was like to feel different than your closest relatives, but he never felt as though he didn't have a place with them.

Drew gave him a small smile, turned off the alarm, and unlocked the door. His pulse sped up as he did it. There was excitement there, brewing beneath the surface, because damned if he didn't enjoy spending time with Justin.

A few seconds later, he pulled the door open and Justin came inside. He smelled slightly of spaghetti sauce, and as Drew closed and locked the door, he wondered if Justin served it tonight.

"I'm sorry," Justin said before he had the chance to speak. "I know this is odd. I shouldn't be here. It's late, but I got off work and needed to burn off some energy. I drove by and saw that you were here, and now I am too." He winked and gave Drew a sexy half-grin that got the attention of his cock. He was trying to be playful, which Drew liked about Justin. There were no two ways about it, he did it for Drew, but Jesus, was now the time to fuck around with each other? The answer to that was *no*.

"If you are heading out, it's fine. I just—"

"No," Drew interrupted him. It didn't matter that a few moments ago, he'd wanted nothing more than to go home. He was here and he'd stay here as long as Justin needed him to. "I'm not going anywhere. You're welcome to stay. I have a mountain of shit to do, so unfortunately, I can't join you, but it can't hurt anything for you to get a workout in since I'm here. Exercise, shower, whatever you need. I'll just be pulling my fucking hair out running numbers."

"Don't do that." Justin nudged him with his arm. "It's nice hair, even if you do cover it up with that fucking hat all the time."

Drew adjusted the cap on his head. "I like hats. You don't like my hat? I think I look sexy in it."

"Cocky, cocky, cocky," Justin admonished. "I'm giving you shit. It looks good on you. You're the jock everyone wants to fuck."

A shrill of excitement zipped through him. He hadn't gotten to do nearly enough exploring and he wanted to do that with Justin. At the same time, the thought of being fucked left an uneasy feeling settling at the base of his spine. Not because he didn't ever want that but because he sure as hell wasn't ready for it yet.

They stood there for a second, looking at each other. Drew could see in the way Justin stood, the way his shoulders slumped slightly, the softness around his eyes, that he had a bad day. He wanted to ask him about it but didn't know if he should. Did Justin wonder what Drew was thinking? Was he thinking about sex, or had it just been a passing joke?

It was Justin who broke the silence first. He nodded his head toward the office. "Relax and go do your paperwork, Cinderella. I'm going to lift weights. Get ready to show you up the next time we work out together."

Drew's body went lax, while at the same time he thought about how much he enjoyed the simplicity of this man. "You're cute when you're delusional, Sleeping Beauty." He stepped forward and placed his hand on Justin's stomach. Felt the hardness of his abdomen beneath his hand. He was strong; it was there in the firmness of his body. He had nothing to worry about in that regard. "This feels okay." Drew shrugged. "Not quite like mine but…"

"Ooh. Check you out. You flirted first this time. Feeling a little more confident with men? You taken some more test drives I don't know about?" The last question didn't seem to have the same playfulness as the rest of what Justin had said. Or hell, maybe he was imagining things.

"No," he said, his voice serious as well. He wasn't sure why he wanted Justin to know that he hadn't fucked around with anyone since they'd met up again at Shanen's, but it was important to him. "Now get your ass in fucking gear. I'm beginning to think you really came because you wanted to see me, and not for my excellent equipment. Or would it be that you did come for *my* equipment?" Drew wasn't typically that big of a flirt, but something about Justin brought it out of him. Maybe because Justin did it so well, or because the dullness in Justin's eyes went away when he did. Justin was a flirt; that was obvious. He liked it, and Drew liked the look on him.

Justin stepped closer, then closer again. The Italian herb smell got stronger, and Drew didn't drop his hand from Justin's stomach. Hell, he gripped his fucking shirt and he had no clue when that had happened.

The other man leaned in, his mouth so fucking close to Drew's ear, he felt his lips brush it when he started to speak. "I didn't get to see enough of your equipment. You ran away, remember? So how do I know if it's excellent or not? But I can assure you, mine is." And then the motherfucker walked away, leaving Drew standing there, rock hard, chuckling loud enough for Drew to hear him as he went.

"I hate you!" Drew called out.

"I'm crushed!" Justin replied, and Drew turned just in time to see him disappear into the men's locker room.

Well hell. Looked like he had to find a way to do paperwork he didn't want to do, with his dick perked up for the man stripping in his locker room right now.

CHAPTER ELEVEN

JUSTIN HAD NO idea what in the hell he was doing here. The second he'd stepped up to the door, he'd almost turned around and walked away.

But he hadn't. He'd texted and now here he was, an hour later, muscles burning, sweat dripping down his body and his mind on the man in his office down the hall.

There was a part of him that felt guilty for how much thought he put into Drew. There were a hundred other things he should be thinking about instead of a man with long, lean muscles, a tight ass, a cute blush, and a kind smile. But, goddamn, it felt good to think about other stuff. To joke and flirt and just let everything else go. To try and forget—even if only for a few minutes—what he was going through. What they were all going through.

Justin stood up, walked away from the machine he'd been using and then went over to work his shoulders. It was funny how the ache of lifting weights dimmed the rest of the shit going on in his life. He never would have thought it, but Drew was right about that. It gave him something else to concentrate on and it burned some of the pent-up energy inside of him.

After finishing five reps of fifteen on his shoulders, Justin made his way to the locker room. He didn't want to abuse Drew's hospitality by staying too late. Drew couldn't want to spend all night at the gym. Hell, he likely could have already gone home if Justin hadn't been here.

Justin made quick work of his clothes, probably stalling because he didn't want to go home, while telling himself it was because he needed a shower. Five extra minutes couldn't hurt.

He stepped under the warm spray and immediately began soaping his body. His dick got a little excited when he rubbed his balls, and even though Drew had been right that lifting was a good way to release tension, he still believed he was correct too, and that sex was an equally good way. Maybe better.

It didn't take Justin long to clean up and wash his hair. Before he knew it, he'd turned off the shower, dried off, and dressed in a pair of jeans and a T-shirt from his bag.

And he had nothing to do besides go home.

He really fucking didn't want to go home.

The house smelled like sickness. It hurt to breathe it in. To see his father.

Justin grabbed his bag and made his way back into the gym. It had to be close to two in the morning, but as he stepped into the room, he saw Drew in the back corner, close to one of the mirrors, cleaning it.

He had his back to Justin, one arm stretched up as he wiped down the glass. He wore a pair of basketball shorts that looked fucking hot on his ass, a T-shirt, and that black fucking hat, backward on his head.

He wanted him. Christ, he really fucking wanted him. From the second he'd seen Drew in that club he'd wanted to fuck him, to be fucked by him, to suck his dick to the back of his throat, and nurse the fucking thing like it was his only way to get sustenance.

Blood rushed to his cock, making it painfully hard in no time flat. He turned off his brain. Didn't let himself worry about anything in this moment other than himself and Drew. And fuck, he hoped like hell that Drew wanted the same thing he did.

Justin set his bag down and started walking Drew's way. He looked up, and their eyes met in the mirror. Drew smiled at him, and then Justin realized Drew saw the hunger in his stare. The smile slipped from his face, but not as though he didn't want the same thing. No, because he was just as fucking hungry as Justin was.

Drew turned, just in time for Justin to crush their mouths together. He heard the bottle drop, felt Drew's hands on his sides as he dug his fingers in, and opened his mouth for Justin to sink his tongue inside.

Christ, he wanted to fucking ravage him. To lose himself in this because it felt so much better than anything else did right now. Justin knew his way around sex, around pleasure. It was so much easier to navigate than pain and loss.

Drew held his sides tighter, his fingers digging in harder as Justin's mouth made a trail down his neck. As though he just realized it, Drew's hold loosened and he said, "Fuck…sorry."

"What for?" Justin nipped at his neck and then sucked hard. "You can be rough with me. It's a whole lot more fun that way."

The second the words were out of his mouth, the pressure was there again, Drew squeezing him hard. He'd probably have marks there, little bruises from the pressure of his fingers, and damned if Justin didn't want them. If he didn't want Drew to brand him, leave evidence there of something that felt so fucking good.

Justin rubbed his cheek against the always-present scruff on Drew's face. He pushed himself closer to Drew and thrust his dick against the other man's. Ate Drew's moan, and then let his hand roam down Drew's body, to palm his cock. "I want to get on my knees for you. Want to suck you till we both lose our fucking minds. Want to bury my face against your sac and breathe nothing in but your scent. I've been wondering what you taste like, what you smell like. Tell me you want that too."

Drew thrust into his hand and gritted out, "Oh fuck. You're going to make me come and we haven't even gotten to the good stuff yet."

Justin smiled into Drew's neck, let his teeth graze over his skin. "This isn't good? There you go hurting my feelings again. Now make me feel better and tell me you want it."

He pulled back so he could look into Drew's steel-blue eyes but still kept his hand on the other man's erection.

"I want it," Drew rushed out. "Jesus, I fucking want it. Did you really think there was a possibility I didn't? Now *my* feelings are hurt because you obviously think I'm insane."

Justin pressed a quick kiss to his lips and he realized he was smiling again. Drew was good at making him do that. "I'll make it up to you." And then he dropped to his knees. Drew leaned against the mirror behind him. His hand slapped down on the mirror to the right of him.

Oh fuck. He couldn't have planned this any better if he'd tried. Justin turned, watched them in the mirror as he pulled Drew's shorts and underwear down. His thick cock sprung free, bouncing against his belly. A pearl of pre-come glistened on the tip. His pubes were darker than the dirty-blond hair on his head. His balls were full, big, and hung a little lower than Justin's did. He reached out, cupped them, tested their weight as Drew hissed above him.

And then he dropped his hand and leaned in, nuzzled his face between Drew's legs the way he promised he would…and inhaled. It was musk and man. Sex and desire. He loved this. Loved everything about pleasuring a man. "You smell just as good as I thought you would."

"Fuck. You're killing me. Put your goddamn mouth on me before I go out of my mind."

Didn't he know that's what Justin wanted? To drive him crazy, make him soar, and then bring him back to earth. To pull him to the edge, only to retreat just so he could tease him into a frenzy again. "Watch me. Look in the mirror and watch me worship this pretty fucking cock of yours."

Justin let his tongue sneak out. He flicked the head of Drew's erection. Tasted his pre-come as he licked at the head. He'd always loved giving head. No, it wasn't his favorite place to have his mouth, but it was right up close to the top. He'd always loved rimming. Loved driving a man crazy with his tongue between his cheeks. They'd get to that next time.

He looked up at Drew and put his tongue out, teased the tip of his prick, taking just a taste, before he sucked him as far back as he could. Drew shuddered above him, his eyes firmly on the mirror beside them, watching.

"You're so damned sexy looking up at me from your knees. Suck me again. Want to feel your mouth," Drew told him and Justin gladly obliged.

He held on to Drew's sides, relaxed his throat muscles, and took Drew's cock deep. It hit the back of his throat. Justin swallowed around it as Drew cursed and groaned. He was proud of his deep-throating abilities. Loved the fact that he could swallow around Drew's erection.

His hand tightened in Justin's hair, a gentle sting that urged him on even more. Justin loved the feel of his hard cock in his mouth. Loved the salty taste of Drew's skin. Loved the stretch in his lips to accommodate Drew's girth.

He pushed forward, buried his face in Drew's pubes, and felt the rough hair of his thighs against his hand.

His own dick throbbed, but right now, all he needed was to drive Drew crazy. To show the man what he'd missed out on the first night they met.

"Jesus fucking Christ. I'm going to lose it. Gonna fucking blow," Drew gritted, obviously trying to hold off. Justin just sucked harder, swallowed around the swollen head again. Drew's grip intensified. He watched them in the mirror, thrust his hips, and then his dick jerked in Justin's mouth. Hot, thick come jetted down the back of this throat. Justin swallowed before Drew cried out and shot again. Justin took it all, sucked his balls dry before pulling off and licking his lips.

"You taste good," Justin told him.

Drew trembled. "My legs are going to give out. Holy fuck, I've never come so hard. I've never had head like that before."

Justin chuckled as Drew pulled up his shorts and then slid down the mirror and landed on his ass. He was breathing heavy, his hat sort of sitting awkwardly because he leaned against the glass. He had that blissed out, *I-came-so-fucking-hard-I-could-die* look on his face, and it was almost as good as coming himself.

Almost.

Sexed out Drew was fucking hot.

"I'll reciprocate. I swear. You just have to give me a minute. Jesus, you're good at that."

Justin's pulse throbbed though he didn't know why. The compliment settled into his bones. He felt...relaxed...satisfied...happy. "Move." Justin playfully pushed him over and then sat down. Their arms brushed together as they sat there in silence just...*being*...and it was exactly what he needed. Coming here was exactly what he needed.

IT HAD TAKEN Drew a few minutes to come back to earth. His body had been jittery, his legs jello like that had been his first time getting his dick sucked. But Jesus, no one's mouth had ever driven him as wild as Justin's just had.

When he felt grounded again, they'd just started talking—about movies, and holidays, and traveling. "No...are you serious? You've never been out of North Carolina until now?" Drew couldn't see how that was possible. He'd always loved traveling, and even if he hadn't, his parents had dragged him and Jacob all over the world before they hit the age of eighteen.

"Yep. I'm sheltered. We can't all grow up rich kids like you did." Justin nudged him with his arm. He was a nudger, Drew noticed. He did that a lot. They still sat side by side on the floor of his gym, leaning against the mirror. It had been damn near an hour since they started talking but neither man had moved yet.

He didn't want to even look at his phone to see what time it was. He could pretty much guarantee he wasn't getting any sleep tonight...and he was actually okay with that. He enjoyed talking to Justin. It was like a new burst of energy from how he'd felt in his office earlier. He wanted to get to know Justin. To find out what got him excited, and what made him tick. To find out who he really was.

"No reply about the rich kid comment? You know I'm giving you shit, right?"

Drew nodded. "Yeah, I know." Despite wanting to know everything he could about Justin, he felt like he knew him a lot better than he really did. "If you could travel any place, where would you go?" It felt like such a cheesy question, but he really was curious. He loved Ireland and Scotland, himself. He'd actually considered moving to one of them when he left law school, but hadn't.

"United States?" Justin asked. "I'd say, Seattle. I don't know what it is about Seattle but I've always wanted to go."

"I actually haven't been there. I love San Francisco, though. It's probably my favorite city in the U.S. From what a lot of people say, Seattle reminds them of Frisco in some ways, so I'd probably like it. What about outside of the U.S.?"

"I don't know." Justin shrugged. "I haven't thought much about it."

"Really?" Drew asked, not sure why he was surprised by the answer.

"I mean, there's the obvious—France, London, Scotland, Ireland. Everyone wants to go to places like that, but there's no real reason behind it."

"I love Scotland and Ireland. I think you would too."

Justin looked down, and picked at the carpet. "Tell me about it," he said softly, almost vulnerably.

Suddenly, it was incredibly fucking important to make Justin fall in love with whatever he said. To make him feel it, breathe it in as though he was living it. "Okay," he replied. "Hmm...I think we'll start with Scotland. Edinburgh is incredible. I like to climb Arthur's Seat which is outside of the city. When you get to the top of the hill, there's a beautiful view of Edinburgh. It's peaceful up there, being surrounded by nature and seeing the bustling city below."

There was a heavy pause in the air and then Justin closed his eyes and asked, "What would we do next?"

Those words did something to Drew. Tied him up, stole his breath. Made him feel like he was somehow giving Justin something he needed. That had never been important to him before, but right now, he wanted nothing more.

"We'd want something a little more upbeat after that. We'd go to the Royal Mile. The Palace is on one end and the castle on the other. We'd go from pub to pub, restaurant to restaurant, eating good food and drinking good beer. We'd laugh with locals, and meet new people."

"Unhealthy food?" Justin asked and Drew laughed.

"We're on vacation so it would be okay. We'd get so drunk that day we'd stumble to our hotel, but we'd feel okay when we woke up the next morning. We couldn't feel shitty before going to The Isle of Skye. It's a small fishing village where we'd explore medieval castles. We'd have to work off all the bad food you made me eat, so we'd hike some of the cliffside trails. They're beautiful. I love all the green and seeing the ocean."

"I made you eat, huh? This is your trip," Justin teased before Drew continued.

"The coast is really beautiful there. I'd take you sailing. I love sailing. You'd be tired after that so we'd go back to our room. The next day we'd go see Stirling Castle and the Wallace Monument before we found a quiet pub to drink more beer and eat more food."

"Then what?" Justin asked sounding almost...wistful, like he really fucking needed to be doing the things Drew told him about.

"I think Loch Lomond. It's a freshwater Scottish loch. We'd take a boat out and go water skiing."

He felt Justin's hand on his leg and stopped speaking. Drew looked down as Justin let his fingers dance up and down Drew's thigh—up and down, he walked them along Drew's leg. Rubbed it with his thumb. It was such an intimate action. In some ways it almost felt more intimate than anything he'd done, which he was aware made no fucking sense at all.

"Thank you for taking me to Scotland. I needed to get away." His voice was so damn honest, so raw, that Drew felt it in his chest.

He didn't know what in the hell they were doing here. They knew nothing but each other's first names when they'd jerked each other off in that club. Then Drew had bailed on him because he was still getting used to moving forward in exploring his bisexuality. Now they'd discovered a connection between them. One that made things a little sticky, and one that they needed to navigate carefully.

Yet, they weren't doing that, were they? They'd somehow dived head first into...*something*. He didn't know quite what it was, but it felt like more than spending time with his sister-in-law's brother. A guy who had a hundred things going on in his life that made whatever this was even messier.

But Jesus, he wanted to know what this was. Wanted to enjoy spending time together because he enjoyed Justin. He felt the need to ease some of the pain Justin was dealing with. "Hey," Drew said.

With the back of his head still against the mirror, Justin turned and looked at him. They were only a few inches away, and he wondered if Justin would feel his breath when he spoke. "You need to get away, just need a fucking break or whatever, I'm here, okay? I know that sounds dramatic. Jesus, who the hell am I to you? But I want you to know I'm here. Whatever you need."

Justin gave him a small, teasing smile. "You like me."

"I do," he answered truthfully. What was the point in being

anything other than honest? He liked everything he knew about Justin so far.

"No weirdness?" Justin asked. They were still only a few inches away, facing each other as they sat on the floor.

Again, he went with the truth. "Maybe a little. I'd be lying if I didn't admit the family connection worries me slightly. It'll make things worse between Jacob and me...but that part we can't do anything about. That's on him, but I worry how our friendship could affect you. I know you're still trying to get to know Landon and Shanen. I would hate for Jacob to overreact and for it to cause problems between you and Shanen."

Justin nodded. Blinked, his thick lashes creating a brief shield between them. He knew that was something that had to worry Justin too.

"What about the rest of it?"

Drew's brows pulled together. "You being a guy? No. Not really. Like I said, regardless of how little I've explored it, I've always known I was bi. It's hard in the way that I feel like I'm fumbling a bit. Everything is new, and in some ways, I feel like I'm a virgin again. But I have no problems with what we're doing and who I am."

Justin's fingers started moving again. His eyes tilted down, watching them, but Drew continued to watch him. "I can't make you any promises. My life's a fucking rollercoaster right now. And I know you aren't asking for any either, but I feel like I need to say it. My home is in North Carolina. I'm losing my father. I can't commit to anything beyond friendship."

"And blowjobs?" Drew winked at him, trying to lighten the mood.

"I'll also throw in fucking, if we get the chance to work up to that. Oh, and if you think I give good head, it'll blow your mind when I eat your ass. There's a fine art to ass eating. I'd be happy to impart my knowledge to you."

Drew's balls tingled at that, even though it wasn't something he'd ever really thought about having done to him before. It felt incredibly intimate...having someone's tongue on your ass, a little different, and definitely intriguing. "Really?"

"Oh yeah. There's nothing like it."

The tingle in Drew's balls got stronger. He suddenly couldn't keep his mouth off Justin, so he leaned in and kissed him. He'd kissed quite a few men by now, but there was always the brief second when their lips touched when he thought about how different it was. It felt equally as good as kissing a woman, but it was just...different.

He swept his tongue inside Justin's mouth, and then let his hand cup Justin's dick. He was already hard, straining against Drew's palm. He wanted to taste him the same way he'd tasted Drew. Wanted to drive him fucking crazy. Wanted to help him forget.

"I'm going to blow you now," Drew said against his lips. "I'm feeling a little bit of performance anxiety, though. I don't have a lot of experience. I'm not nearly as good with a cock in my mouth as you are."

Justin leaned back and winked at him. "Then we'll have to practice a lot."

Drew smiled, perfectly okay with that. He grabbed one of the towels he'd had earlier, but hadn't used. "Ass up." He patted Justin's leg. There had to be a better place for them to do this, but right now he didn't care.

Justin leaned back, and lifted his ass. Drew shoved the towel beneath it, so he wouldn't be sitting on the bare floor, and then pulled his jeans and underwear down. The second Justin's dick sprung free, he realized how much he really wanted that cock in his mouth. Wanted to taste it, to memorize every inch of it with his tongue.

He didn't take the time to pull the jeans past Justin's knees before he lay down beside him and swirled his tongue around the purplish head of Justin's prick.

"Oh see? You're already fucking good. Suck the crown," Justin instructed him and Drew did. He put the head of Justin's erection in his mouth and nursed it. He tasted pre-come on his tongue. Smelled soap from Justin's shower and wished it didn't cover up the natural scent of him.

Justin pulled Drew's hat off, and shoved it down on his own head. Drew smiled around the cockhead in his mouth before he sucked Justin deeper. He felt the veins beneath his tongue. The soft skin covering his hardness.

"Balls need love too. Give 'em a little attention, Drew. Lick them."

So Drew did. He let his tongue make a trail down the seam of Justin's nuts. He tongued them, sucked them. Felt Justin's pubes scratch against his face, and goddamn that felt good.

"Yeah...like that. Christ, you're a fucking liar. You're good at this. Tell me you like it. Tell me you like having my balls in your mouth."

Oh fuck, did he like Justin's dirty talk. Drew pulled back. "Yeah, I like it. We're definitely going to have to keep doing this. Wanna taste your cock again, though."

"Then do it. It's all yours." Justin ran a hand through Drew's hair as he took Justin's dick. He couldn't go nearly as deep as Justin could, but as far as Drew could tell, he didn't seem to mind. He went fast, then slow. Made himself choke once or twice but just kept going. There was something about this that made him feel...powerful, causing Justin to make noises and take deep breaths and fist his hair.

He used his hand on him, stroking Justin's thick cock as he sucked it. Justin kept touching him, running his hand through

Drew's hair, brushing his thumb over Drew's cheek.

He pushed on Drew's head, so he took him deeper.

"Christ, you're killing me here. My balls are so fucking full. Gonna let go."

Drew almost pulled off, but at the last second, he sucked harder and took Justin as deep as he could go. He flinched at the first spurt of thick come on his tongue, but then he swallowed it down. Justin blew again, giving him another mouthful and this time, the swallowing came automatic as he drank Justin down.

"I needed that. Give me a kiss," Justin told him and Drew leaned forward and did it. He knew Justin had to be tasting himself on Drew's tongue and that only excited him more. He was half-hard in his shorts.

Their tongues wrestled before Justin pulled away much too soon. "That was fucking awesome. You were worried for nothing…" and then, "I don't mean to come and run, but it's late. I should go soon." He lifted his ass again, pulled his jeans up, then sat back down. He touched Drew's head and then Drew found himself leaning it against Justin's thigh. "We'll catch our breath and then I'll go."

"That was the first time I've swallowed." Drew wasn't sure why he'd just told Justin that.

"There it is," Justin said softly, brushing his thumb over Drew's cheek. "You blushed at the bar the first night we hung out. It's cute. Don't be shy, though. Who wouldn't want my come?"

Drew playfully rolled his eyes…and then closed them. Lack of sleep was catching up with him. It was probably four in the morning by now.

Justin still wore his hat and had his hand in Drew's short hair when he spoke. "I was talking to Nick tonight." Drew let his eyes slip open only to see that Justin had his closed.

"He was talking about Bryce… How they met and became friends. How they just started talking and how good it felt. I don't think I realized it at the time...but I think that's why I came here. To talk, just like he said, because it makes me feel good."

Drew felt himself smile, but couldn't find it in himself to reply. Justin didn't say anything either, and before he knew it, there was nothing but darkness.

CHAPTER TWELVE

"D REW? UM... IT'S time to wake up..." Justin's eyes popped open at the soft, female voice saying Drew's name. Drew still had his head in Justin's lap, and Justin had a hand in Drew's hair. His neck had a kink in it from sleeping sitting up against the mirror.

"Oh shit. What time is it?" Justin rushed out.

It was then that Drew's eyes shot open. They took in the woman, then Justin. A small burst of panic exploded in his eyes that made Justin's already uneasy gut roll.

He leaned up and as he did, Justin pushed to his feet.

"Um... It's five thirty. We open at six. I'll just... Go... clean... the... locker rooms...."

"Thanks, Robyn. I appreciate it," Drew replied as he stood, and the woman scurried away.

"I can't believe I fell asleep!" Justin picked up his bag, afraid to look at his phone. He'd left Joy at home with his father. With his *sick* father and he'd come here after work and spent the night? "Fuck...*Fuck!*" He nearly yelled it the second time. "I have to go. I can't believe I did this. What the hell is wrong with me?" He went to run a hand through his hair, which made him remember he was wearing Drew's hat.

After sleeping on the floor with him.

Drew with his head in his lap.

When no one knew he was bisexual. "I'm sorry. I hope everything is going to be okay with you here. I called and told Joy I was making a stop after work, but I shouldn't have been out all night."

"Hey…no. Go. Don't worry about it." Drew crossed his arms, not as though he was annoyed, but more like he didn't know what to do with them. He was a little embarrassed. Justin could see it by the way Drew wouldn't look at him and that slight pink in his cheeks. Or hell, maybe he was just trying to figure out what he was going to tell Robyn, the same way Justin didn't know what to say to him.

"It's normal for two buddies to fall asleep at the gym together, right? Just another night?" Justin tried to joke but it didn't quiet the silent cursing he was doing at himself. He was supposed to be taking care of his dad, and now he not only had a job getting in the way of that but his dick, too.

"I'll tell her…. I don't know exactly what to tell her, but I won't deny who I am. That's not what this is about for me. I've never been in the closet. I just don't think I took my bisexuality seriously."

Justin suddenly wanted to ask him if he did now, but instead he only stood there like an idiot, when he really needed to get the hell out of here.

"Go. We'll talk later." Drew tilted his head toward the door.

Justin began to turn away but then stopped and walked back over to Drew. "Thank you for letting me talk…work out…" He got a little embarrassed when he thought about the Scotland thing. He'd never done something like that. Never needed it. "Thanks for just letting me be. I feel like I'm always thanking you for something."

"You have nothing to thank me for," Drew replied. "I wouldn't have done it if I didn't want to."

Which Justin had no doubt was true. He didn't quite understand why he felt so comfortable around Drew, and why Drew seemed to feel the same about him, but he couldn't deny that it was there. "I'll call you when I can. It depends on how everything is going, okay?"

"No problem. Take care of yourself and your family. That's the most important thing."

Justin nodded. Paused. Took the hat off his head and put it on Drew's. "So fucking hot." He winked and then turned. Drew followed him over, unlocking the door so Justin could leave. His stomach was in knots the second he walked out.

He didn't want to look at his phone, but as he walked back to the car, Justin pulled it out of the bag and…nothing. No missed calls. No messages. No texts.

The near constant ache in his gut twisted and tightened intensely. This was a good thing. Nothing was wrong. They'd probably fallen asleep and didn't notice that Justin was acting like a teenager, getting his dick sucked when he had responsibilities.

Justin tapped his thumbs against the steering wheel as he drove back to the house.

Ridiculously, he checked his phone every couple minutes to see if there was a message, something he missed, but just like it had been when he first looked, there was still nothing when he pulled into the driveway, dodging the potholes he now knew by heart.

He grabbed his bag out of the passenger seat before making his way to the porch. He pushed the key into the lock, and slid the door open quietly as not to wake up his dad. It was a good thing that he apparently slept in today. He hadn't been getting enough sleep. It was always restlessness for him.

But the second he opened the door, he realized he was being quiet for no reason. His dad sat at the table, Joy across from him sipping from a coffee mug. Unexpected anger splintered through him, breaking apart his insides. "Sorry I didn't come home last night. I didn't mean for you to have to stay," Justin managed to grit out over his anger. An immature part of him had wanted them to be worried about him. For it to have mattered that he hadn't come home.

"It's okay. We managed. I'm sure you needed a night out." Joy looked at him and smiled kindly. And she was right. He had needed a night away. It had felt good, almost freeing, which was why he didn't understand the way his pulse pounded at her statement. Didn't understand the sadness that bled into him as he stood there looking at the two of them.

"Did you have fun?" his dad asked before reaching for a glass of water in front of him. His hand shook too badly for him to steady it. "Goddamn it," he cursed softly as Justin stepped toward him to help. He didn't get the chance, though. Joy reached out and steadied the drink before he could and damned if the pain and anger didn't burrow deeper into his core.

"Do you have straws? That would make it easier. Then we could just scoot it closer to you," Joy told him.

"No," Justin answered. He hadn't thought of that. He should have. It was such an obvious answer. "I'll get some today."

"Okay. Thank you." Joy gave him another smile before scooting closer to his dad. "Let me help you, Larry," she told him, and his father did. He let Joy lift the glass to his lips and help him drink.

Justin watched the two of them for a moment, and damned if he couldn't see the love between them. Had it always been there? Had he wanted to be with Joy while he was with Justin's mom? Wanted Shanen and Landon instead of him?

"I'm just…going to go take a shower. I'll be out soon," he told them both before he went for the bathroom, trying to figure out what in the hell was wrong with him.

DREW WASN'T SURE what made him head over to the firm. Maybe it was spending time with Justin, knowing what was going on within his family that made him think about his own. They were lucky. They'd always had what they needed. They'd always had each other, yet he and Jacob didn't treat each other like family most of the time. He couldn't put all the blame on Jake either. Drew didn't try to make things better. Hell, he let his frustration at his brother keep them at arm's length, just as much as Jacob did.

"Good morning, Mr. Sinclair," Jacob's secretary said when he walked through the door.

Drew winked at her. "Morning, Deb. And it's Drew. Please." He'd asked the woman a hundred times over the years to call him Drew, but she couldn't seem to do it. But then, he'd asked his own family to call him Drew instead of Andrew more times than he could count so if they couldn't call him what he wanted to be called, why did he think she would be any different?

"It feels strange to call you Drew."

"It feels strange to be called Mr. Sinclair," he countered and the older woman smiled.

She laughed at him. "I'll give it a shot. Your brother just got out of a meeting, so you came at the perfect time. I'll let him know you're here."

"Thank you." Drew stood around while Deb called back to let Jacob know he was here. Jake would likely wonder why in the hell he'd come, much like Drew was wondering himself.

It was only a few seconds later when Deb told him he could go in. Drew made his way around her long, L-shaped desk and toward the heavy double doors which led to Jacob's office. "Hey. Is this a good time?" Drew asked after closing them inside together.

"It's as good a time as any," Jacob replied. He sat behind his desk, wearing a black suit to Drew's sweat pants and T-shirt. Their hair was the same shade of dark blond. Jacob's was a little more styled than his. They looked alike in so many ways, but in others they were so different.

Drew sat across from him in the high-backed, brown leather chair. Jacob shuffled a few papers, stacking them neatly on his immaculate desk, and he found himself chuckling. "You'd have a heart attack if you went into my office at Invincible."

"Huh?"

"I was just thinking about how different our offices look."

"I would suppose that would make sense considering how different our jobs are."

Okay. Not really what he was going for there. Drew was pretty sure his messy office had nothing to do with his job.

"Is everything okay?" Jacob asked after a few moments of silence. "Mom and Dad?"

Because why else would he come and see his own brother? Jesus, what was wrong with them? "Oh yeah. Everything's fine." He shifted in his seat. It shouldn't be this fucking awkward to talk to his own brother.

"Okay…did you need something? I'm not trying to be rude, but I have work to do."

It was that statement that made the question tumble out of his mouth. "Why don't we get along better?" They'd never spoken about it before. It was much easier just to ignore the tension that was always around them.

Jacob frowned and then shook his head and rolled his eyes. "We get along fine."

"Shut up." This time it was Drew's turn to shake his head. "We do not and you know it. We've never gotten along—even before what happened with Iris. You've always disliked me."

"That's not true and *you* know it." Jacob straightened the same small stack of papers for the second time. "We might not have ever been close, but we were fine. We're different, and we always have been. You chose to try and set yourself apart from the family, not me."

Drew's blood pressure shot up. This had been a mistake. He should have known it from the second he walked in. He should leave right now but he knew he wouldn't. It was long past time they did this. "Set myself apart from the family? Why because I wanted to be happy? Because I didn't want to work a job I didn't love for the rest of my life? What the fuck does that have to do with anything? Jesus, Jacob. Do you even hear yourself? You've never given a shit about me. You've always written me off. Can you imagine if we worked together?"

"Me?" Jacob shouted and then took a deep breath as though to calm himself. God forbid he let emotions out. Which was odd, because he did with Shanen, but only her. "*I've* never given a shit about *you*? You've always thought you were too good—this free spirit, who would never be tied down to the kind of things that made our family who we are. And if we want to talk about not giving a shit about someone, I didn't have an affair with a person you were in a relationship with. You're crazy if you don't realize I know you did it just because you could. Because you don't want to follow the rules and you didn't think Iris and I were right for each other. You told me that, Andrew. Before you went after her, you told me she wasn't right for me and why was that? Because you wanted her? Because I was too stuffy for her? Why would she want to tie herself down to someone like me?"

It was as though a heavy boot stepped on Drew's chest. Jesus, did he really think that? Did he really think Drew would go after someone Jacob was with? That he wanted to hurt his own brother?

"You've always wanted to show you're better than me," Jacob added.

Drew shoved to his feet. "Me? I always wanted to show I'm better than you? You're delusional. I told you I was concerned about Iris because I believed it. Because I wanted you to be happy, and I thought you were just with her because we'd known her all our lives." He didn't add in the fact that Iris had often flirted with him, both before and after she and Jacob had gotten together. He knew it would somehow just come back on him and he also didn't see the point in possibly hurting Jacob by telling him that part of the truth.

"You're happily married to Shanen so it looks like I was right. And how many times do I have to tell you it wasn't an affair? It was a kiss. You wouldn't be with Shanen if it hadn't been for that kiss. Hell, maybe you should be thanking me for it." The second the final words cleared his mouth, Drew wanted them back. What he should have pointed out was the fact that Jacob had never looked at Iris the way he looked at Shanen. That he'd been wrong, made a mistake, even though he had told Iris no. Even though he'd stopped the kiss not long after it started. Because he did feel like shit about it. Even though he'd told her no, he still felt guilt. But Jacob hit all his buttons. It was hard not to lash out against his brother. "Shit," Drew cursed. "Jacob I—"

"I assume you can see yourself out? I'm done talking to you." With that Jacob stood, walked out of the room, and Drew knew he'd just fucked up.

CHAPTER THIRTEEN

THE HOUSE WAS too quiet without the familiar hum of the oxygen tank. He'd hated it when his dad first got it and he still did, yet without it, the house was eerily silent.

Justin had considered going to the gym to work out today, but the truth was, he knew he was too on edge to be around anyone. It's why he'd stayed home, but now part of him regretted the decision while the other part knew he was right.

If there was anywhere he should be right now, it was at the chemo center with his dad. When Justin had woken up to take him today, Larry told him that Joy had offered to take him for his weekly treatment. Justin probably should have argued the point. Probably should have said it was his responsibility, but damned if there wasn't a fucked-up part of him that had been relieved. If he never saw another doctor or nurse the rest of his life, it would be too soon.

So he sat here, his leg bouncing up and down, a powerful tornado of guilt and sadness twisting and turning in his head...and waited.

As hours passed, the more agitated he became. He cleaned things that didn't need to be cleaned. Called his mom to check in while pretending everything was okay.

When his phone rang with Joy's number, he was afraid to answer it. Wanted to throw the fucking thing out the window because the heaviness in his gut, in his chest, told him something was wrong. Well, many things had been wrong, but this was more.

"Hello?" Justin's heart beat in his throat.

"Hey, buddy. I have a favor to ask you." Buddy. His dad hadn't called him that since he was a kid.

"Yeah?" Justin tried to ignore the clenching in his gut. "What is it?"

"Can you head over to Joy's and meet us there? We…we have to talk about a few things."

There wasn't a doubt in his mind what those things were. This was the moment they'd all been expecting—just not yet. "I…" He didn't want to go. Wanted to pretend none of this was happening. Wanted to go back to the way things were, but he couldn't do that, could he? He couldn't pretend that he hadn't been dealt blow after blow. That his problems were nothing compared to the man who was losing his life. None of them were winning in any of this. "Okay. I'll be right there."

But still, he didn't want to go. His fucking hand shook as he ended the call. Justin leaned forward, elbows on his knees, and the palms of his hands against his eyes.

His dad was going to stop chemo. He didn't have to go to Joy's to know that. He was going to let go and there wasn't a damn thing they could do about it. You could know something would happen, maybe know it should happen, but that didn't mean it wasn't a shock to the system when it did.

They'd gone in for his chemo treatment, and now he had to meet them at Joy's. There was no reason for this to be happening other than that fact that his father or the doctor thought it was time.

"Fuck," he gritted out, shook his head, and then pushed to his feet.

Before he could talk himself out of it, run, hide like a fucking kid as though that would make anything go away, Justin went for the door and got in the car to head for Joy's house.

SHANEN ALREADY SAT in one of the chairs when he arrived. Jacob stood behind her with his hands on her shoulders.

Landon was on one of the couches, with Rod beside him. He had his arm around Landon and Landon clutched his knee as though he was afraid to let go.

His dad was on the other couch, and his first thought was *There it is*. The familiar hum of the concentrator on the tank was back. It was comforting in an odd way.

"Hello, Justin." Joy hugged him but he couldn't find it in himself to squeeze her back. "We called Landon first because we knew it would take him longer to get here. Shanen just arrived."

He nodded, as though it mattered. She walked over and then found her seat beside his dad. "You can sit down," she said, but Justin shook his head.

"I'm okay." Really he fucking wasn't. He felt like he was cracking apart. Like he would burst at the seams at any second, and lose his goddamned mind. He couldn't do this. Jesus, he couldn't fucking do it. He hadn't expected it to be so soon. His dad hadn't had much time with Shanen and Landon yet. Didn't he deserve more time with them?

Justin leaned against the wall just as his dad started speaking. "I wasn't going in for chemo today. I had an evaluation with my oncologist."

"What?" Justin interrupted. "Jesus, Dad. Why didn't you tell me?" That's what Justin was supposed to be here for—to help take care of his dad. He should know those things.

"Us," Landon added, and even though Justin wanted to be angry, he knew Landon was right. They all should have known, not just him.

"The evaluation is something new, isn't it? You haven't had that scheduled for very long." Shanen's voice wobbled when she spoke. She was right, though.

"Yes. I've been feeling a little off the past week. I've...had brief periods of confusion, but it was almost as though I knew I was confused. That I knew I should know more than I did."

"What?" Blood ran through Justin's ears so loudly, he could hardly hear. "Why didn't you say anything?" Here he'd been going about his life and his father was getting worse? He was confused?

"Because I didn't want to worry you."

"That's a bullshit answer. That's what I'm here for! I'm supposed to know those things." He *needed* to know them. Needed to know he still had a spot in his father's life.

"I'm sorry." Larry shook his head. "I don't know how to do this. I don't..." He shook his head and couldn't continue. He buried his face in his hands. Guilt stole Justin's breath. Jesus, he was fucking angry. When he first came here, first met Landon and Shanen, he thought he'd gotten past most of the anger but he hadn't.

"It's okay." Joy wrapped an arm around him, and suddenly Justin was angry at her too. For being here. For supporting him. For not being angry at him for what he'd done to her.

His dad shook his head and then looked up—first at Justin, then Shanen, and finally Landon. "The news wasn't good. We did a scan and the cancer is growing. It's spread to my..." When his voice cracked, he cleared his throat. "To my lymph nodes. A lot of them, and that's not the only place. It's.... It's time to stop the chemo and just...try to live the best life I can from here on out. I should feel a little better for a while. We can...we can do more..."

This time when he stopped, Justin knew he couldn't continue. He stood, frozen against the wall, unable to speak. Unable to move. Despite knowing this would happen, he was still devastated. Shocked. Like he got a call that his father was in a car accident, or something else they hadn't expected. No matter how much you tried, you could never really prepare yourself for something like this.

Landon leaned forward, face in his hands much like Justin had done at the house. Rod held him, kissed his neck. Whispered quiet words to him. Shanen started to cry. Jacob walked around the chair, pulled her to her feet and wrapped his arms around her.

Justin was alone, though. He crossed his arms, watched the veins in his hand as he fisted it, as he wished he wasn't alone on an island in the middle of nowhere.

"Justin. I—" His dad started, but Justin shook his head, silencing him. He couldn't do that right now. Not in front of everyone. These people who had known and loved each other for much longer than they'd known Justin. "So what are the next steps? What do I need to know? I can talk to Nick and tell him I have to leave the restaurant. He'll understand." Facts. He was resorting to facts because they were much easier than emotions.

"I was going to suggest he could stay with us?" Shanen piped in. "We have more space. I'd like to help take care of him. Of course you'd be welcome too, Justin. I—"

"No. Why does he need to leave our place? That's why I fucking came here. I can do it. I can take care of him. Maybe you don't think so, but I can."

"That's not what I meant," Shanen continued and damned if he didn't know she hadn't. "I was just thinking it would be easier. I know you're on the couch. We have the extra room and the means to...."

"Nope. Don't need your money." The whole time his brain was telling him to shut up. That she didn't mean it the way he made it sound, but his heart overpowered it.

"Don't," Landon interrupted. "I know you're hurting, Justin, but we all are. Don't take it out on her. I won't allow it."

His chest ached. His hand twitched. He wanted to slam his fist into Landon's face, yet at the same time he respected the hell out of him. He was protecting his sister, and no matter that they also shared blood, Shanen would always be more to him than Justin could be.

"Hey, it's okay," Rod told Landon. "We're all dealing with this the best way we know how."

"I know you didn't mean it," Shanen told Justin. "I just think…"

"Shanen. Not right now." Jacob shook his head at her. Everyone started speaking over each other, and then getting louder and louder to be heard. *But this? What about that? Justin can. Dad should. Mom will…* They kept going and fucking going until Justin thought he would lose his damned mind.

He opened his mouth to tell them all to shut up, when his father spoke first. "That's enough!" Larry had pushed to his feet, his voice stronger than Justin had heard it in a long time. "I can't handle this. Can't handle the arguing. Not right now." The room went silent. Rod stood with his arm around Landon for support. Jacob held Shanen for the same thing. Joy was strong and steady beside his father. Justin waited on the outskirts, alone as they all listened to his father speak.

CHAPTER FOURTEEN

DREW SAT ON his couch flipping through the channels. There wasn't shit on TV. He wasn't much of a television person anyway. He'd rather be *doing* something. He wanted to go for a jog but it was raining like crazy outside. It had been clear all morning and then suddenly heavy, dark clouds rolled in and it had been pouring for a good hour straight. It wasn't as if he'd never jogged in the rain. Sometimes he did but he wasn't in the mood for that right now.

After pushing the power button on the remote, he tossed it to the coffee table. Just as he pushed to his feet, there was a knock at his door.

As he walked over, he adjusted the ever-present black baseball cap on his head. There was another knock, and Drew cursed whoever was being so damn impatient before he pulled the door open.

The second he saw Justin standing there, soaked to the bone, his dark hair plastered against his head, his arms crossed, and his eyes looking down, he knew something was wrong. He trembled even though it wasn't cold outside, but a humid rain. Drew's heart broke for the man. He hadn't been lying when he told Justin to come to him if he needed something. He had an intense urge to be there for Justin in a way he hadn't experienced with anyone before. "Get in here. You're drenched."

He reached for Justin, who pulled back. "I don't want to get your floor all wet." His voice was distant, alone, and damned if the pain in Drew's chest didn't double.

"I don't give a shit about my floors. Com'ere."

Justin stepped out of his sopping sneakers as Drew pulled him inside. He didn't let go of Justin's hand as he led him to the stairs, and up them. His hand was cold in Drew's but he gripped it just as tightly as Drew held him, maybe tighter. He wanted Justin to know he could hold on as tight as he needed to.

"Fuck. I'm getting water everywhere. I'm sorry," Justin said as his wet socks padded against the carpet.

"It's water. It'll dry." They continued down the hall. He really fucking wanted to know what was going on but part of him was scared to find out too. It was hard seeing someone he cared about dealing with so much pain. And he did care about Justin, he realized. He cared about him a lot.

Drew's bedroom was at the end of the hallway. He pushed the double doors open. Directly across from the door, the back wall was nearly all windows, looking out at all the green and trees of the property behind his house. The bed was on the left wall, his dresser the right, and the bathroom between the dresser and the windows. "You can get undressed in the bathroom. I'll grab you something to change into. Or, if you want, you're welcome to take a shower. Towels are in the cabinet."

"Okay."

Drew watched as Justin made his way around him, and headed for the bathroom. His shoulders curled, sagged as though the weight of the world rested on them. He left the door open, and even though Drew couldn't see him, he knew Justin was undressing because he heard wet clothes being removed. Jesus, what had happened? There were too many things to choose from—something with his dad, his relationship with Landon, or with Shanen.

Drew rummaged around in a drawer and pulled out a pair of sweats and a T-shirt for Justin. He went toward the bathroom, but kept out of view and said, "I have some clothes for you."

"You've had my dick in your mouth. You can come in." Justin's voice was slightly lighter than it had been a moment before, but he thought it was a façade. He could still hear the sadness hiding behind it, making each syllable sound heavy, weighted down.

"Good point." Drew went into the bathroom and tossed the clothes onto the counter. Justin had a towel wrapped around his waist, as he leaned against the glass-enclosed shower. Jesus, he was sexy as hell—gold kissed skin. A patch of dark hair on his chest. He wasn't overly defined, but Drew could see the muscles in his stomach. He let his eyes drift back up as Justin's Adam's apple bobbed when he swallowed, and as much as Drew wanted to take in the view, there was a part of him that wanted to just…hold Justin. And holy fucking shit, was that different from what Drew was used to thinking about someone he was having sex with. Or in their case, hopefully having sex with.

"Are you okay?" he finally managed to ask.

Justin answered with, "I'm sorry to just show up like this. I didn't know where else to go. You're the only thing here that feels like mine."

Goddamn if those words didn't do funny things to him. Made his chest feel full and his pulse kick up. "Hey, you don't have to apologize for coming here. That's what friends are for. I'm glad you came. I want you to come here." Drew shrugged, feeling a little silly. "I'm honored that you feel like you can count on me."

Justin cocked his head slightly and looked at him. Drew could see his chest rise and fall with each heavy breath he took. He didn't know what in the hell the man was thinking, what he saw as he studied Drew so intensely, but something was there, in his wide, dark eyes. Worry or confusion or sadness or desire. Maybe a mixture of all of them. Drew was pretty sure a cocktail of the same things swished around inside of him.

And then Justin stepped forward—took one step, then another and another, closing the space between them. He didn't stop until only inches parted them. Drew could feel Justin's breath. He smelled like fresh rain and Drew wanted to inhale him deeper.

He placed a hand on Justin's hip, pulled him even closer.

He brushed his thumb over Justin's hipbone. His skin had warmed up. It was slightly wet from the rain but he felt good, too fucking good. They were playing with fire. He already felt the singe, but damned if he didn't want the spark to ignite brighter. If he didn't want to go up in flames with this man.

"Will you fuck me? I want you to fuck me." Justin leaned forward, ghosted his lips across Drew's neck, making him shudder. Drew's dick went hard in two seconds flat, as Justin continued. "Want to feel your dick inside me, stretching me out."

His teeth brushed Drew's neck and if they weren't careful, he'd blow his fucking load without even touching Justin.

"I know you haven't gone there with a man yet, and maybe I shouldn't ask you to, but I am. I want you to drive me wild. Make me lose my mind. Make me come with your cock so deep inside me, there's no room for anything else."

Did Justin think he didn't want that? There wasn't a possibility of him saying no. His whole body was blissed out, eager and needy for exactly what Justin had said. "Fuck, yes. I want that too." Drew looked down. His sweats were tented, as was Justin's towel. He tugged the end, watched it fall open before it hit the floor.

Justin's erection bounced against his stomach. Stood long and fucking proud and Drew wondered what it would feel like inside of him too. He'd played around, fingered himself a few times, but never taken anything more than that. He was definitely curious despite his nerves.

Drew rubbed his finger over the slit in Justin's dick, smearing the pre-come there. "I might ask you to return the favor sometime. I've always wanted to know what it feels like to be fucked."

Justin smiled a wicked grin that automatically made Drew do the same. "It's fucking amazing. And just say the word. I'd love to break in that ass for you." Then he nodded his head toward the bed, pulled away, and Drew followed.

JUSTIN HADN'T COME here to have sex. Those thoughts hadn't been even a blip on his radar as he'd found himself driving to Drew's. The only thing he'd known was that he was sad. So fucking sad and afraid and pissed off. Alone. He'd never felt lonely before all of this started. Before he'd realized what he was doing, he'd been driving to Drew's because the loneliness slipped away when Drew was around.

But as he'd stood in the bathroom, heard the sincerity in Drew's voice as he'd told Justin he was honored that he felt like he could count on him, Justin realized he really did feel that way. He knew he could depend on Drew and then the want became too much to ignore.

He wanted to fuck.

To come.

To lose his motherfucking mind with the man.

And he knew Drew would make him lose it.

He turned around when he got to the edge of Drew's bed. "You have entirely too many clothes on for fucking."

"Then why don't you take them off of me?" Drew countered.

His fucking pleasure. Justin put his fingers in the waistband of Drew's grey sweats and pushed them down his legs. He got a surprise when he did. "Look at you, going commando. Are you sure you weren't expecting me?" Justin teased.

"I was hopeful." Drew took over and kicked his legs free.

"Wishes do come true. Lift your arms."

Drew did as he said. Justin pulled the T-shirt up his chest and over his head, taking his cap with it. The second he was free of it Justin leaned forward, held Drew's right arm up as he licked a path down his collarbone, over his shoulder and then nuzzled his face in his pit. He smelled clean, like soap and man.

"Holy shit." Drew trembled and pulled back slightly.

"Depending on the kind of sex you've had, this might be a little dirtier than that."

Drew frowned, and Justin realized his nose wrinkled when he did. "I can handle it. I want it."

"Good," Justin told him before he nuzzled his face in Drew's armpit again. "I like crevices. Like this…" And then he started to kiss his way down Drew's side before kneeling in front of him. "And right here." He licked the space where Drew's leg met his crotch. "And here." He ran his finger down the crack of Drew's ass. "But we'll get to that another time."

Drew moaned when Justin pushed his face into his pubic hair again. He breathed Drew in. Squeezed his ass, dug his nails in.

"Jesus," Drew moaned. "You're determined to fucking kill me. Get up here. I want to kiss you."

Justin let Drew pull him to his feet. Their mouths clashed down on each other. Their tongues dueled. Hands were everywhere, arms wrapped around each other, scratching and gripping and pulling. Christ, Justin was ravenous for this man. Insane with need. His body was on fire. His dick throbbed and his balls ached.

He grunted when Drew pushed him backward. Justin fell on the bed, Drew on top of him. They thrust their dicks together, hairy legs rubbing against each other. Sweaty, hard bodies slapping together.

"You feel so goddamned good beneath me. All this skin on skin, male body against male body. This is new," Drew told him.

"Didn't make it to the getting naked and sweaty together part yet, huh? I'll show you how good it can be."

And then their mouths were on each other's again. Justin grabbed Drew's muscular ass. It was little and tight and damn did he want his mouth on it. Wanted his tongue to trace it and his teeth to bite into it.

He let his fingers dig in and squeezed the globes, every once in a while teasing Drew's crack with his finger. Every time he did, Drew let out a throaty moan. Oh yeah, he was definitely curious about bottoming. Justin couldn't wait to be the one to show him just how fucking incredible it could be. But right now, he really fucking wanted it. Really needed to turn everything else off and let Drew make him feel blissed the fuck out.

"Make me feel good, Drew. Christ, I need you to fucking take me." Justin rolled them. Drew laughed as Justin ended up on top of him, but then he kept going. He crawled up to the head of the bed, lay on his back and spread his legs wide so Drew could see his hole.

When Drew didn't move, didn't speak, there was a brief moment that his chest went tight. *He's never fucked another man...* What if he realized he was attracted to men, yeah, but he wasn't sure if he wanted to be balls deep in them? As quickly as that thought dive-bombed into his brain, it drifted right out again. Drew looked at him with hunger, with naked desire.

"Jesus," he said as he began moving toward Justin. "It looks so fucking small. So goddamned tight." He kneeled between Justin's spread legs. When he reached out and rubbed the pad of his thumb over Justin's asshole, he shuddered.

"Oh fuck. I could see you clench when you did that. Do it again. You are so fucking sexy."

Justin clenched his hole again before saying, "Then why don't you put something in me?"

From his spot between Justin's legs, Drew looked up at him and grinned. "I'm going to. Now be quiet and let me play."

CHAPTER FIFTEEN

JUSTIN SAID HE wanted to lose his mind, but Drew was pretty sure he would be the one to lose control. Even looking at Justin's small, pink hole he wanted to come undone. How tight would it feel around his dick? How hot would he be inside? He really couldn't fucking wait to find out.

Drew put his finger in his mouth, getting it nice and wet before he rubbed it against Justin's wrinkled pucker. He clenched it again and damned if it wasn't the sexiest fucking thing he'd ever seen. He couldn't wait to watch his dick disappear inside.

For now, he'd settle for a finger. Drew let the tip of it push inside Justin's hole.

"We don't have to do the one finger, two fingers, three fingers stretch, you know."

"Shh," Drew told him. "I'm exploring, remember? Let me fucking explore every part of you." And then he pushed his finger all the way inside. Justin moaned a delicious fucking moan, and Drew felt the urge to beat his fists against his chest because he was the one making Justin feel this way.

He fucked Justin with that one finger. With his other hand, he cupped the man's sac, played with his tight balls, and watched his dick jerk against his belly in anticipation.

Justin's dick leaked, dripped against his stomach in a long line. He watched as Justin stroked himself once, before putting his finger in his own pre-come and then sucking it off his finger.

Lust went off like a firework display in Drew's gut. "Oh God. I feel like a fucking virgin. Jesus, that was hot." He leaned forward, spit on his finger and then used two to fuck Justin's pretty, pink asshole.

"Christ, yesss… Right there. Right fucking there," Justin said over and over as Drew pleasured him. He took over, stroking Justin's dick with one hand and continued finger-fucking him with the other.

His dick was so damn hard it hurt. Angry and pleading to sink inside Justin.

"Fuck me," Justin told him. "I need you to fuck me, Drew."

Damned if Drew didn't need that too. He pulled his fingers out, leaned forward and licked the new drops of pre-come leaking from the head of Justin's dick. There was a part of him that felt as though he was on unsteady ground because he'd never done this before. Never fucked a man, but then…he was confident in it too. This had always been there, waiting inside Drew for him to see where it would take him.

It took him to this moment with this man and he wouldn't have it any other way.

He leaned toward the bedside table and rummaged through the top drawer. He felt Justin's hand on his ass, rubbing the globes and spreading his cheeks. For just a second, he froze up. He'd never had someone look at his asshole before, but if the fucking thing made Justin feel half of the desire Drew did when he looked at Justin's, they were good.

His heart sped up a bit. "Shit," he said as he kept looking in the drawer.

"No…no, no, no. I don't like the sound of that."

Drew didn't either.

"Please tell me you have condoms. Who the hell doesn't keep condoms?"

"I'm out! I didn't know I was out. It's been a long time since I brought someone home. I have to have at least one buried in here. I don't have lube either."

Then Justin was sitting up, trying to squeeze around Drew to look in the drawer. It made the edge of the bed dip and Drew almost tumbled off. "Move." He swatted at Justin's hand. "You're making it harder."

"This wait is making me softer! Find the motherfucking condom, Drew. We can do it without the lube, though, seriously man, we're going to have to have a talk about your stock."

"Shit. Shit, shit, shit." Drew continued looking. Almost fell off the bed again and then, "Oh, thank God." He pulled a condom out and checked the date. "Yes! We're good." And they both started laughing like crazy. It was wild, frenzied laughter. Happy laughter. Completely comfortable laughter.

"Come on!" Justin pulled Drew back on the bed the right way. "If I hadn't had a view of your ass the whole time you would have had to get me hard again. Seriously? You should always have a spare box of condoms."

"Leave me alone. I saved the day. I found one." Drew lay on top of him and then lowered his head. Their mouths came together again. Drew pushed his tongue into Justin's mouth and thrust against him. This was different. He wasn't stupid enough not to notice that. He'd never laughed like that in bed with someone. Never had this much fun. Drew wouldn't deny the confusing things he felt.

When he pulled away, Justin said, "Think you have it in you to save the day again? I really need a fucking orgasm."

"I do," Drew told him. "Get on your hands and knees. I want to watch my dick slide into your ass when I take you."

"Oh, you're bossy. I didn't know."

Drew pulled back, kneeled behind Justin. He opened the condom wrapper and sheathed his aching prick. He used his own spit to slick himself as best he could. He did the same to Justin's hole, and then he was there, pushing the head of his cock inside. He went slow, watched that tight fucking ring stretch to accommodate him.

He saw Justin's hands clench the pillows, heard him breathe heavily. "You good? I can go find something for lube if you—"

"I'm good. Fuck, it feels good. Get me a little wetter and you got it."

Justin dropped his head. He had a beautiful fucking arch to his back.

Jesus, he couldn't fucking believe he didn't have lube. He let another drop of spit land on his dick, rubbed it on himself and on Justin's hole, before he started to push again.

Fuck, it was tight. So goddamned tight and hot. And sexy as hell, watching Justin's hole stretch. Watching it grip his dick, swallow it as Drew pushed slowly inside.

The second he was buried to the hilt, they both let out a deep breath.

"I think I'm going to stay right here forever. For the rest of my fucking life, because goddamn, I don't think anything has felt as good as being inside of you."

"Might be awkward at family get-togethers," Justin replied and then softer, he added, "Just fuck me, Drew. Please."

The *please* almost did him in. Their laughter from earlier was gone now, the room heavy again. Drew wanted to make all of that shit go away. Wipe it out of Justin's mind as best he could. For now, this was the only way he knew how.

He held on to Justin's hips, pulled almost all the way out and then slammed forward again. Over and over he pummeled Justin's hole. With each thrust, he watched his own prick disappear and then pull out again. It was so fucking sexy, his balls wanted to unload right then and there, but he would make this good for Justin. He wouldn't let himself ruin it before Justin had the chance to come.

"I've never felt something this tight. You feel so good, Justin. I want to make you feel good too." Drew leaned forward, thrust harder. He wrapped his hand around Justin's erection and started to stroke.

He fisted him tightly. Rubbed his other hand down the perfect fucking arch in his back.

"Right there. Christ, yes, just like that," Justin gritted out.

Drew kept fucking—stroking and fucking. His balls burned. They were so fucking high and tight that he didn't know how much longer he could last when Justin thrust back against him, cursed, and then come spurted from his cock, slicking it up. Another jet pulsed from his dick as Justin's ass clenched Drew's cock and he couldn't hold back anymore. He slammed deep, his own orgasm ripped out of him as he filled the condom with come.

They fell in a heap in the middle of the bed. Come spilled from the condom, down his leg and onto his blanket but he didn't have the strength to move. They didn't speak, nothing but heavy breathing filling the room.

Drew didn't know what to say. *Are you okay?* felt ridiculous. *Hey, why did you come over?* was even worse.

It was Justin who saved the day this time. "So," he said after a few minutes of silence, "How was your test drive?"

Drew let out a loud laugh; his cheeks hurt from smiling so fucking big. "It was perfect. I'm wondering why in the hell I took so long to take the ride."

But really, as emotional as it sounded, he was glad it hadn't happened earlier, so it could be Justin he experienced it with.

JUSTIN KNEW HE needed to say something to Drew but he wasn't sure where to start. It was a whole hell of a lot easier just to talk about fucking.

But it was more than that too…he needed to talk to someone about the things going on inside of his head and he thought maybe he needed that person to be Drew.

Drew took the condom off, rolled over and tossed it into the trash. As he was about to stand up, Justin reached over, grabbed his wrist, and shook his head. He could see the understanding in Drew's expressive eyes. He nodded and then lay back down beside him, this time on his side, looking down at Justin with his head propped up on his hand.

His blue eyes entranced Justin. He had a little laugh line beside his mouth. He must have trimmed this morning because his scruff was a little lighter than it normally was. Christ, the man was fucking gorgeous.

"What is it?" Drew asked. "You can talk to me."

"I guess...I guess the time has come. Dad and his doctors decided it was time to stop chemo. Everything has been all sorted out." And by that, he meant he had no fucking say in anything. Should he have a say? He wasn't sure. All he knew was his dad and Joy had organized everything before they'd even spoken to Justin and his siblings. "He'll move in with Joy because she'll be able to take better care of him."

"What about you?" Drew asked and Justin let out a deep breath. He'd needed that more than he thought he should. He selfishly needed someone to think of him—but was it selfish? Landon had that in Rod. Shanen had it in Jacob. Even his father had it in Joy. And...well, he guessed he kind of had it in Drew now, too.

He lifted his free hand and let his fingers play with the hair on Justin's chest. It felt good...comforting, so he said, "I'm welcome to stay there as well."

"But you won't."

No, he wouldn't.

"And I can understand your feelings on that. I think in some ways it would be a good thing if you did. They're your family—even Joy, but I can see why it would be awkward for you as well. Just don't miss out on time with him, okay? I don't want you to have any regrets."

Justin didn't want to have any either. He'd told that to Landon when they first met, but damned if it didn't mean a lot to have someone say that to him. "I'll still see him, and I'll think about it. I'm just...I'm so fucking angry about all of it. I'm angry that he's dying and angry about what he did. I'm angry he took time away from my siblings and I...and sometimes, I'm angry at them for being around. What kind of man would feel that way?" If anything, Landon and Shanen had the right to think that about Justin, not the other way around.

"The human kind. I don't think it would be realistic *not* to feel those things," Drew told him. "Emotions are a funny thing, but they're yours and you have a right to feel all of them. What matters is how you react to them."

Justin felt an unfamiliar fullness in his chest. He liked this...having these talks with Drew. Having someone there to talk to at all. "Has anyone ever told you you're a smart guy?"

"Of course. How could they not?"

They both chuckled. When he'd shown up here, he hadn't thought he would be able to laugh at all today, but this wasn't the first time they'd done that together. Drew made those things easier than they should be.

"What happens next?" Drew asked, steering them back to shit that fucking hurt.

"We wait," Justin replied, hating those words. "Hopefully, he'll get some of his quality of life back, before things get worse. You just never know. It could be a week, or he could have months. When things do get harder, hospice will make things easier on him. It's all set up so like I said...we just wait..."

With his fingers still rubbing Justin's chest, Drew said, "I'm sorry."

"Thank you."

"What are you thanking me for?" he asked.

For approaching Justin at Shanen's house that day. For letting him drink and taking him home. For breakfast that day. For the gym and their talks and for letting Justin barge into his house wet and depressed. "For everything."

Drew looked down at him and didn't reply. Justin's gut began knotting, the relentless twisting and turning there getting tighter and tighter. He wasn't sure what was wrong or what Drew's brows pulling together as he looked at him meant.

Or why it mattered so fucking much.

"We might have a problem here, Justin, and I'm not sure what to do about it."

Discomfort slid down his spine. Everything else in his life felt so fucked up, everything off its fucking axis, and he needed this piece of it to be level. To counter everything else. "What is it?"

"Jesus." Drew sat up, and so Justin did the same. "I feel like a tool saying this but I think I'm starting to feel something for you. Something a little more than just a friend, or a guy who I can now say I'm fucking." He tried to grin but it didn't ring true…and if Justin were being honest, he didn't know how to reply. They'd skirted around this subject at the gym the other night.

"See? It's almost like I just gave you a note that said, 'Do you like me? Check yes or no.'"

Justin knew he should say something but he wasn't sure what. He thought maybe he was on the same page as Drew, but could he trust that? Could he trust his emotions when they were so scattered right now? When they were so heavy with pain and fear and the potential loss he would endure?

"This isn't like me," Drew added.

"I know." And somehow Justin really did know. That this thing between them was a little different.

"But I'm also a grown-ass man, and I realize that everything you have going on in your life is a whole lot bigger than me. So you keep doing what you're doing. You take care of your family and sort out your life. I'll be your friend and maybe that's all it'll ever be. Or I'll be your lover and that's all it'll ever be. Or…who knows? We have time to figure everything else out later. I just thought you should know where I'm at."

That was exactly what Justin needed to hear. Hell, how could he even let himself be thinking about anything more than just seeing what happened, while he was losing his father? "Once you get ass, you're never the same," Justin teased, and Drew rolled his eyes at him. "Speaking of ass, mine hurts like a motherfucker. We need to get you some goddamned lube!"

He stood up and Drew did the same. He rubbed his strong hand against one of Justin's cheeks and said, "You talked about eating ass last time. Maybe you can give me a few pointers and I'll kiss it and make it better?"

That got his cock's attention. He felt blood start to rush there.

"I can't believe I just said that. That was fucking cheesy."

"That was fucking sexy," Justin countered. "We can definitely work something out."

"I'll hold you to that." Drew nodded toward the door. "Get the sweats on. I want to show you something."

They both free-balled it in sweatpants as they made their way downstairs. Drew led him to the back of the house, to another set of stairs that led to a basement full of, "Workout equipment? Why am I not surprised?"

"Because you're smart. Come on. That's not why we're here." They went to the back of the room where Drew had a punching bag hanging from the ceiling. "You're pissed? Take it out on this. It's what I do. Hell, I should probably go a few rounds myself. I got into it with Jacob recently."

Justin really didn't understand the animosity between them but what did he know about having a brother? He just found out about his. "What happened?"

"Talk later. Hit now." Drew grabbed a pair of gloves and tossed them at him, and that's what they did. They took turns punching the bag. Sweat dripped into Justin's eyes from swinging so passionately. His arms felt like wet noodles, but damned if it wasn't exactly what he needed. Drew was pretty good at helping him with that.

CHAPTER SIXTEEN

DREW CHUCKLED AS Justin snored softly beside him. They'd spent the day around the house yesterday. After boxing, Justin had used his shower and then they'd eaten dinner, which Justin had teased him about because it had been healthy.

It was after dinner when Justin had called his dad, apologized for walking out, and told him that he just needed to clear his head. Who the hell wouldn't? Drew knew he would. His head was spinning just experiencing it through his friend…the guy who he was pretty sure he wanted to be more than just friends with. The man he'd fucked. He hadn't expected that…of course he hadn't, and it had nothing to do with the fact that Justin was a man either. He wasn't saying he was in love with the guy. All he knew was he felt good around Justin. He wanted to be there for him, to support him. He wanted to spend more time with him.

Drew decided early morning after the emotional night they'd had wasn't the time to think about all of this. He rolled over, grabbed his cell phone from the bedside table, and snuck out of the room to make a call. He was halfway down the stairs when Robyn answered. "I have a favor," Drew told her.

"Shoot."

"Is there any way you can cover for me today?"

Robyn laughed. "You're the boss, Drew. You get to tell me to do those things, remember?"

He wasn't good at that kind of stuff and that was okay with him. "I don't work that way. I'm not going to push my work off on others. I have a lot of accounts that need to be gone through today, so it's not going to be fun work. Are you sure you're okay with it?"

"As long as you're doing something fun," she replied.

"I hope to be." He really wanted to try and help Justin get his mind off everything he had to deal with.

"You know it's killing me not to ask you for more details about the guy you were here with, right? Justin? I have a feeling he's involved and this is the first time you've asked me to cover for you at work."

Drew walked into the kitchen and began getting coffee started. "Who knew you were such a gossip?" He hadn't gone into a lot of details when she'd woken them up at the gym, and Robyn hadn't asked, though he'd known she wanted to.

"You know that's not it...but we're friends too...okay and I'm nosy as hell."

They both laughed and he hit the power button on the coffee pot. He crossed his arms and leaned against the counter. "I'm bisexual. It's not something I'd explored in great detail until recently but I've always known it. Justin and I are friends. He means something to me." He couldn't really say they were seeing each other even though it felt like they were. Dating had to be the last thing on Justin's mind. "It's complicated, though. He has ties to Jacob, so if on the rare chance any of my family come in, I'd appreciate it if you didn't say anything."

"You know I wouldn't do that, Drew, and I'm happy for you. Now let me off the phone so I can get ready for work. My slave driver boss called me at six a.m. on my day off."

"Brat," he told her as Justin rounded the corner into the kitchen. He wore another pair of Drew's sweats. They hung low on his hips, the shape of his erection clearly defined beneath them. He didn't have a shirt on; his right arm raised to scratch his head, as he yawned. His eyes were partly closed, and he looked sleepily mussed and sexy as hell. "I have to go. I'll talk to you soon." Drew set the phone on the counter and said, "Good morning, Sleeping Beauty."

"This early, I'm more like one of the seven dwarfs. It's Grumpy to you. Why the hell are we up this early? Oh shit. Coffee. That smells so fucking good."

Drew pulled two mugs from the cabinet and set them on the counter. It was Justin who filled them both.

"Cream and sugar?" Justin asked and Drew hooked a finger in the waistband of his sweats.

"I got the day off. I don't know if you work but if not, what do you say we go and do something today? Just fucking go and try and leave all the other shit behind, even if it's only for a few hours."

Justin paused. Looked at him. Cocked his head a little. His eyes were questioning and he looked confused and Drew didn't know why that was cute as hell. Jesus, he liked this man.

"Are you trying to take me on a date, Cinderella?" Justin asked playfully.

"Eh." Drew shrugged. "Figured it might help me get in your pants again."

"Such a horny slut. First you jack me off in the middle of a goddamned club. Then you blow me at the gym. Yesterday you fucked me senseless and it's still not enough for you? You're insatiable."

"Hey! You approached me in the club and I'm pretty sure you were the one on his knees for me first at the gym. Actually, I'm also the one who said it wasn't a good idea to fuck around the first time you came to my house. I'm a goddamned gentleman. You're the horny bastard here. Not me."

Justin smiled and winked at him. "Never said I wasn't."

Drew squeezed Justin's hip trying to figure out why just standing in the room with him felt so fucking nice. "As long as we're on the same page."

Justin paused again before he softly said, "We are," and Drew had a feeling they weren't just talking about who was the horniest anymore. "And yeah. Let's get the fuck out of here. Selfish as that makes me feel, I need it."

"That doesn't make you selfish. It makes you human."

Justin rolled his eyes as though he didn't believe him. When Drew tried to speak, Justin pressed a quick kiss to his mouth instead. "Be quiet or I won't let you in my pants later. Coffee, breakfast, and then let's get going."

He walked to the fridge and Drew knew that for now, he needed to let it go.

JUSTIN HAD A million things he should be doing right now. Talking to Nick and letting him know what was going on with his dad. Spending time with his father. Talking to his brother and sister. Driving an hour and a half to the Eastern Shore wasn't on that list, yet that's what they'd done.

Once there, they walked on a quiet beach, wearing jeans and hoodies because it was pretty motherfucking chilly. Most people were smartly in their homes, avoiding the clouds above in case they opened up the way they did the day before.

And there was nowhere else he wanted to be.

He shoved his hands into the pockets of the jeans Drew lent him and kicked a twig in the sand. "Tell me about the guy. The one you kissed. You said he was a friend of yours."

Drew adjusted his hat, and Justin had a feeling he was stalling.

"Yeah…he was my best friend. Honestly, I don't know what in the fuck I was thinking. I should have known it was a bad idea. We were graduating. The next year we'd be off in college. I think I already knew I didn't want to be a lawyer, even then. Shit was changing too fast for my taste, and he was stability, ya know? He represented home—high school sports, drinking too much, and just being young and having fun. I kissed him, he punched me, and that was the end of that friendship. It scared me off a little bit. The next time I kissed a guy, I made damn sure the idea of kissing a man didn't make him want to commit bodily harm."

"He stopped being your friend?" Justin asked.

"He did. I tried to talk to him a few times over the summer, but he wasn't having it. I went to one college and he went to another one. Now I only see him once in a while when he comes back home to visit his parents."

"Damn. That's harsh." Justin leaned closer and bumped into him. "FYI, there will be no bodily harm when you kiss me. Unless you want to try some of the kinky shit, but I have to admit, I don't think pain is my thing."

"Always flirting with me. What am I going to do with you?" Drew teased back.

"You like it," Justin countered and then, "So your first love was a man. Huh. I find that interesting."

"I don't know that I loved him. I was a kid. He was familiar. I wanted to bone him."

"Were you a virgin?" Justin asked.

"No. I slept with two girls in high school—a girlfriend and a hookup. I guess maybe I did have feelings for him, but I didn't understand them. And I don't think it was love. Like I said, he was familiar and I wanted that at the time."

Justin nodded because what Drew said made sense. "What about you?" Drew asked.

"I was a good boy. I actually didn't have sex for the first time until the summer after I graduated high school."

"No shit?" Drew asked, the surprise evident in his voice.

"Partial lie. When I lost my virginity is true, but I sure as hell didn't want to be a good boy. Christ, I think I jerked off more than any guy at my school. I also knew I was gay so I had no interest in sleeping with women. There weren't a whole lot of options for me."

"Who was your first?"

Justin shrugged. "Just a random guy I met at a club. He was older. Wanted to fuck a twink, which I was at the time. I didn't want to be a virgin forever, and there you go."

"Damn that sounds…"

"No, no. If you're going to say it's sad, it really wasn't. It is what it is. We both got what we wanted. Look at you. You really are Mr. Fairytale, happy endings."

"No, I'm not." Drew playfully pouted before Justin asked him something he'd been thinking a lot about.

"How do you think your family will react when you tell them you're bi? Will it be a big deal?"

"Hmmm," Drew said and then it was his turn to kick a small branch that made its way to the beach. "That's a good question. I think they'll be surprised and likely a little confused. I doubt bisexuality is on their radar but I won't have to worry about being disowned or anything like that. My family doesn't really work that way. Jacob doesn't really care who I am or what I do as long as it doesn't get too close to his perfect world, and my parents will just see it as another way I'm different from the rest of them, I guess."

The softness in his voice made Justin think maybe he was a little sadder about that than he wanted to let on. Not just the part about his parents but about Jacob, too. "What's the deal with you and Jacob? There has to be more to it than you're letting on."

"You're awfully chatty today."

"I'm always chatty."

"True," Drew conceded. "Let's see. I already told you we've never been close. We're extremely different but I think part of that is typical sibling stuff."

Justin had an idea of what Drew would say before he said it. "Let me guess. There was a woman?"

"There's always a woman."

"Or a man." Justin looked over at him and cocked a brow.

"Another truth. But yeah, there was a woman. Jacob was in love with her…or he thought he was. I'm not sure. He didn't look at Iris the way he looks at your sister."

Justin almost stumbled at the mention of Shanen. Drew reached out and grabbed hold of him, then pulled him closer, wrapping an arm around his shoulders. "So yeah. He loved Iris. She kissed me. I didn't stop her as quickly as I should have. Don't get me wrong, it didn't get out of hand, but it took a minute for me to get my head straight and stop it. She admitted we kissed before I had the chance. None of the details mattered—that she kissed me, that I said no. For him it was just me trying to take something or someone that was his. Jesus, I think...I think he really believes that I wanted to hurt him for whatever reason."

Then he was a fucking idiot. That wasn't Drew. There was no doubt in Justin's mind about that. "He should get to know you better if he thinks that."

Drew glanced over at him, pulled Justin's head closer, and kissed the top of it. "Thank you. I'm not perfect, though. I've thrown it back at Jacob in anger. I'm not innocent. We're like oil and water, the two of us."

Justin wondered how Jacob would feel if he knew about the two of them. That they were friends...that if Justin was at home, back to his life, and he'd met Drew, that they would've likely considered themselves to be in a relationship right now.

They continued walking down the beach while the clouds kept getting darker, but it didn't deter them.

It was a few minutes later when Drew said, "Can I ask about your dad?"

"Yep," Justin replied because he knew it was coming...and somehow it was okay because it was Drew asking.

A few seconds later, Drew added, "I think I just did. Nothing specific. Just tell me about him."

So Justin did. He talked about his dad coming back into his life and how he'd become his best friend. How he'd taught him to ride even though he didn't love it with the same passion that Landon did. They talked about camping and sports and his father's support when he came out. There had never been a second that his father had a problem with his son being gay.

And it felt good. Really fucking good, even though his father had been lying to him the whole time.

CHAPTER SEVENTEEN

Somehow, they beat the rain. They'd spent hours on the beach, part of it cold and trembling, but it hadn't started to pour until they made it back to the truck.

The drive home was much like the drive there had been. They talked and laughed and gave each other shit. Before they got into town, they made a stop at a Whole Foods store to grab something for dinner. Drew knew they both understood that they made the stop there because the chance of running into someone he knew was less likely. He wasn't sure how he felt about that…or if it should matter. He just knew things needed to be easy right now and keeping this between the two of them, protecting it, felt easier than anything else.

After they parked and got out, Justin nodded to the building beside the store. "I'm going to run into the drug store and grab a few things you're sorely lacking. I'll meet you when I'm done." He winked and then jogged away, wearing Drew's hat. He forgot Justin had stolen it from him in the truck.

He chuckled to himself as he made his way into the store to grab what he needed for the teriyaki chicken stir-fry he planned to make tonight, while Justin got to shop for condoms and lube.

Forty minutes later, they pulled into the driveway of his house.

"It's relaxing out here," Justin told him as he waited for Drew to unlock the house.

"It is. I love it. No one bothers me here. You should try out the hot tub on the back deck. Maybe if the weather clears up." He liked that Justin seemed to feel comfortable at his home, that it was a place for him to get away from everything.

Drew started dinner while Justin made another call to his dad from the kitchen table.

"No, I wasn't at work today. I met a friend and we hung out." Drew looked over his shoulder at Justin's statement, and Justin shrugged as if he didn't know what to say. The truth was, it shouldn't matter if the two of them were friends. It shouldn't matter if they were fucking either. And maybe it wouldn't.

When Justin got off the phone, they finished cooking together, and then ate. Justin teased him about eating healthy and missing fried foods, and Drew told him he was lucky he didn't force a protein shake down his throat. The rain started coming down again, so the hot tub idea was shot. "I'm going to take a quick shower," Justin told him.

"Go for it. There are clothes in my drawers. You can wear anything. I'm just going to do a few things down here and then I'll be up. I'll take one after you."

It was so strange, how they'd stumbled into what basically felt like a relationship. Or the start of one at least.

Justin went upstairs and Drew rinsed the dishes and loaded the dishwasher. Before heading upstairs, he grabbed them both a beer.

The shower was still running when Drew got to his room. He called out, "I brought you a beer," loud enough for Justin to hear him.

"Great. Wanna bring your ass in the shower with me next?" Justin replied, making him roll his eyes and chuckle.

He set the beers down and made his way into the bathroom. Justin's long, lean body stood beneath the spray, water on the glass making it harder to see him, but Drew definitely saw enough. "Jesus, you're fucking bossy."

Justin turned his way. "Hey, I asked. I didn't demand. But even if I did, would you really argue? I mean, we're naked. Well I am, and if you hurry your ass up, you will be too."

Okay, so he had a really good point there. Drew pulled his T-shirt over his head and dropped it to the floor. "I'm coming, I'm coming."

Justin paused, then opened the shower door, and goddamn Drew's dick went hard on the spot. "Not coming yet, but you will be soon."

There wasn't a doubt in Drew's mind that he was right.

He finished stripping out of his clothes and then stepped into the enclosed shower with Justin. It was big enough that they could fit without touching and he suddenly wished he'd designed a smaller shower.

"Get cleaned up. I already did." Justin nodded toward the showerhead and stepped back a little. Drew took his place, standing backward and dropping his head back to get his hair wet.

He hissed, pleasure shooting through his body when he felt Justin's hand wrap around his erection. "I'm not going to get anything done if you do that."

"But it's such a pretty cock, I can't help but want to touch it." He stroked and Drew's knees damn near gave out. "And this." He rubbed his palm over Drew's pubic hair. "I hate it when I get a man out of his clothes and find out he shaved. Trimming is fine, but who doesn't want rough hair scratching against their face when they're sucking dick? I love burying my face in it, almost as much as ass."

Drew's arm shot out and he steadied himself on the wall. "You keep touching me and saying shit like that to me, and my balls are going to empty before we get a chance to do much. Fuck, that feels good." And it did—Justin's rough hand against him. His deep voice talking to him. Drew's fucking toes curled into the floor of the shower.

Justin stepped back and held his hands up. Drew immediately wanted to pull him back. Why had he opened his mouth?

"Fine. I'll be good. You have three minutes. I'm not making

promises after that."

Drew grabbed the soap and took care of business. He cleaned his body, listened to Justin suck in a deep breath as he watched Drew soap up his balls. The second he finished with his whole body, Justin was on him.

Their mouths crashed together and their tongues wrestled. Justin pulled him closer, undulating his hips and making their dicks rub against each other. They stumbled, fell against the wall, and laughed against each other's lips.

"You make me crazy." Justin spoke close to his mouth. "It's like you take me somewhere else. All the outside stuff is on pause and I just get to live in the moment. How do you do it? How do you take me away from all of it?"

Justin's mouth ravished his again before he had the time to answer. He wanted to tell Justin he felt the same way. No, he didn't have the same things going on, but Justin made him crazy, wild.

They thrust their hips together as they ate at each other's mouths. He felt that sweet burn in his balls, the slight tingle that begged to explode into a full-on orgasm.

Drew grabbed Justin's ass, squeezed the globes as they made out like kissing each other was their air.

"I want to play with your hole." Justin squeezed his hand between Drew's ass and the wall. "I want to watch my finger disappear inside you. Lick you. Spread your cheeks apart and feast on you."

"Oh fuck." Drew's dick jerked against his stomach and he damn near blew his load. "You're making me feel like a fucking virgin here."

"Have you ever had anything in your ass?" Justin asked before licking a path down Drew's collarbone. "I know you haven't been eaten out."

No, he hadn't been eaten out but that was about to change, and he couldn't wait. "I've fingered myself. Played around. It feels fucking amazing. I want to feel your fingers stretching me. Want to know what it feels like to be rimmed by a self-proclaimed master at ass eating," Drew teased and there was more laughter. But the truth was, even before he'd fingered himself he was always fascinated by the idea of ass play. As much as Drew liked to do the fucking, he foresaw a very versatile future for himself.

"Prepare to have your mind blown," Justin told him.

"You're confident." He liked that about him.

"I'm honest about my abilities. Now turn around and let me work my magic. I can't wait to get a taste of you."

Drew turned and Justin pushed him over to the back of the shower, keeping them out of the spray. He put a leg between Drew's, telling him to open them, which he did.

Drew let his arms lean against the wall to hold himself up, as Justin's hands moved down his ass.

"You have a nice butt. Do you work out?" Justin asked.

Crazy motherfucker. "Sometimes. I'm not real big on the gym."

He held his breath when Justin kneeled behind him, suddenly more thankful than he could explain that it was this man with him right now. That it was this man he'd met at the club and who was going on this ride with him.

"Liar," Justin said before he bit into Drew's right cheek. "Put your ass out a little more, baby."

Drew froze at the term of endearment. He didn't have to look behind him to know that Justin did too. That the word *baby* had slipped out accidentally.

It was Drew who recovered first. He did as Justin told him, pushing his ass out more and then he shook it. "Don't leave me hanging. Jesus, I need to feel your mouth on me."

That was all it took to get Justin back in the game.

Drew cursed when he felt Justin's finger rub against his rim. He started softly and then increased the pressure. Then his finger was gone and it was replaced by his warm, wet tongue in quick, short strokes lashing across his pucker.

The pleasure started at that point and then shot throughout Drew's body, ricocheting around.

He gasped, groaned, pushed back farther wanting Justin's tongue inside him.

Justin reached between Drew's legs, fondling his nuts, playing with them and teasing them as he worked Drew's asshole with his tongue.

"Fuck, Justin…So good. That feels so motherfucking *good*." It was like all of his favorite things put together giftwrapped just for him.

"I knew you'd like it."

He felt Justin smile against his crack.

"Hold yourself open for me and I can really play."

It didn't occur to him to be embarrassed about having someone back there. Drew grabbed his ass cheeks and spread them wide just as Justin dove in. He licked at Drew's hole, long slides of his tongue, from his taint to the top of his crack.

"I knew you'd taste good," Justin said and then he dove in again. He buried his face deep—licked hard, soft, up, down, in circles, his hand playing and teasing Drew's balls the whole time.

When he pulled away, "Jesus Christ, get back here," ripped out of Drew's mouth. His cock leaked. His balls were heavy. He wanted to come. No, he needed it.

"Who's the bossy one now?" Justin asked and then his finger was there, working inside Drew's hole. He pushed it in deep, pulled out again and then started over. "Such a tight, little hole. I can't wait until I get to fuck it. Tell me you're gonna let me, Drew. Not tonight but soon."

Hell, he'd let Justin take him right now if he wanted. He could fuck Drew every day, all day, just live with his cock in Drew's ass if it felt half as good as a finger. "Yeah, I already told you that. Any time. Any place. I want your dick inside me."

At that, Justin ravenously went at him again. A guttural growl came from Drew's throat as he was eaten and finger-fucked at the same time. He fought to hold it off as long as he could but then his balls let loose. He came, long spurt after long spurt shooting from his slit and coating the shower wall.

He fought to catch his breath, his chest heaving as he let the wall hold him up.

"Well shit. I didn't think that through. I didn't get to eat your come."

Drew couldn't find it in himself to laugh, not this time. All he could think was, *I'm a goner.*

CHAPTER EIGHTEEN

IT HAD BEEN early but they fell asleep after their shower. Or at least, Drew had. He came so hard his head nearly popped off so Justin understood the exhaustion. But there was more to it than that. There was a heaviness to the air all of a sudden, that Justin tried to ignore. Drew had tried to return the favor after their shower, but Justin had waved him off. Who in the hell said no to an orgasm?

The room was dark, he had his back to Drew, their two full beer bottles unopened.

He wished he could turn his brain off. He'd told Drew that everything felt like it was on pause when they were together, and though that was true most of the time, the pause button always came off eventually. And this time, he had thoughts of Drew in the mix.

What were they doing?

Was this as real as it was starting to feel and if so, how in the fuck had it happened?

And Christ, how could he be thinking about another man when so much was going on? When he was losing his father.

The bed dipped. Drew rolled over. He wrapped an arm around Justin's waist, and the warmth felt fucking perfect there.

"Stop," Drew whispered against his neck.

"Stop what?"

"Overthinking things. Worrying. The only thing you need to consider is your family. That's first. Everything else will wait."

And somehow, that helped. The weight eased off of him. "How

did you know I was thinking?" he asked.

"I'm not sure." Drew kissed his shoulder, his neck, sucked his earlobe. They both lay on their right sides, as Drew ran a hand up and down Justin's top leg. He pushed it forward, and Justin read what he was saying. He bent it at the knee, sliding it off the other leg to give Drew access to his hole.

"I'll put my mouth on you next time. I'll do it all goddamn day if you want, but right now, I really just need to fuck you."

Damned if Justin didn't need that too.

The lube and condoms were next to him on the bedside table. He grabbed them both and handed them to Drew.

He kept in the same position on his side as Drew pulled away and suited up.

Justin heard the condom wrapper open. Knew Drew was rolling it down. The lube was next, and then Drew lay beside him again. He peppered more kisses along Justin's shoulders as his lube-wet finger breached Justin's ass.

A heavy breath pushed out of his lungs as though it had been trapped there for years. "Just put your dick in me, baby. Fuck me."

Drew worked his way inside him, stretched him in the best fucking way, and then his arm went around him again. He wrapped it under Justin's armpit, and then gripped his shoulder.

Then, he fucked. Long, slow strokes, his front smacking Justin's ass each time he thrust. With each pump, he gripped Justin's shoulder tighter. He wanted Drew's finger marks there. Wanted to be bruised. To bear Drew's mark.

His cock dragged back and forth across Justin's prostate. His dick throbbed, it was so hard.

They were quiet as Drew fucked harder. Squeezed tighter, but still went so goddamned slow. It was as though he was trying to draw it out.

He loved the feeling of being full, of Drew filling him.

Justin let everything else go. Just felt Drew fucking him. Surrendered to this moment, with this man.

"So hot," Drew whispered. "So motherfucking tight. Can't get enough of you."

Drew drilled him with precision. With skill. When Justin wrapped a hand around his own cock, he knew it wouldn't be long before he came.

Justin jerked himself off with slow, greedy pulls. "Christ, you fuck me good. I'm gonna come."

His balls pulled up, let loose and pleasure rolled through him as he came hard all over his hand.

He felt Drew tense behind him and then his teeth were there, biting into the muscle at the top of Justin's shoulder as he fucked through his orgasm.

They didn't speak for a few minutes. Justin didn't know what to say, which honestly didn't happen to him much. It was Drew who spoke first. "Well shit. I didn't think that through. I didn't get to eat your come." He repeated what Justin said in the shower.

He couldn't have said something more right as they both laughed and held each other, just living in the moment.

JUSTIN KNEW HE was overreacting but this felt very much like a set up. Of course it wasn't. What would they be setting him up for? But still, as he sat in a room with Landon, Rod, Shanen and Jacob, he couldn't help but feel like the odd man out.

Shanen paced her living room, obviously on edge when Jacob grabbed her hand and smiled at her. That easily Justin saw some of the weight drain from her shoulders. It was obvious they were in love. It was obvious Jacob would do anything for Justin's sister. Still, he couldn't help but feel a little animosity for the man because of his relationship with Drew.

Drew was the best man he knew—honest and caring. He couldn't understand how someone couldn't see that when they looked at him. Especially his own brother.

How would Jacob feel if he knew about Justin's relationship with Drew? How would any of them feel? He couldn't see Landon caring, or really Shanen either. Her only problem would likely be how it affected her husband.

He had no business wondering about that anyway. He didn't live here. He had a home in North Carolina. School, work, his mom. Soon, he'd be gone, which didn't leave his relationship with Drew much of a relationship at all.

"I just thought we should all touch base, a bit," Shanen began. "The next few weeks…or hell, months are likely to be challenging ones. God," she shook her head. "We have no idea how much time we have with him. I wanted more time." She buried her face in her hands. Her shoulders began to shake. Justin went to push to his feet, but Jacob pulled her into his arms. He held Shanen while she cried. Rod whispered in Landon's ear, as Landon sat with his elbows on his knees, looking down.

It was so similar to sitting in Joy's house and hearing that his father would stop chemo that he immediately felt the anger rise inside him. Felt it squeeze a fist around his chest as he watched them…as he longed to be that fucking close to someone. It was then he realized it wasn't anger at all. It was jealousy.

He didn't have what they did.

Hell, he didn't have much of a family either. He loved his mom and they were close, but she was all he had. The people in this room didn't have the same history with Justin that they had with each other. They would always be closer to each other than they would be to him.

"I'm sorry." Shanen pulled away from Jacob and wiped her eyes. "I swore I wouldn't do this."

This time, it was Justin who found his eyes glancing down. He looked at the carpet. Moved his foot across it, making the fibers move in the opposite direction.

"I just think we need to be united right now. Spend time with Dad, and try to make whatever time he has left as happy as we can make it."

Justin's gut twisted and turned, guilt creeping in. "You're right. I apologize for losing it before. I just…I just don't know how to do this." How the fuck did he lose his dad? How did he find his place in this other family if his father wasn't around, and should he even try?

"No," Landon cut in. "Don't be sorry. This whole situation is fucked. We're all just doing the best we can."

"Landon's right," Shanen added. "I didn't mean to insinuate that this was about you."

Justin looked up and he could see the sincerity in both their faces. He heard it in their voices as well.

"You didn't," Justin told her.

"Good. I just…I know how important this is to him—to know his family is together and by his side. I want to give him that, and I think we all deserve it for ourselves as well. We don't want to have any regrets."

And that was the crux of why Justin was here in the first place. Why he buried his anger at his dad, and dropped everything in his life to come to Virginia. He didn't want to have any regrets either.

CHAPTER NINETEEN

D REW HAD TO bite his tongue not to ask Jacob or Shanen how things had gone at their house today. Likely, Shanen because he hadn't talked to his brother since their meeting in his office the other day. It all felt so fucking petty when he thought about what Justin was going through. He'd tried to call him earlier, but Justin had gone straight from Jacob's to work.

He wondered how much longer Justin would be able to keep the job at Nick's. He had a feeling Justin did it just to have something else that was his own.

What he did know was that he'd wanted to be there for Justin today. He'd wanted to support him and that feeling didn't come as a shock to him. He wasn't sure how he'd let himself get so wrapped up in Justin, but he had, and damned if he didn't know it wouldn't turn out well. His life was here. Justin's was in North Carolina.

"How are things at work, Andrew?" his mother asked as they sat around the table eating dinner. This was the second dinner like this they'd had recently and he wondered if seeing a family lose someone made them want to hold fast to their own.

Shanen spoke before Drew had the chance to respond. "You know, I've been thinking about signing up. I just have so much going on right now, but it's important to me to take good care of myself. Especially with everything going on with Dad."

"I'm so sorry, dear," his mom said. "Jacob told me that he's going to stop treatment."

Shanen shook her head and Drew could tell that she definitely didn't want to talk about it. "I appreciate that. You were asking about Andrew, though. I didn't mean to change the subject."

The last thing Drew wanted to talk about was himself but his reasons were a whole hell of a lot more selfish than Shanen's, so he spoke a little bit about work and about giving Robyn more responsibilities. He hoped one day he would be able to open a second gym, and maybe she would run it.

"That sounds wonderful," his mom replied. His dad of course didn't have much to say. Drew's career wasn't important and that was that. It was only a few seconds later that his mother added, "Okay...I've tried not to pry but what about dating? You've been awfully busy lately. I'd love to see both of my boys settled down with a nice lady."

Drew wasn't sure why but his eyes darted toward Jacob. His brother paid attention to his plate, taking a bite of his food and obviously not at all interested in the conversation. It pissed him off. Jesus, it fucking pissed him off. They were brothers. It shouldn't be this way.

"Leave the boy alone," his dad said. "He's young. Let him have fun." His dad had always had his back in that regard.

Shanen smiled at him like she was interested in the answer as well. Jacob still paid no attention to him at all, and Drew decided to just go with his gut. What was the point in continuing to keep it to himself? When Justin left, there was a very strong chance that he would eventually date another man. "If I ever do settle down, it might not be with a woman."

Jacob's head shot up. His eyes went wide and latched straight onto Drew. He was shocked and that made sadness settle into Drew's bones. These were the kinds of things siblings should talk about. His brother should have been one of the first people Drew told when he realized he was also attracted to men.

"What do you mean?" his father asked, obvious confusion in his voice.

Drew pulled his eyes away from Jacob and he looked toward his parents. "I mean it might not be a woman. It could be. But it could just as easily be a man." Although none of that felt right to him in this moment because there were no women he was interested in and he thought he wanted it to be one man, specifically. Even though he knew what would eventually happen, it was hard to see past now, and now was all tangled up with Justin.

"You're gay?" his dad asked.

His mom swatted his shoulder. "He's not *gay*, sweetheart. If he were gay, there wouldn't be a chance that he'd date a woman. You're bisexual? I read this big article about it in a magazine the other day—how so many more people are realizing they're bisexual, gender fluid, and other sexual identities and orientations."

"Wait. Gender what? Gender fluid? What the hell does that mean?" His dad nearly choked, and damned if Drew didn't suddenly want to laugh. This conversation was definitely out of his father's realm of comfort.

"There are a lot more sexual orientations and identities than you realize, dear. Didn't that young singer girl who sticks her tongue out all the time say she's pansexual? Or demisexual?"

This time it was Drew who almost choked. He grabbed his stomach as he coughed. In a million years, this wasn't how he saw this conversation going. That his mom would start speaking about people being pan or demi—he was glad for it, though.

"I can get you the article if you want." His mom patted his father's hand.

"No, I don't think so, dear. I'd like to hear from Andrew, though."

Drew. I want to go by Drew. Why was that so hard to understand? He was Drew. He felt more himself being called Drew. "Yes, Dad. I'm bisexual. I'm attracted to both men and women."

"Are you dating a man right now?" his mom asked, and Jesus fucking Christ he wanted to say yes. He wanted to tell them he was dating Justin. That he wanted to support Justin when they got together to talk about his dad, and wanted them to know how fucking incredible he was. That he turned his whole world upside down to come here. That he was one of the most unselfish people Drew knew and that he was afraid he didn't have a place with Shanen and Landon.

But he couldn't do that, could he? Not without Justin being on the same page. "I just think it's time you know." It was the easiest answer he could give. "It's who I am, and I want my family to know me."

"Well, personally, I think that's fantastic," Shanen said. "Landon is committed to Rod but he identifies as bisexual. And I don't know if I've told you, but Justin is gay."

I know, Drew wanted to tell her. *I know because I want to be with him. I want to support him, to be by his side.* Instead of speaking his truth, Drew cleared his throat and replied, "What a coincidence."

For the first time in minutes, he looked his brother's way. Jacob watched him, his eyes narrow...penetrating...but they weren't angry. Questioning, yes, but for the first time in years, Drew didn't see any anger there, and he didn't know what that meant.

IT WAS STRANGE, the changes that came with stopping chemo. There were the parts that always weighed heavy on Justin's mind—the fact that the end was coming soon, but there were good parts too. In the following weeks his father regained some of his strength. He was more like the dad he'd grown up with. Not the same, of course, but the difference was sharp. Stopping treatments showed him how hard they had actually been on his body. It was sad how sick people got from the medicines that were supposed to help heal you.

He didn't vomit daily anymore. He had more energy. His body didn't seem so fucking worn out. They talked more and laughed more. Sometimes, he could almost let himself forget. He enjoyed their time together. Justin went to Joy's and saw him daily, not willing to lose anymore moments than he had to.

But his nights? He'd spent a lot of them lately in Drew's bed. He'd head over after work, or after leaving Joy's, or the gym. They'd eat food that Justin would tease Drew about, even though he enjoyed Drew's cooking. It had become their thing to joke about health and packing meals into his fridge that he labeled with different days of the week.

They spent time in the hot tub, and watched movies, and Drew would fuck him senseless. He was a quick study, learning fast what Justin liked. How to drive him crazy with his tongue, fingers, mouth, or dick.

Today was going to be a hard day, though. He knew it ahead of time and he'd been a stubborn SOB and stayed home last night—well, not home, but at the house he used to share with his dad. But now as he got ready to meet his dad's family for them to go out for a ride, he suddenly wished like hell he was with Drew. Wished like hell that Drew could come with him. That he would have the man by his side.

Maybe he'd known he would feel that way from the start, which was the exact reason he didn't stay with Drew last night. He shouldn't depend on Drew so strongly.

"Fucking ridiculous," Justin mumbled to himself as he stood. He didn't know what his problem was. There was no reason he needed Drew there with him as he went out with his dad's family.

He was a grown man, and they didn't have the same kind of relationship Shanen had with Jacob or Landon with Rod.

Justin finished getting ready and then left. He kept the car quiet as he made his way out to where Landon said to meet. It was out of town, the parking lot of an abandoned building.

The ride was beautiful as he followed quiet, winding roads surrounded by trees.

It was about forty-five minutes into his drive when he saw the worn-down building off to the left. It had a large parking lot, with only a couple motorcycles, cars, and, "Holy shit." Drew's truck was in the damn lot. He was fucking there, and suddenly Justin's chest felt full. Not quite as empty as it had a few moments before, which should probably worry him more than it did.

Justin pulled into the lot, parked, and got out. "I feel like I'm always the last one to arrive," he said smiling.

"We won't hold it against you." Rod winked at him and smiled. He wore dark eyeliner again. He did most of the time, and it fit him. He could see what Landon saw in the other man, not just because he was attractive but because he was a good guy.

"Hey, Dad." Justin wrapped an arm around his frail parent and pulled him into a hug. His eyes met Drew's over his dad's shoulder, and Drew gave him a small shrug and a half-smile. Justin felt that smile bone deep.

What in the hell had he said to get invited? It wasn't as though Jacob would have asked him, though Drew did say Jacob had been acting a little differently toward him since Drew apparently told his family he was bi.

As soon as he pulled away from his dad, Shanen was there. "It's good to see you, little brother." Her words were like a stun gun to the chest. Yes, it was true. He was her younger brother but she'd never called him that before.

"Thank God. It's nice not to be the baby anymore," Landon added, and Justin felt an ease that he hadn't felt in months. He didn't know where it came from. If it was the fact that sometimes, they could pretend their dad wasn't sick now, or what. But what he did know was that he liked it.

"The baby is supposed to be the spoiled one. I can handle that," Justin teased and everyone laughed.

"Justin, you remember Jacob's brother, Andrew, right?" she asked and damned if it didn't suddenly feel like the craziest thing in the world that no one knew they were spending time together. At first it had been because he had so much on his mind, and Drew's rocky relationship with his brother. The fact that Justin wanted something in this town that was his and his alone, but now the alone part didn't feel so good. He didn't know how Drew would feel about it, so he held out his hand.

"Good to see you again, Drew," he said as Drew smiled and they shook.

"I mentioned what we were doing, and Drew wanted to come and hang out to see Dad ride," Shanen added.

"You're going to have to force me off that thing once I get on," his dad said and Justin could see sincere joy on his face. In the light in his eyes and the strength behind his smile. He needed this. Needed it so fucking much and Justin was glad as hell Landon was giving it to him.

"This is where I taught Rod to ride. He only tried to kill himself once," Landon teased and Rod rolled his eyes.

"Don't blame the student, blame the teacher. Isn't that the motto nowadays?" Rod asked and again, there was a round of group laughter.

It felt...good. This moment, with these people felt really fucking good. It made him realize how much he hoped it could last, that he would still have family here when his father was gone.

"Okay, let's do this," Landon said once silence washed over them again. Justin watched as Landon took one of the helmets that sat on his bike. He turned toward their father in the wheelchair. He lifted his chin so Landon could strap the half-helmet on him and damned if Justin didn't see Landon's hand shaking. He felt the same tremble in his own. He shook it out, tried to get ahold of himself. When he looked up again, his eyes met Drew's, who held on to him with such unwavering support that Justin could feel it despite the distance between them.

"Looking good, Dad," Landon told their father before strapping on his own helmet. He held his hand out to their dad, but he shook his head.

"I got it. I need to do some of this by myself." He still wore his oxygen, something he would have to do until the end. When he shakily stood, he put the backpack on that carried the tank. Landon stayed close to him as they slowly made their way to the bike.

Landon got on first and started the bike. Their dad got on behind him. "Hold on tight," Landon told him, so much fucking pain and sincerity in his voice that it damn near stole Justin's breath.

This was part of their goodbye and it was beautiful. He was honored that he got to see it.

When Justin glanced at Drew again, the other man was still watching him. Everyone else had their eyes on Landon and his dad. Drew was the only one looking at Justin.

"You ready for this?" Landon asked.

"I am. Thank you."

And they began to ride. He made trips up and down the large lot—fast, slow, driving straight lines, and swerving around for fun.

It was as though all the weight in the world was suddenly on Justin's chest, living inside of it, swelling until it crushed every single piece of him.

He was watching his brother with his father. Watching them bond, and knowing how fucking much they needed this. Feeling like shit because he wanted to be a part of it too. Wanted to connect with them over something they both loved so much.

Everyone was silent. Everyone watched them. Justin looked down, his fucking eyes stinging. He wiped them quickly, determined not to let a tear fall. Joy and Shanen were crying—smiling and crying as they watched Landon and his dad on what would be his last ride. What was likely the first time the two of them had been on a bike together since Landon was a child.

Justin couldn't make himself look at Drew. He felt his friend's eyes on him. Felt the support and…Christ, the fucking strength he somehow managed to give Justin just by being here.

It was a few minutes later when Landon steered the bike back toward their group.

They hardly had the time to come to a stop before Drew spoke, "If Larry is up to it, I think you should take one more ride. Maybe Justin could take Rod's bike out, and the three of you could ride together."

The statement was like a stun gun to his heart—a shock that made it beat again when Justin hadn't realized it stopped. Maybe it had been dormant for months but now it was there again, beating life in his chest, because of what Drew just suggested.

"I think that's the best idea I've heard all day," his father replied and Justin let out a deep, relieved breath that his dad wanted him to be a part of this.

He looked at Landon, who nodded, because it was important to him that Landon felt okay with it. This was their moment. He didn't want to take it away from them.

His eyes found Rod's next. Some people didn't want others to ride their bike, but Rod just winked at him and grinned, like he knew a secret that Justin didn't know.

In that moment, everything else melted away. The weight in his chest got lighter until it weighed nothing. Justin hadn't realized it until Drew made the suggestion, but he needed this.

He thought maybe all three of them did.

And it was Drew who had known to give it to him.

CHAPTER TWENTY

"THANK YOU," JUSTIN told Rod when the other man handed over his helmet.

"That's what family is for."

Rod's words hit him straight in the chest. Almost stole his breath. No, it wasn't Landon or Shanen, but hearing Rod say he was family meant the world to him.

"It is." He nodded at Rod before strapping the helmet on. It had been a while since he'd ridden a bike. He knew how. His father had definitely made sure of that, and Justin did have a motorcycle license too. He wasn't sure why he'd always kept it up, even though he wasn't as avid a rider like his dad, but he was glad he had.

He threw his leg over Rod's bike. Felt the rumble of the engine when he started it.

"Do you want to ride with me?" he asked Shanen, but she shook her head. She had a sad smile on her face that looked so much like a feminine version of their dad.

"No. This is just for you boys," she replied.

He looked over at Landon, who gave him a smile and nodded. Without words, they were on the same wavelength. Maybe that was something most brothers shared. He didn't know but he felt damned proud to feel it in this moment.

They both drove toward the street. They stopped at the edge of the parking lot. It wasn't until their dad gave a silent, "Let's do this," that the men pulled from the parking lot and onto the road.

The wind blew, making the orange, green, and brown leaves fall like rain on them. The leaves danced across the twists and turns in the road. They didn't ride fast, but they didn't need to. That's not what this was about. Justin and Landon were side-by-side—two brothers taking a last ride with their dad.

Amazingly, no cars passed them going the opposite direction. None pulled up behind them. In this moment, it was as though the world belonged to the three of them. He wondered if it would have been like this if their father had stayed in touch with all of his kids. If he would have grown up riding with his dad and his brother. What kind of relationship would they all have had?

And as much as the not knowing hurt, as much as he wanted to be angry at his dad, he managed to keep it locked inside him, hopefully for good this time. They couldn't change the past. They only had the present, and Justin wanted nothing more than to live in this moment.

There were no guarantees in life.

They rode for what was probably too long. Landon eventually pulled over for a small break, and to swap places.

"Thank you," Justin told him.

"He's a father to both of us. We should both get this," Landon replied, and then they were going again. Justin felt his father's tight grip. He hadn't been hugged by his dad with this much strength since he was a kid. He hadn't thought his father had it in him anymore, but he did, and Justin would remember this moment for as long as he lived.

When they made it back to the parking lot, he wanted nothing more than to go to Drew. To hold him. To thank him. To have the support he needed so fucking much.

"Thank you. Thank you both. That was the best ride of my life," their dad said.

"Mine too," both Justin and Landon said in unison.

The whole time, he felt Drew's hot stare on him. Felt it in his chest. *There are no guarantees in life...* And there weren't. All you could do was live in the moment because the next one wasn't promised.

Drew nodded as though he could read Justin's mind. His wide, expressive eyes told him it was okay. If it caused problems, they'd work them out later.

Maybe it was because he was going through so much emotionally, because he was so raw and exposed—an angry fucking wound that couldn't heal—just kept getting ripped open again. Maybe he was just needy for something to hold on to. Maybe that would change when his father passed and Justin was able to go back home. He didn't understand the reason. The only thing he did know was in this moment, in all these pieced together moments that would make up the rest of his time here, he needed whatever it was Drew gave him. The stability. The support.

Justin walked over to him and stopped not a foot away. "Hi," he said lamely.

"Hi." Drew smiled.

And then Justin stepped closer. He wrapped his arms around Drew's shoulders. Drew held his waist, his fingers dug into his hips. Their foreheads dropped against one another, Drew wearing his hat backward like he always did. Justin closed his eyes and whispered, "Thank you," over and over and over again.

EVERYONE WENT QUIET, but Drew didn't pay attention to them. He didn't let himself think about his brother, or anyone except for Justin.

Justin needed him, he'd be there. That's all there was to it.

A moment later, it was Justin who pulled away first. Drew had no idea what he planned to say—that they were friends? That they were seeing each other? *Were* they officially seeing each other? He was curious about that himself. As far as he was concerned, it wasn't anyone's business but theirs, but he also wanted it out there. Wanted the title.

It was Shanen who spoke first. "Oh...wow... This is a nice surprise." He liked her a lot. She was a good woman.

"At the party you said—" Landon started, but Justin tossed him a look that Drew assumed was a warning. What in the hell had they spoken about at the party?

"How long have you been seeing each other?" Joy asked. "Or I guess I should ask, are you seeing each other?"

Drew wanted an answer to the same question.

"He's a friend," Justin answered. "A good friend. He's made..." Justin glanced back at Drew. "He's made things here easier."

And as much as Drew was glad for that, as much as he wanted to make things easier on Justin, there was a part of him that had hoped for more. This felt like more than friendship to him, and even though he'd told Justin not to worry about that now, part of him wished they could.

"Good." Larry nodded. "Thank you for being here for my son."

"It's my pleasure," Drew told him, this throat slightly bitter, when he had no right to be. They'd made a step in the right direction. That's all that should matter.

They were all quiet again. Drew hadn't expected Jacob to say anything. Not here in front of Shanen's family. He knew his brother wouldn't be happy, but what could he do? Drew couldn't let himself be bothered with that. Still, he could feel the tension around them. The questions...and maybe the concerns.

"I'm tired," Larry said from his wheelchair. "I think I need to go home."

Still, no one moved. Was it really that big a deal? Did it really matter if they were seeing each other or not? Drew didn't get it.

"I think we need a night out." It was Rod who broke the silence. "I think we all deserve a good time. I want to dance with Landon. You should all see me dance. I'm fucking incredible."

A chorus of laughter followed Rod's words and Drew was thankful for them.

"I think that's a great idea," Landon replied.

"Me too," Shanen added.

"Yeah, I'd like that. What do you say, Jacob?" Justin asked, "Let's go out. Have some fun with the family." Justin was doing it for Drew. He appreciated it, but it wasn't necessary. Drew would go regardless.

"I'm game." Drew put a hand on Justin's shoulder and squeezed. Now that he could touch him in front of everyone, he didn't plan to stop. Drew always wanted his hands on Justin.

Until he left, at least.

It felt like a goddamned eternity before his brother finally replied. Drew's jaw was tight; discomfort slid down his spine as he waited.

"Yes. Of course. That would be great," Jacob finally answered, before he asked a question. "Andrew, would it be okay if I rode back with you?"

He had no idea what his brother was up to, but he assumed it had to do with something Drew was doing wrong. Butting into Jacob's new family, maybe? Still, he told his brother yes. They made quick plans to go out that evening, and to invite Nick and Bryce.

Joy and Larry were going home, and as they all said their goodbyes, Drew leaned close to Justin's ear and whispered, "That was a surprise, Sleeping Beauty."

He hoped Justin knew that he meant what happened between them and not his brother. He knew by Justin's reply that he did. "For me too, Cinderella."

Drew kissed his cheek. "I'll pick you up later. It's time for my lecture."

"Fuck him if—" Drew silenced him with his mouth. Let their tongues wrestle. It felt really good to kiss him when and wherever he wanted, even if it was temporary.

When their kiss was over, he let his mouth trail to Justin's ear again. "We'll go out and dance, but it's going to take everything in me not to stick my hand down your pants like I did the night we met. I'm hard just thinking about it. I'm not sure we'll even make it upstairs by the time we get home. I might have to fuck you right there against the front door."

A low rumble reverberated from Justin's chest. "I'm looking forward to it."

"Me too," he said before they parted. It was a few minutes later that he sat behind the wheel of his truck, Jacob in the passenger seat.

The second they pulled out of the parking lot, it was Drew who spoke. "I won't apologize for it. It was a coincidence that I met him. At the time, I didn't know who he was. I refuse to feel guilty about this. I know it's hard for you to see clearly where I'm concerned, but this isn't about you, Jacob. It's about me and Justin. I—"

"You're in love with him," Jacob interrupted.

If Drew had been standing, a feather could have knocked him over. His first instinct was to say, *Yes,* followed by, *How did you know?* He settled on a different version of the latter. "What makes you say that?"

"Because you're my brother and I know you. I see it in the way you look at him. It was killing you not to go to him when he was watching Landon and Larry drive. Your pain matched his and something like that only comes from loving someone. I know because I feel Shanen's pain the same way."

As much as Drew wanted to tell him yes, to say thank you, a slow anger simmered beneath the surface. It got stronger and stronger as his hands tightened on the steering wheel. "You know me? Fuck you for saying that, Jacob. My whole life you've accused me of thinking I'm better than the family. Of wanting to be different and not respecting the rules or making my family proud by following in Dad's footprints. In *your* footprints. You fucking accused me of going after Iris because I wanted to hurt you. That's not me. You can't claim to know me when you've believed those things about me."

He saw red. Was afraid of crashing the truck, he was so angry. How dare Jacob try to pretend they were close? That they knew each other. "Do you know what it feels like to have your brother believe those things about you? To hate you for no reason? To resent you so fucking much? And why?"

"Because I was jealous!" Jacob yelled. His voiced filled the truck. "Because I was jealous," he said again, more softly.

"Why?" Drew asked. "What did you have to be jealous of?" He hadn't expected that. He wasn't sure what to think about it.

"I don't know… I'm not sure I realized it at first, but I think that's what it is. I've tried to tell myself I'm not, but the truth is, I've always envied your ability to be yourself. To do what you want no matter what anyone expects of you. To have your own dreams. I love what I do. I love being an attorney…but it was Dad's dream that became my dream. You've always had your own. People gravitate toward that about you. I'm the boring one. I'm the one who does what's expected and follows the rules. I took that out on you."

"I…" Drew started but he didn't know what to say. How did he respond to that? "I thought you hated me," he settled on.

"No," Jacob shook his head. "I think I hated me, but I took it out on you. Especially after Iris because that fed my insecurities. She chose you over me. But things are better. Being with Shanen makes me feel better in ways I never imagined, but old habits die hard. I'm sorry for that. For how I've treated you."

Drew's brain was still a mass of confusion. His heart beat heavily as he tried to figure out his thoughts. He'd been with Shanen a long time now and that hadn't made their relationship better. "Why now? What's the difference now?"

It took a moment for Jacob to answer. Drew waited, let him sort through his thoughts. "I don't know, exactly. I haven't shown it but I've been coming around for a while. Like I said, being with

Shanen has helped, even though I've treated you like shit because of her. I would tell myself not to, that I was wrong, but being wrong meant I had to take a look at myself. At the *why* of my actions and that's a scary thing."

He took a deep breath and continued, "But then when you announced that you're bisexual the other day, I just kept thinking that I didn't know you at all. I was your brother and I didn't know you. That's something we should have spoken about. It's something I should have known about you, and I didn't because I hadn't treated you fairly."

Jesus, Drew couldn't believe this was real. That this conversation was really happening.

"But today I watched you with Justin. You found a way to come because he needed you. You looked like you would have taken every ounce of pain from him if you could. You just wanted to make it better for him, even if in some way it hurt you, because of me, and I realized I *do* know you. We're alike in that because I feel the same way about Shanen. I want nothing more than to make this better for her. You went into a relationship with him knowing what he was going through. That takes a big man."

Drew wasn't so sure he deserved all the praise Jacob gave him. It felt nice, but he'd never meant to fall for Justin. He was supposed to be a hookup. From there, he just wanted to apologize for walking away, but spending time with Justin changed things. "I didn't expect to fall for him. It just happened, but I'm selfish too. I want him to feel the same way. In between every fucking thing he's going through—losing his dad, gaining siblings, not knowing his place in his new family, leaving his home and his life behind—I also want him to carve out a spot for me. For him to be able to work out his feelings for me, when he has so many more important things in his life. I tell him it's okay, that it's not important but really I want it from him."

Drew tensed when Jacob reached over and squeezed his arm. It was a show of support, but not one his brother had ever given him.

"That's not selfish, Drew. That's human and it's okay. Regardless of anything else, you're putting Justin first."

He turned and looked at his brother, shocked on too many levels to comprehend. He thought about Justin and their family. What they were going through. How they'd been able to forgive Larry because they were family and sometimes that's what you did. You forgave. You moved on. He hadn't been perfect himself. "About time you called me Drew," he teased and Jacob smiled.

"It is."

"I'm sorry about everything. About Iris and—"

"It happened. It's in the past. I know she was the one to kiss you; I was just being an asshole."

And it was a start. Things weren't perfect, but it was definitely a start.

CHAPTER TWENTY-ONE

IT HAD BEEN such an emotional day and Justin couldn't wait to go out tonight. This would be the first time he did something like this with his siblings. They probably should have planned something earlier, spent more time getting to know each other, but they were still testing the waters.

He smiled at his choice of words. It looked like Drew wasn't the only one on a test drive. They all were in a way, as they navigated the new territory they'd been thrown into.

Justin stood by the window of the small house. When he saw Drew pull into the driveway, he went straight for the door, ready to just let fucking loose. He deserved that. They all did.

When Justin got to the truck, he looked inside the open door and wasn't surprised to see Drew with his black hat on backward. He also wore a black, V-neck shirt that clung to his arms and across his muscular chest, and black jeans that Justin could tell were just loose enough to hang off his slender hips but tight enough to show off his ass. Drew had his signature scruff that Justin found so fucking hot, making him doublethink his earlier thought that going out was a good idea. He'd much rather stay in and fuck the night away.

Drew gave him a cocky grin. "You like what you see."

"I do."

"Wait until I stand up and you get a glimpse of my ass. It's fucking sexy in these jeans."

Justin didn't doubt that. "It's fucking sexy all the time and if you stand up now, we're not going to make it out of my driveway tonight. Hell, we might not even make it back into the house."

Drew gave him a husky laugh, his cheeks colored a light shade of red. He loved that Drew blushed. He'd never really thought about something like that turning him on before, but it did.

"As good as that sounds," Drew told him, "and believe me, it does sound good, I think you need to get out tonight. I think maybe you're not the only one who needs it, too."

Justin nodded, knowing Drew was right. He adjusted himself before he sat down in the truck and closed the door. "Don't blame me if I'm sporting a hard-on all night."

"I wouldn't think of it." Drew smiled and leaned over. It was like he was the positive electron and Justin the negative, making the strongest spark of static electricity. Justin couldn't keep himself from leaning over as well and letting Drew press a quick kiss to…his forehead? Huh. He'd expected the lips. He'd never had a man other than Drew kiss his head.

"You don't look so bad yourself," Drew added.

"Not so bad? That's all I get?" he teased.

"For now. I'm not sure this is the right time for all that I want to say." Drew put the truck into reverse and started to back out.

It was there, the question on his tongue, wanting to know what Drew had to say, but Justin had a feeling the other man was right. He had a feeling it might change everything and he didn't know if it was the right time to throw more into the mix. But still… "I need to thank you again for being there today. I didn't realize I needed that and with what's going on with my dad and my family…I don't think I have it in me to sort through my thoughts right now. That's shitty and unfair but—"

"But nothing," Drew interrupted. "I get it."

And as much as he hated the words, as much as he didn't want to say them, Justin knew he needed to repeat what they both knew. "I live in North Carolina. I own a home there. I'm enrolled in school there. My mother is there." She was his family. Yes, Shanen and Landon were too, but she was the one who had always been there. She was the one who would always have his best interests at heart. "Being in Virginia is temporary."

He could see Drew's fingers tighten on the steering wheel. Could see the slow tic in his jaw, and damned if it didn't make him want to take the words back…but he couldn't. They had to be realistic.

"I know that." Drew didn't look at him. A searing pain ripped through Justin's chest. He wanted to fix it. Wanted to let go of everything else tonight.

He reached over and squeezed Drew's muscular thigh. "I'm here now, though, and the only reason things feel remotely okay is because of you. Can we just focus on that? Just let everything else fade to the background and try to live in the moment?"

It took a few seconds, but Drew's right hand slipped off the steering wheel and gripped Justin's. "Yeah…yeah we can."

Because right now was the only thing in this world that was promised.

DREW COULDN'T BELIEVE he was in a gay bar with his brother. His straight-laced brother who currently had his arm intertwined with Rod's as they gave each other shots.

What the fuck was this life?

"Next is a blowjob for you, Jacob! Blowjobs loosen everyone up," Rod told his brother and then looked over at Landon. "For you it's a real one. We'll save that for later, though." Rod winked and Landon rolled his eyes, nothing but love and affection on his face.

"Losing your touch?" Bryce asked. "The Rod I know wouldn't wait until later. He'd be dragging Landon off to some corner somewhere."

"Don't give him any ideas!" Landon playfully hit the other

man's shoulder. Drew liked Nick and Bryce. They were fun men to be around—Bryce loud and sarcastic, Nick a little more subdued, but incredibly kind.

"Why not? It's a good idea," Bryce countered. "It's what I'm planning on doing with Nick in a few minutes. There's always time for a blowjob."

"Smart man," Justin whispered in Drew's ear as he wrapped his arms around him from behind. When they met in this bar, jerking each other off, not knowing more than first names, he never would have thought they'd end up here. Together. With their families. Drew being in love for the first time in his life, because he was, he realized. There wasn't a part of him that doubted his feelings.

"Oh! That reminds me of that old Jell-O commercial!" Rod grinned.

"There was a commercial about Jell-O and giving head? How'd I miss that?" Bryce asked.

"No! The *always time for* part. All you had to do was spell blowjob instead. That should have been my joke. I totally would have thought of it. Who's losing their touch now?"

The group all laughed. Drew felt Justin's laugh vibrate through him, and it made him smile.

"Don't you have a business to run or something?" Bryce teased him back.

"Rods-N-Ends is in great hands without me," Rod replied.

Wait. "Rods and what?" Drew asked. "What's that?"

Landon leaned closer to Drew to reply. "He owns an adult toy store, called Rods-N-Ends. It's where we met and where he met Nick and Bryce too."

Somehow the knowledge that Rod owned a store for sex toys didn't shock Drew in the least.

"Landon was quite the fan of his hand, when he met me. He used a lot of lube." Rod nudged Landon, who pulled Rod into his arms.

"Nope. The first time I needed lube. All the other times I just went because of the sexy-ass man who ran the store." He pressed a kiss to Rod's forehead much like Drew had done to Justin in the truck.

He looked around at the three couples—Jacob and Shanen, Landon and Rod, and Nick and Bryce, and wondered if this would be their lives if Justin lived here. If he and Justin would be committed like the six people here with them. If they'd meet up for drinks on the weekends and have cookouts together.

As if Justin could read his mind, he squeezed Drew tighter.

"Feel free to stop by the store sometime. I'll give you guys the family and friends discount."

"I think we have it under control," Justin replied to Rod. "But thanks."

From there they continued to talk and hang out. He liked these people a lot, he realized. Rod liked to make people laugh. Drew could tell it was his way to try and make people feel better. Landon was strength and love. Nick was the definition of kindness. He reached out to catch someone when they almost fell and he spoke about a food drive he was doing for a homeless shelter in town. Bryce looked at him like he was the most important person in the world, and also with respect. He could see a streak of loyalty in Bryce a mile long. Shanen was sweet and caring and kept his brother steady.

They were a good group of people and Drew was honored to know them all.

Jesus, he didn't know why he was getting so emotional lately—why the world suddenly looked different to him—but he had a feeling it was because of the man behind him.

"Dance with me, Cinderella," Justin whispered in his ear, and Drew nodded.

Justin hooked one of his fingers through one of Drew's and led the way through the crowded bar. People danced and talked and drank around them. They weaved their way through bodies as Justin headed for the same corner they'd made out in the first night they met.

The music was fast, but they moved slow. They kept their arms wrapped around each other, grinding their dicks together as they swayed.

"This has been a good night," Justin said against his ear. "Spending time with Shanen and Landon. Getting to know their significant others. I'm happy for them. I know your brother—"

"It isn't an issue." Drew cut him off. He didn't want Justin to feel as though liking Jacob was a betrayal. "We came to an agreement together. We're working on our relationship, partly because of you."

"Yeah?" There was awe in Justin's voice. "I'm not sure what I did but I'm glad. You're too good a person for anyone not to see that."

Drew's pulse quickened. "You trying to get in my pants?"

"No. I thought that was already promised."

Drew smiled as he let his hands run up and down Justin's back, loving the feel of the muscles there. Being with him felt as natural as breathing. "Yes, it is."

"I'm scared," Justin said softly. "I'm scared of losing my father. I'm scared of not having a place with my siblings when he's gone."

"I know," Drew whispered, his heart breaking. He wrapped his arms around Justin tighter, greedy for him. To comfort him, to fix whatever it was that hurt him. "You will, though. They love you. I see it. And even outside of Shanen and Landon, you have friends here. People who care about you—Nick, Bryce, Rod…"

"You," Justin added.

"Nah, I'm pretty much over you." Drew tried to keep the mood light, when really he wanted to tell Justin he was all fucking in. Maybe it was soon and maybe he was somehow just wrapped up in his first relationship with a man, but this didn't feel like a test drive to Drew. It felt like the real deal.

"Then I guess I better take advantage of you while I have the chance. Can we go home and get to the fucking now?" Justin asked. Drew was all on board with that idea as well.

CHAPTER TWENTY-TWO

Neither Justin or Drew drank much and they'd stopped quite a while before they danced, so he felt comfortable with Drew driving them home.

They were both quiet as they drove, and Justin wondered if Drew was thinking about them the way he was. About their surprising spiral into what would likely be a very real relationship if they didn't have completely separate lives in separate states. What was it about the man that ensnared him so completely?

Before he knew it, they were pulling into the driveway of Drew's home and just like every time he saw it, Justin was struck by how beautiful it was. He had never felt like the little house he'd shared with his father was home, but there was something incredibly comforting about being at Drew's.

They got out of the truck, and as they approached the porch, the sensors made the light click on. It reminded Justin of the first time he'd come home with Drew. When he was drunk and being ridiculous, and how far they'd come since then.

When Drew went to put the key in the lock, Justin nestled his body against Drew's back. "You were right. Your ass does look fucking sexy in these jeans." He rubbed his dick against Drew's jean-covered ass, just as Drew hissed and the keys went clattering to the porch.

Justin grabbed his hips. Let one hand slide down to cup Drew's erection as he continued to thrust his prick against him. "Butter fingers."

"How in the fuck am I supposed to concentrate when you do

that?"

Justin pulled Drew's hat off and put it on his own head. "I didn't do this the first time we stood on your porch together and I seem to remember the same thing happening."

Drew dropped his head backward to rest on Justin's shoulder. "Yeah, but I was wishing you would. Jesus, what do you do to me?"

"I don't know, but whatever it is, you do the same thing to me," Justin answered honestly. He pulled back and kneeled behind Drew. He rubbed Drew's firm ass with one hand while he found the keys with the other. Then he was back on his feet, arms on either side of Drew's body while Drew fumbled with the lock, and thrust his dick against Drew again.

Drew had one hand flat on the door, his forehead pressed against it. His breath came out in heavy, quick gasps as Justin grinded against him.

"Please..." Drew whispered and Justin's dick hardened even more.

"Your ass is hungry for me, isn't it? You want my cock deep inside you. Christ, I want that too, baby, but not tonight. You promised to fuck me the second we walked through the door. The first time I take you will be in your bed where I can do you right. Worship your tight, little hole with my fingers and my mouth before I take it, before I show you how fucking amazing it feels to have a dick buried deep inside you. My dick." He nipped at Drew's ear.

"Yes...God, yes."

Justin finally managed to get the lock and pushed the door open. Drew stumbled inside, pulling Justin with him. The second they were closed in the house, they were on each other—kissing and tearing at each other's clothes.

"Jesus, I can't get enough of you. You're on my fucking mind all the time. I want my dick inside you every goddamned second," Drew said as he pulled Justin's shirt over his head, taking the hat with it.

Justin fell back against the door. His hand knotted in the longer hair on the top of Drew's head. His tongue flicked over Justin's nipple. "The way you taste," he said before licking again. "The way you smell." He nuzzled his face in the crease of Justin's arm. If he went just a little bit more, he would have his face right in Justin's armpit. "The way you feel." Drew palmed Justin's dick and he knew the damn thing was leaking all over behind his fly. "You drive me fucking wild."

"Christ." Justin closed his eyes as Drew delivered torturous pleasure. "How in the hell did you get control of this?"

"Because I'm good," Drew whispered against Justin's collarbone.

"So am I." Justin turned them, made Drew's back slam against the door as their lips crashed together. He expertly worked Drew's pants as his tongue plunged deep into his mouth.

He was a predator, devouring his prey. He wanted to eat the man alive.

Justin dropped to his knees and shoved Drew's pants down, before he stepped out of them. The second his thick, veiny cock sprung free, Justin sucked the motherfucker to the back of his throat, tasting salty skin and pre-come.

"You don't play fair," Drew gasped out as he guided Justin, pushed him closer until Justin had no choice but to breathe in Drew's pubes.

And he fucking loved it. Loved the wild, hungry side of this man.

When Drew's hand eased off, Justin pulled back. Drew's cock popped out of his mouth, glistening with saliva. "So you want me to stop?" Justin teased.

"Fuck, no."

"That's what I thought," Justin told him before he went after him again. He alternated between deep-throating Drew's prick, sucking his balls, and nuzzling his face in the crease of Drew's leg and breathing him in. "Spread your legs," he told Drew before sucking a finger into his mouth. When Drew did as he was told, Justin let that finger find Drew's pucker, and pushed it inside.

"Oh fuck. Jesus, that feels so damned good."

"I can't wait until it's my cock pushing into your virgin hole. Gonna treat you right, baby. Gonna love you good."

"Do it now," Drew rushed out.

With the tip of Drew's cock in his mouth, Justin looked up, trying to read Drew, to see if he really meant what he said.

"Jesus, you are so fucking beautiful. That's where you belong, looking up at me with my dick in your mouth. I belong there for you too, Justin. But right now, I really need you to take me. I really need to know what it feels like to have you fill my ass. To make it yours."

Drew stared hard, his blue-gray eyes dark and stormy with emotion. Emotions that made Justin's heart beat too fast and his chest both light and heavy at the same time.

"You said you're gonna love me good, and I want that now. I want sweat-slicked bodies colliding together as you show me what it's like to have someone make love to me."

How could he say no to that? Especially when he didn't want to?

Justin stood and smiled at him. "You owe me a fuck against a door."

Drew returned his smile and Justin held out a hand for him, before leading him up the stairs.

CHAPTER TWENTY-THREE

DREW HAD WANTED this from the beginning of the night. Had planned for it to make sure he was ready. This wasn't a new desire for him. He'd always wondered what it felt like to be fucked, but the burning need his desire suddenly took on was new. He couldn't wait. It was Justin he wanted. Justin inside him.

When they got to his room, Justin swatted his ass and nodded toward the bed. "Lay down on your stomach. Spread your legs for me."

Drew nodded and then did as he was told. The lamp beside his bed was on. Justin opened the drawer and pulled out lube and a condom, tossing them on the bed.

Drew watched as Justin finished undressing. He was so damned beautiful—all golden skin and tight muscles. His dick stood tall against his stomach. His balls full, two tight little globes ready to bust. "Are you sure you're going to be able to last?" Drew teased him to lighten the mood.

"If you make me embarrass myself, I'll never forgive you." Justin winked at him before climbing onto the bed and kneeling between Drew's legs. "Look at this ass." He rubbed Drew's cheeks, pushed them together and then pulled them apart. "Oh yeah. I'll find a way to make sure I can last. I'm not going to want to leave you once I'm inside."

Yes. That sounded perfect to Drew. Suddenly needy, his hole ached to be filled. He pushed his ass toward Justin. "Then get inside me, baby. Show me what I've been missing."

"Shh," Justin told him. "I'm getting there. I'm admiring the view." He leaned over and kissed the back of Drew's neck. His lips were warm, his breath hot as he kissed his way down Drew's shoulders, to the swell of his ass. "Arch your back a little bit. Put your ass in the air. Show me where you want me. Let me see that pretty hole."

Fucking hell, Drew had to bite his lip so he didn't come. "Okay, so it might be me who can't last," he teased before doing as Justin said. He pushed his ass out. Spread his legs more. Arched his back and wondered how he looked this way. Completely out of his mind with lust, offering his ass to the man behind him—wanting him to take it, to fill it, to fuck it, to slam into him, pound him deep and hard until he didn't know anything other than Justin. Until he didn't even know his own fucking name.

And he would love every second of it.

"Christ, look at you laid out for me, like a fucking gift. Such a tight, pretty hole." Justin rubbed his thumb against Drew's pucker, making him shudder.

"Then do something with it." He was fucking ravenous for him. Wanted Justin to devour him. "I want to feel you stretching me."

"Christ, that's hot. Knowing you're so greedy for my dick. I'm going to taste you first. Get you ready with my mouth."

Drew held his breath as Justin lay between his legs. As his strong, rough hands spread his cheeks. Finally, with the first flick of Justin's tongue against his hole, he breathed again. "Yes. Like that. Give me more." Who the hell would have known getting rimmed would feel so incredible? It was so damn intimate, the feel of Justin's mouth on him. Of Justin's tongue probing his hole. Every time the man did it to him, he lost his mind.

He humped the bed, grinding his dick into the white comforter as Justin devoured him—hard, soft, finger, no finger, then tongue fucked him until Drew was a gasping, needy mess writhing beneath him.

"I'm going to open you up for me now." Justin kissed his right cheek, and then his left before he kneeled again. He grabbed the lube, and Drew heard it open before Justin squeezed some on his fingers.

His stomach was a mass of nerves and excitement. As much as he wanted this, he was about to take a cock for the first time. He was about to take Justin's cock.

Drew flinched when he felt Justin's slick, cold finger at his asshole. Closed his eyes as it pushed in and then... "Yes..."

"Look at you, taking two fingers like a champ."

That made Drew open his eyes and look over his shoulder to see Justin concentrating on him. He used his left hand to pull Drew's cheek apart, to open him more as his eyes were firmly on where his fingers were fucking Drew's ass.

He felt the difference—the stretch as Justin used two fingers on him for the first time, but all he could think was that he wanted *more, more, more.*

"I'm going to go for three now, okay, baby?" Justin asked. "Christ, if you could see this. It's like you were made to be opened up by me."

As sappy as it sounded, Drew wondered if he might be.

Justin used his free hand to grab the lube and squirt more on his fingers, and then there was more stretching, burning as he worked a third finger inside Drew's hole.

"You're doing good. So fucking sexy." Justin slid his fingers in and out, twisted them, spread them. It was slightly uncomfortable...but not. It was like the burn made things better, made him want more, but there was another part of him that felt like something foreign was happening. Like something was going inside a part of him that something didn't usually go into.

Still, Drew wanted more.

"So good. So damn good but I want your dick. Give me your dick, Justin."

Justin growled above him and then pulled his fingers free. Drew felt open…embarrassed, but he didn't have much time to think about it. Justin ripped open the condom. Drew watched over his shoulder as his lover rolled it down his red, throbbing prick.

He squirted more lube on his dick. "Lift up a bit." Justin swatted his hip and Drew did, so Justin could slip a pillow under him, making Drew higher.

Justin angled his dick down toward Drew's hole and started to push inside.

Justin was bigger than his three fingers, stretching Drew's hole wide as he tried to work his way inside. It burned, really fucking burned. For a second he almost said never mind, but then Justin rubbed his back and whispered. "You're doing good. So fucking good, baby. I almost have my crown inside. Damn, I wish you could see this. Wish you could see how fucking gorgeous it is watching my cock breach you."

Drew closed his eyes, and relaxed, Justin's words filling his brain as his cock pushed farther and farther until he filled his ass too. They both released a deep breath at the same time. "Give me just a second." Justin's voice was hoarse, on edge. "You're so hot inside. If I move this is all over. Just let me get used to you."

Justin breathed out.

Drew in.

Justin in.

Drew out.

And then with his hands flat on the bed, one on each side of Drew, as he held himself up, Justin started to move. He pulled almost all the way out, before slamming in again. It was fast and hard. He railed him the way Drew wanted, but there was a tenderness to it too. He was careful and loving as he fucked Drew for the first time.

No, as he made love to him. Because that's what they were doing, making love.

When he lay down on Drew's back, giving Drew his weight, he

thought it couldn't get any better, but then Justin's arms went under his, so he could hold on to Drew, moving slower now. Pushing in, digging his hips into Drew's ass, before slowly pulling out again, and Drew realized that it could get even better.

"Are you good? Is this okay?" Justin asked, his voice tight like he struggled to rein himself in.

Each time he thrust, he rubbed Drew's prostate sending a shot of pleasure through him. "Yes...better than good."

Their bodies slapped together the way Drew had wanted. They were slick with sweat. His balls ached, begged for release. His cock wanted friction, which he got each time Justin slammed into him, making his dick rub against the bed.

"I'm a hair-trigger here, baby. What do you need? I want you to come," Justin told him.

"Take me harder. Give me your mouth," Drew told him and then Justin was gone. He pulled out. Drew almost lost his fucking mind needing him back. When Justin flipped him over, he got it. He held his legs back and open. Justin's dick impaled him again.

Justin's hand found Drew's cock and stroked. The second their mouths fused together in a scorching kiss, his balls let loose. Three long spurts of come shot from his slit, between their bodies. Justin kept thrusting. Kept fucking. Kept loving, his chest rubbing the thick, white semen into Drew's and then... "Fuck!" Justin tensed, and went tight as he thrust through his own orgasm.

They lay together, tangled in each other, nothing but sweaty limbs, come, and deep breathing.

"That was incredible," Drew said when he finally caught his breath. "How could I have waited so long to do that?"

Justin looked down at him, all fucking emotion. But then, as though he realized it, he winked and grinned. "Because you were waiting for me, of course." And then he lay down with his head on Drew's chest, his thumb brushing back and forth over one of his nipples. "I know I should want to do nothing but pass out right now, but I know I can't sleep. Talk to me. Tell me about the house."

So Drew did. He told him how he wanted something that was his. Something he created for himself, and he knew Justin would understand that.

They talked about how much longer Justin had in school and how he couldn't wait to be a paramedic. They talked about first kisses, and Drew admitted he'd been arrested at sixteen for drinking in an empty house. They talked and laughed and held each other, and he thought maybe he would never get tired of talking to this man.

CHAPTER TWENTY-FOUR

"How's everything going, son?" Justin's father asked as they sat on the back porch of Joy's house. Justin came over to spend some time with him today, and Joy had left to give them some space. He'd stopped by every day for the past week and a half, since they went on the motorcycle ride, but this was the first time they'd had an extended amount of time just the two of them.

"I'm good. How are you feeling?" Justin already knew the answer to that. It was scary how fast someone could start to deteriorate. He knew when chemo stopped, there were no definites—a week, a month, three months. He'd looked so much better after he stopped the treatments that Justin had hoped they'd get more time, but it was almost like after that ride the other day, everything started to go downhill. He looked more tired. Slept more. Got weaker. He was tired of fighting. Justin could see that even though he didn't want to believe it.

Before he could reply to what Justin had asked him, his dad started to cough and Justin's heart dropped to his feet. He stood up to...hell, he didn't know what in the fuck he would do. It was a cough, but his dad waved him off.

His hand shook as he held a white cloth to his mouth and when he pulled it away, Justin's heart wasn't in his feet anymore. It was ground to dust.

A splotch of blood was in the middle of the cloth.

"Jesus." He didn't know what to say. Should he call someone? Did that happen often?

"It's okay," his father replied, but it wasn't. It really fucking wasn't okay.

"I..."

"Sit down, Justin." But he couldn't. He didn't think he could move at all. His dad was coughing up *blood* for God's sake.

"Please," he asked again and as much as Justin wanted to run, to pretend this wasn't happening, he sat. If his father couldn't run from this, Justin damn sure wouldn't either.

It was like the world suddenly turned off—no wind blowing or birds chirping—the only sound was the constant buzz of the oxygen tank.

"Tell me about Drew," his dad finally broke the silence.

"Drew? You just coughed up blood and you want to talk about Drew?" Justin snapped like a live wire. He hadn't meant to, didn't want to, but he couldn't hold back. "Has Joy seen that?"

"Yes. So has the hospice nurse. She started coming in about a week ago. Things are moving faster than I expected."

Justin's leg began shaking, bouncing up and down uncontrollably. He leaned forward, put weight on it with his elbow to try and stop it but it didn't fucking work. *Things are moving faster than I expected.* "How long?" he finally croaked out.

"We still don't know. You can never say for sure. Did I tell you how much it meant to me to ride with you and Landon together?"

"No." Justin shook his head.

"Well it did. I—"

"I meant *no* I can't do this. We're not going to sit here and start saying our goodbyes!" That's what he was doing by asking about Drew and speaking about their ride and Justin wasn't ready yet. He just fucking wasn't. He shoved to his feet, and made it to the porch stairs before his dad's voice stopped him.

"Do you know how much I love you, Justin? That Shanen and Landon being in our lives doesn't diminish that at all? You're my son, no matter how things happened with your mother and I. Or Joy and I. Despite the fact that I regret disappearing from Landon and Shanen's life, do you understand there isn't a second of raising you that I regret?"

Justin's hand squeezed the railing. A sharp piece of wood dug into his finger. He was frozen, rooted to where he stood, his back to his father.

"I never should have cut ties with your brother and your sister, but I also loved every second of being *your* father. Of watching you grow. I'm damned proud of the man you are. You're a better man than I ever was. I robbed you of knowing your own brother and sister." His voice cracked, his breathing was ragged, but Justin still couldn't turn.

"I robbed you of a relationship with them. I robbed them of a relationship with you, and yet here the three of you are. Supporting me. You walked away from your life to come here with me. Do you know how incredible you are? How much respect I have for you?"

Justin dropped his head forward, and a single tear rolled down his face. He'd needed to hear that. Needed to hear all of it, so fucking bad it hurt. He'd wondered those things so many times since he found out about Landon and Shanen. Had his dad wished he was with them all those years? Did he have more in common with Landon? Did he wish he was with them instead—his original family and the woman he obviously still loved? It didn't matter that he was a grown man, those worries plagued his heart on a daily basis.

"Don't be like me. When I'm angry or hurt, I run. There's nothing I want more than to know you'll have a relationship with your siblings when I'm gone. You're all better people than I am, and you'll all need each other. They love you. It doesn't matter that they were raised together. They're your brother and your sister and they love you."

Justin closed his eyes, a mixture of pain and hope in his chest. "I love them too," he whispered.

"I know you do. I see it—you think you don't belong, that you don't have a place with them, but you do. Now sit down and tell me about Drew. I want to hear about the man you're in love with."

It was a truth that Justin tried to ignore. He turned, and walked back to his empty chair, and sat down. "Maybe I am. I don't know. I can't think about that right now."

"You should. No matter what's going on in your life, always make time to think about the things that make you happy."

Justin looked over at his father, surprised at those words. "Listen to you, giving life-affirming advice all of a sudden."

His dad laughed, husky and raspy. It was obvious how out of breath he was, so Justin made the choice to speak so he didn't have to. "He does make me happy. I have a good time with him. He means a lot to me, and I'm not sure how that happened."

"Most of the time, we're not sure. People don't plan falling in love. Maybe there's hope there, or the possibility, but it's not a plan."

Maybe he was in love with Drew. Regardless, how were they supposed to make this work? "I have a life back home. I belong there."

"Your mother will understand."

Justin's head snapped up at that.

"You feel guilty, even if you don't realize it. You feel like you'd be choosing this place, these people over her, and that's not the way it is. You aren't me. I loved your mother, but I didn't love her the way I should have."

Because he'd always been in love with Joy. Justin knew that, and he thought his mom did as well.

"This isn't the same thing," his dad added.

Justin shook his head. He couldn't do this. Couldn't sort through all of these thoughts and emotions right now, so instead he did as his father asked, and he talked about something that made him happy. Someone who made him happy. "He owns a gym, did you know that? He started law school, but didn't finish because he wanted to own a fucking gym. I like to give him shit because he eats too healthy. He's kind to people and makes them feel at ease. He designed his own home. He's the kind of person who's good at everything, but he doesn't act like he's better than anyone else. He listens, he lives his own life, and he just wants to be happy."

His dad nudged his arm. "He sounds like someone else I know."

Justin wasn't so sure about that.

They talked for a little while longer. He told his dad that Drew had traveled all over the world, that they'd gone to the beach, and how Drew had told him all about Scotland. As time went on, his father's replies got slower, more time between them. When Justin looked over, he realized he'd fallen sleep in the middle of their conversation and his gut clenched. He wiped his eyes when he realized another tear snuck out, before he stood up. He pushed his father's wheelchair into the house. He didn't wake as Justin lifted his frail body from the chair and laid him in the bed.

He started to shake again. Wanted to rage. Wanted to tear the fucking world apart. It wasn't fair, none of it, but then what in life ever was fair?

The second Joy came in, Justin said, "He's coughing up blood."

"I know." She nodded.

"I have to go." He pushed out the door and went straight for his car. His bag was in the back with his uniform for his shift tonight. Justin sped from the driveway and that's the direction he went in. He squeezed the steering wheel too tight and his heart beat too hard the whole drive to the restaurant. He shouldn't be there. He knew that, but he also couldn't leave Nick in a bind at the last minute.

When he parked in the lot at the restaurant, he sat in the car, trying to catch his breath.

His dad would die soon.

He would die. This was all real.

And his dad also thought Justin was in love with Drew, and maybe he was, but was it real? Or was it just because his heart was so raw and butchered that he clung to the one thing in his life that felt good?

Justin jumped when there was a knock on the passenger window. He looked up to see Nick, and unlocked the door before Nick opened it. "Jesus Christ. You scared the shit out of me," he said.

The man looked sad, his kind eyes sympathetic.

"Joy called Landon and he got in touch with me. She said you looked upset when you left."

Upset? "No shit. My father is coughing up blood and he fell asleep in the middle of a conversation. He didn't even stir when I lifted him and put him to bed. I think upset is an understatement."

Remorse slammed into him as Nick's eyes got even softer. He didn't deserve for Justin to take his mood out on him. "Fuck...I'm sorry. I shouldn't have snapped at you. I just need…"

"You need to go home. Or go to Drew. You don't need to be here and that's okay. You need to take care of yourself, or better yet, let Drew take care of you."

"I have a shift. It's my responsibility to—"

"To be okay. That's your only responsibility. And as your friend, because I consider you that, the only thing I'm worried about here is you."

Jesus, he liked this man. He liked all of the people he'd met here.

And he also knew Nick was right. He had no business being in the restaurant tonight. "Tomorrow I can—"

"No," Nick told him. "You take some time. If you ever need a job again, I'll be here for you, but working here isn't what you need right now. And this isn't what you want, either. Landon says you were going to school to become a paramedic."

He hadn't realized Landon spoke about him. His chest warmed at the thought. "Yes. I wasn't sure what I wanted to do for the longest time. I went back to school when I was almost twenty-five."

"Bryce was the same way. It's funny how some of us just

know—like me, I always knew I would be a chef. Bryce didn't fall in love with motorcycles until later in life, but both our loves are just as real."

They spoke for a couple more minutes before Nick got out of the car and Justin drove away. He was losing it. He was fully aware of that fact. He drove without thinking, and when he walked into the gym and saw Drew, some of the heaviness in his soul bled out.

Drew walked over and gave him a small smile. "I have some spare time. Come work out with me." Just by seeing him, Drew had known he wasn't okay. He'd known that Justin needed him…and he did. He really did.

Justin smiled back, and followed Drew, the whole time knowing he was so incredibly fucked when it came to this man.

CHAPTER TWENTY-FIVE

DREW LOOKED ACROSS the hot tub at Justin. He was low in the water, his legs stretched out in front of him. His head was tilted backward against the headrest, and he had his eyes closed.

One look at him showed his exhaustion—the dark circles under his eyes and the slump of his body. He'd been like that every day since he came to see Drew at Invincible, since he'd found out his dad was coughing up blood.

He was pulling away. Drew could feel it. Part of him resented Justin for it but he understood it too. He had to do whatever needed to be done to protect himself. To get through this in whatever way he could.

The only time he completely laid himself bare was when they were in bed—when Drew was inside of Justin, or Justin inside of him. He loved it when Justin took him, loved the connection he felt. It was different, being inside of someone compared to feeling someone inside of your body. He was a part of Drew in a way no one ever had been.

"We should do something. I think you need to get away."

Justin shook his head before the last word had even left Drew's mouth. "I don't want to be around anyone."

"You're around me."

At that, Justin opened his eyes and some of the playfulness was back in them. They were bright and smiling when he said, "I don't want to be around anyone other than you, smart ass." Justin closed his eyes again. "I like your house. Feels like a home."

Drew felt like he'd just fucking conquered the world, hearing that. He was so fucking in love with this man. Felt him inside his bones. "It is a home and you know you're always welcome here. You like me," he teased moving closer to Justin. He didn't stop until they were touching. He wondered if Justin remembered saying the same thing to him, *you like me,* and when he smiled, his eyes still closed, Drew knew he did.

"I know I do. We're ridiculous."

"So? I like it." He wrapped his arm around Justin, and the other man let his head relax on Drew's shoulder. The air around them was cool, but the steam of the hot tub made it feel okay. He leaned back, relaxed, and held Justin.

"Get me out of here," Justin said after a few minutes of silence. "Take me away."

"I thought you said you didn't want to be around anyone other than me?" As soon as the words left his mouth, he realized what Justin meant and damned if it didn't make him even more lost in the man.

The second he opened his mouth, he realized they really were a little ridiculous, but maybe that was the best way to be. Crazy and ridiculous. Bizarre and silly. Pretending they were traveling the world, even though it was all in their minds. "Ireland is close to Scotland. It's a short trip. At first I was thinking Kinsale. There are a lot of shops and pubs there, but a lot of people too."

"That's okay." Justin shrugged. "I can handle it for a few hours since we're in Ireland."

"Okay," Drew replied. "We'll explore Kinsale then. I'll buy you the best Irish beers there are, and you know the Irish know their beer."

His eyes still closed, his head still on Drew, Justin chuckled.

"We'll leave there early and head to County Antrim, in Northern Ireland. I love hiking the Causeway Coast Trail. I'll make you walk the Carrick-a-Rede rope bridge."

"What's that?" Justin asked.

"The only way to get to the island from the cliffs."

Justin's eyes popped open and he looked at Drew. "We have to cross a rope bridge to get to an island?"

Drew chuckled and kissed his forehead. "Yep. It's over a chasm. The bridge swings too, but don't worry, I'll protect you. It'll be worth it when we get to the island. It's gorgeous. We'll find a quiet spot just to take in the scenery. It's fucking beautiful. The water is so damn blue and everything else vividly green. We can see across the water to Rathlin Island and on to Scotland."

"This is fun, but will we be having sex on this trip?" Justin asked. "I want to fuck you in Ireland."

Drew could handle being fucked in Ireland. "Yes, I'm getting to that. We'll take a boat to Cape Clear Island. It's cool listening to the locals speak. Very, traditionally Irish. We'll stay in a room on the island and take turns fucking each other all night. Does that work for you?"

"Yeah." Justin settled against him again. "As long as I get to go first."

"Always have to have your way," Drew teased him.

Justin sighed, paused. "Thank you. That was perfect. We're meeting with hospice tomorrow."

Drew's gut clenched. He wished like hell Justin had told him earlier. "I'm so sorry. Do you want me to go with you?" Rod and Jacob would likely be there, so why couldn't Drew be there for Justin?

"It's okay. I appreciate the offer, though."

Drew closed his eyes, wished the answer had been different.

"I appreciate everything you've done for me."

The thought was nice, but it wasn't enough.

"THE MOST IMPORTANT thing for you to take away from today is that hospice is here to support not only you, Larry, but to support the whole family. I want you to understand we don't shorten a person's life. Our goal is to help you have a higher quality of life during the time you have left. Medication to relieve pain is only part of what we do. There are many techniques we'll use to keep you as comfortable as possible."

Justin listened to the woman speak, but he couldn't look at her. It was too hard to look at her. He wanted to be angry with the woman, wanted to blame her as though she was the one ending his father's life, even though his brain knew that wasn't the case. She was helping them give him something they couldn't give him themselves.

"Thank you," Joy told her.

"How do we do this? We'll be taking care of him, correct?" Shanen asked.

"We want every family member to be as involved as you feel comfortable with. We won't push any of you away, or ask you to do anything you don't want to do. Sometimes we'll be in the background supporting you, and other times you'll need us to take over. Remember that it's just as important to take care of yourself—both physically and emotionally—as it is to take care of Larry. From here on out, we'll be working together as a team. Contact me with any questions or concerns. We'll adjust his care plan as often as necessary." She had a kind voice, Justin thought. He should attempt to make eye contact with her. To speak to her, but he didn't. Instead he listened.

They spoke about what would happen now, levels of care and how things would move forward—his father was quiet. Justin was quiet. Landon was quiet. There were a few questions here and there from Shanen, Joy, Rod, and Jacob as they went over everything they needed to know about in-home hospice care.

Justin forced his eyes up. They found his father's and...he smiled, shrugged, and nodded toward Landon.

Landon shrugged too, and in that moment, it felt like the three of them were on the same wavelength. They were alike, he thought. Not in every way, but in some…and he wanted that. Liked it.

The people in this room would experience something life changing with him. No matter how hard it was, no matter how much they didn't want to do it, they didn't have a choice. Regardless of how well they knew each other, and what had happened in their lives, they were family.

CHAPTER TWENTY-SIX

H IS DAD SLEPT more every day. His pain continued to increase and the more it did, the more pain medication the hospice nurse would give him, which then made him sleep even more.

It was better than hearing him moan, and hurt. Even when he stepped into another room, his dad's struggle to breathe and the hum of the oxygen tank were constantly in his head. Those sounds never went away.

He hadn't left Joy's in days. Shanen, Jacob, Rod, and Landon were all staying there as well. His dad's hospital bed was set up in Joy's room. Rod and Landon were in Landon's childhood bedroom and Jacob and Shanen in hers. No one wanted to miss any time because they all knew that soon he wouldn't have any left. The hospice nurse said it could be hours or days.

How the fuck did you accept something like that? That someone you love could be gone within a week?

He'd spent hours on the phone with his mom. She wanted to come, to support him, but he knew it would be hard for her, and Justin didn't want that.

So instead he lingered in the corner of the room, watching as everyone stood around the hospital bed. There were moments of quiet, of laughter as they shared stories and talked about the past. They asked Justin to share memories with them of their dad from when he was a kid. They smiled and laughed and cried while he did, and he appreciated that it mattered enough to include him, but really he felt like a ticking fucking time bomb ready to explode.

The air in the room was too thick—too heavy with death and

pain and regret, and Justin knew if he didn't get out of there, the bomb would detonate.

"I'll be back," he mumbled.

"Do you want me to go with you?" Rod asked. He appreciated the gesture but waved him off.

He couldn't be around anyone. He needed to be alone.

The second he stepped outside, Justin sucked in a lungful of air, as though he'd been starving for it. There was a chill that did nothing to cool the raging fire inside him.

He didn't think. Didn't plan. Just pulled his phone out of his pocket and dialed.

"Hey you," Drew answered on the second ring.

"It's not fair. Jesus, it's not fucking fair, Drew. How the fuck are we supposed to do this? Why should Landon and Shanen lose him when they just got him back? I feel like I'm going out of my goddamned mind in this house, but I can't leave either. What if I go and he passes and I miss it? What if I'm not there?" He crossed the yard. Breathed like a wild bull. He was frantic and wide-eyed and so fucking angry.

"I'm so sorry. I—"

"Fuck!" Justin cut Drew off. He leaned against a tree, slid down it until he sat in the slightly-wet grass. It must have rained earlier and he hadn't even known it. "I'm sorry. I don't mean to lay all this at your feet. Hell, I was just a guy you jerked off in a club and now I'm putting all my shit at your feet."

"Maybe that's all you were then but you know that's not what you are now. Don't pretend you don't know that, baby. Let me come there. Let me be with you."

"No." Justin shook his head, but he wanted that. He really fucking wanted it. The second he'd told Drew no about talking with hospice the other day, he'd wished he hadn't. "You can't want to be here for this. You shouldn't *have* to be here for this." Who wants to be there when someone dies? He wouldn't put that on

Drew because Justin couldn't help himself from depending on him.

"Jacob is there. Rod is there."

"They aren't allowed a pass. They're in love with my siblings."

"Don't." There was a rough bite to Drew's voice. "Don't pretend you don't know that I'm in love with you. Every fucking thing that Rod would do for Landon, or that Jacob would do for Shanen, I'd do for you. I want to be where you are. I want to support you. Tell me you know that."

And he did. Fuck, he really did.

Justin held the phone against his ear with his shoulder. With the palms of his hands, he rubbed his eyes. This incredible man had just told Justin that he was in love with him. He wanted to say it back. To jump for joy but the pain was still too heavy. It held him down.

"I didn't want to say it. I know now's not the time, and like we said before, I don't expect you to be able to sort your feelings out right now, but I'm tired. I'm tired of pretending I don't know my feelings. I'm tired of skirting around them. I'm in love with you, Justin. I want to be there with you. I want to be by your side. I want to be the one who gives you what you need."

God help him but Justin wanted that too. He thought maybe he needed it. "I'm sorry," he whispered. Sorry he couldn't make himself admit that he felt the same way Drew did. Sorry that he needed him.

"Don't be sorry. Just don't shut me out. I've never been afraid to go for what I want, Justin. You have to know how much I want you. I'm not going anywhere."

Christ, Drew was a good man. Every word out of the man's mouth was real, and Justin knew that…and he felt damn lucky to be on the receiving end of it.

When Justin opened his mouth, the truth that he'd kept hidden behind all the pain came rolling out. "I need you," he whispered. "Christ, I really fucking need you. I keep telling myself I shouldn't. That it's not fair and it's not your place, but I need you, Drew. I need you." He couldn't stop saying those last three words.

Drew's response was immediate. "I'm on my way."

Justin dropped the phone into his lap and closed his eyes.

He was in love with Drew. He didn't know how it happened, but he knew it was okay. His dad was dying, but it was okay to feel something good too. It was okay for him to need Drew. It had to be, because there was no changing the fact that he did.

DREW'S STOMACH ROLLED the whole time he drove to Joy's house. He'd never done this, never seen someone dying…but there was nothing that he wanted more than to be there for Justin, either. To be his rock, his punching bag, his solace to calm the storm that was no doubt living inside of him. How could it not be?

As he made his way there, he picked up the phone and called Robyn. He'd been out running errands when he'd spoken to Justin.

"Invincible, can I help you?"

"Hey, Robyn, it's Drew."

"What's wrong?" she asked immediately, and he found himself thankful to have such a great employee and friend working for him.

"Justin's dad isn't doing well. I'm going to go be with him. I don't know what's going to happen over the next few days, weeks, hell, I just don't fucking know. No matter what, I need to put him first."

Robyn's response was immediate. "Do you remember when I was pregnant with Nathan? I'd just started working for you and I was incredibly sick. I couldn't hold anything down and I was scared to death I'd lose this job. Since his father wanted nothing to do with us, I needed to work. You were great. You did everything in your power to make it easy on me, and also to let me know that I'd always have a job. You were there for me, and you know I'll be there for you. We'll figure everything out here. You just take care of that man of yours."

As much as he appreciated her words, they made his heart pinch at the same time. Justin wasn't really his. There was a good chance he'd be leaving soon. "Thanks, Robyn. You're the best."

He ended the call and tossed the phone onto the seat beside him. Now wasn't the time to think about Justin and their future.

When he pulled into the driveway, the first thing he saw was Justin sitting on the ground, his back against a tree. It was misting out, not real rain but enough moisture in the air that he had to be feeling it against his skin.

He wore a short-sleeved shirt, his arms wrapped around his legs, looking down. Drew's chest went tight, a heavy ache settling in. Justin looked broken. Lost. Scared. And goddamn he wanted to fix it. To bear the pain for him.

When he turned the key and the engine died, Justin looked up, the searing agony in his stare slicing through Drew.

He got out of the truck and walked over, planting his ass in the wet grass beside Justin. He didn't say a word. Didn't have to. Drew just put his arm around Justin and pulled him close. Justin buried his face in Drew's neck and whispered, "Thank you for coming," against his skin.

"There's nowhere else I'd be."

Surprisingly, he felt Justin smile into his neck. "You're good at this. I bet you say that to all the guys…and women."

They both chuckled quietly, but it was a façade to try and hide the chaos he had to be living inside.

"I don't know how to do this," Justin finally said.

"I know, baby." He kissed the top of Justin's head. "We'll figure it out together. I'm not going anywhere."

"I know you won't."

They sat there together, mist coming down from the heavy clouds in the sky. He'd sit out here with Justin all night if he had to.

CHAPTER TWENTY-SEVEN

THEY'D HARDLY LEFT the house in three days. It was cramped—Justin and Drew sleeping together on the floor because the couch wasn't big enough for both of them. Larry slept nearly all the time, the morphine giving him peace. Each time he woke up, one of them would speak to him alone…say their goodbyes. He didn't know what Justin had said when they spoke but he didn't need to. It was between him and his father and no one else.

It was hard for Drew to put together that the man in the bed was the same man he'd watched ride a motorcycle with Justin not long ago. It was hard to comprehend how fast the change could come. How could someone go from living his life to actively dying so quickly? Logically he'd known Larry was dying the whole time, but that day? Watching him with his family, he'd been pulsing with life as he soaked in those last memories.

Drew had thought he would feel out of place here—like a trespasser hiding out on someone else's land, but he loved Justin, and that made him belong.

He looked up to see his brother and Shanen whispering to each other in the kitchen. They leaned against the fridge, facing one another. Shanen's arms were crossed, her eyes were red and swollen. She'd cried off and on ever since Drew arrived.

Drew could feel Jacob's love for her—his support, and it made him damn proud to be Jacob's brother. This would be something that brought them closer together—loving someone while they dealt with death.

It was late morning but the house was dim. It smelled like coffee and pain.

Drew pulled his eyes away from Jacob and Shanen until they landed on Landon and Rod. They were playing a game of cards at the coffee table. The deck had little dicks all over it, and there was no doubt in his mind they were courtesy of Rod.

They whispered when they spoke as well, hushed voices filled with pain.

Joy was in the bedroom, sitting in a chair beside Larry's bed. She rarely left his side. Jesus, the world was fucked up sometimes. They clearly loved each other. Justin had told him about their past, about the way they'd hurt each other and he obviously knew that Larry had left them and disappeared. Sometimes people hurt the ones they love and as much as he wished that wasn't the case, without their tragedy, there would be no Justin. Without Drew's rocky relationship with Jacob, he might not have been in that bar the night of the wedding, and maybe things between him and Jacob would be different now.

Life was messy. It was ugly and painful and hurtful, but sometimes beautiful things were born out of tragedy.

He ran his hand through Justin's short hair. Drew sat on the floor, his back against the wall, Justin's head in his lap, much the way they'd slept that night at the gym. Only then, he'd been the one lying down. The one with a hand in his hair.

Justin breathed deeply, getting a much needed nap as sleep had been scarce.

He heard a gasp from the other room, before Joy said, "Hey you," in a soft voice.

Drew kept his eyes on Joy as she leaned over the bed, her ear close to his mouth. A blanket of pain dropped over the house as he watched her, and knew, fucking knew what she would say.

"Landon, Shanen, Justin, come in here please," she said and Drew's insides crumbled. Turned to dust.

Justin's eyes jerked open, before Drew had the chance to wake him.

Shanen made it to the room first, with Jacob right beside her. Landon next, Rod right there with him for support. When Justin made it to his feet, he turned and looked at Drew with so much raw emotion in his eyes, that it stole his breath.

Drew stood, and then the two of them walked side-by-side into the room.

The man lying in the bed looked like he'd aged a hundred years.... but then as his eyes floated around the room—from Joy, to Shanen and Jacob, to Landon and Rod, and finally coming to rest on Justin and Drew...he fucking smiled. Smiled a smile that made him glow. Made him look twenty years old again.

He had the people he loved around him and Drew couldn't think of a better way to go.

"Remember what I said," he whispered to Justin, who nodded his head.

Somehow, Drew knew those would be the last words he spoke. He watched Larry take in his three children, his eyes fluttering back and forth for what felt like hours. They all watched him as well, silent tears spilling onto the bed. He closed his eyes.

They waited beside the bed, watching his chest rise and fall as he struggled to breathe. Drew's heart broke when he recognized the wet sound of the death rattle he'd read about online. Each breath was rough, raspy, shallower...slower...until he went silent. He didn't breathe at all.

He was gone.

CHAPTER TWENTY-EIGHT

JUSTIN LET HIS head rest against the cold window of Drew's truck. His father had passed away a few hours before. He hadn't cried. He didn't know why, but he hadn't. Everyone else did and he felt like he'd somehow wronged his father because no tears had come.

He was crushed, devastated, cut open with the loss, but he hadn't cried. They'd each taken their turns to say their goodbyes. Joy had called hospice. Justin called his mom. It was as though they ran through a list of things they had to do, but Justin hadn't put crying on his.

"Thank you for being there. That can't be easy, watching someone die. Christ, I feel like all I'm doing lately is thanking you." His voice was raw, harsh even to his own ears.

"Then stop," Drew told him. "You have nothing to thank me for. You would have done the same thing for me."

And he would have. That didn't mean there still wasn't guilt. Or maybe it was just easier to focus on that than it was the pain that gnawed on his insides. Every second it took another chunk of him, ate away at him.

The longer they drove, the more he felt like he was disappearing, like there was a darkness sucking him in.

He'd felt it at Joy's house as well. He'd known he wouldn't be able to stay there. He needed to escape but the need followed him here, where he hadn't expected.

As soon as they pulled into the driveway, Justin was out of the truck. He slammed the door and went straight for the house, Drew right behind him.

Drew didn't fumble with the keys this time. He unlocked the door and pushed it open for Justin, who rushed inside.

"Fuck!" he yelled at the top of his lungs. "It's not fucking fair!"

He was losing his goddamned mind, screaming in Drew's foyer like that but he couldn't seem to stop himself.

"It's not fair. We didn't get enough time to be a real fucking family. I…" Justin's hand knotted in his own hair…and then Drew was there, wrapping his arms around Justin from behind…and it was suddenly like someone was pulling him back. Like Drew was the sun, trying to bleed into Justin's darkness. Like he wouldn't let Justin get lost in it.

"Shh…I got you," Drew said against his ear.

"I need you. Fuck, I need you so goddamn bad right now. I feel like I'm slipping away. Like this isn't real. Like *I'm* not real. Make me feel real, Drew. Make me feel something good." He sounded weak and needy, but right now, that didn't matter. It was okay to be vulnerable here, with this man.

And when Drew's mouth came down on his neck, sucking and kissing him, Justin felt himself being drawn back to earth. It meant the world to him that Drew respected him enough not to ask if he was sure, not to say that it wasn't the time. Justin knew what he wanted, what he needed, and Drew knew him well enough to understand that.

"I owe you a door-fuck. Are you cashing it in now?" he asked and damned if Justin didn't feel himself smile. He wouldn't have thought that he'd be capable of that today.

"Yes. Need you in my ass." Justin was breathless just from feeling Drew's mouth on his neck, Drew's dick nudging his crease. "Just want to feel you for a little while. Nothing but you. The pain will be there waiting when we're done."

From behind him, Drew's fingers worked the button and zipper on Justin's pants. He slid his hand inside and cupped Justin's dick, rubbing it through his underwear. "Don't know how I'm going to live without this when you go."

Justin got a sharp pain in his chest, because the truth was, he would have to leave soon. "We're here now."

Drew pulled his hand out of Justin's pants, turned him around, and jerked Justin's shirt over his head. "So fucking beautiful," Drew told him as he licked Justin's nipple. "Gonna savor you."

He sucked both Justin's nipples, one after the other, making him gasp. He licked both collarbones. Bit his neck. Kissed his Adam's apple.

"You're making me crazy," Justin gasped against him.

"That's the idea." Drew pulled back and tore his own shirt off before his mouth came down on Justin's. They rubbed together, chest against chest as Drew devoured his mouth.

Justin's hands roamed down Drew's back, to his ass, and he pulled away enough to say, "Want to feel your skin. I'm so fucking cold. I need your warmth."

Drew growled into his neck before pulling back. He had his jeans off in two seconds flat, his pretty cock swollen and leaking. Justin let his finger circle his slit, collected the pre-come there and then sucked it into his mouth.

"Oh fuck, that was sexy," Drew shuddered against him and then he lowered himself to the floor. He pulled Justin's pants and underwear down. Justin's dick was so tender, so fucking eager to let go that he thought he'd lose it the second Drew touched him.

But he didn't. He dropped the back of his head against the wall when Drew shoved his face between Justin's legs and breathed him in. He pulled back, stroked Justin's cock, milked it, making pre-come spill from him. Drew pulled Justin's prick away from his body, the come dripping out only for Drew to catch it on his tongue.

"Look at you. So fucking hot. I created a monster." *And then I'm going to leave him...someone else will be able to enjoy him.* Justin squeezed his eyes closed, shook his head, and then Drew shoved to his feet.

"Don't you disappear on me. It's just you and me, baby."

Then they were kissing again. Their arms were wrapped around each other, chests glued together, hands roaming each other's backs as they kissed. Sucked each other's tongues, lips.

Justin wanted to keep going. Wanted to stop so they could fuck. Wanted to do everything all at once and never stop.

"I need you. Christ, I need your dick stretching my ass. Wanna feel you inside me."

"Shit. Condoms. I'll be right back." Drew went to pull away but Justin grabbed his arm.

"I don't want to wait," Justin said, meaning it.

"There's lube. I bought some and put it in the closet, for that fuck I owe you. I haven't gotten to the condoms yet."

"Just take me raw. I've never had anyone raw before." He didn't know why he wanted that so much right now. Why he couldn't let Drew run upstairs or why he couldn't go up with him. Maybe he just wanted this one thing with Drew that he'd never had with anyone else. "I was tested before I came here. I haven't been with anyone other than you."

"I haven't been with anyone other than you since I was last checked either. I go every six months like clockwork."

Justin tried to smile. "Look at you. Looks like you do follow some rules. If you don't want—"

"I want," Drew cut him off. He opened the closet full of coats beside them and pulled out a small tube of lube.

Justin could see his hand tremble as he opened it, stroking his own dick to get it wet for Justin.

He wanted Drew's come, he realized. Wanted it spilled inside him. Wanted a part of Drew inside him that he'd never had inside of him before.

Justin turned, put his hands on the wall, spread his legs, and gave Drew his ass.

It went quickly after that. The head of Drew's thick cock pushed past the first ring of muscle, before sliding in slowly, deeper until he bottomed out.

They were both still. Drew's body was hot and hard against his back. His dick stretching Justin's ass the way he fucking loved. "Make love to me, Drew. Make me feel good."

Drew wrapped one arm around Justin's waist. His hand gripped Justin's cock and he started to stroke. Stroke as he pulled out, and then jackhammered in again. With his other hand, he threaded their fingers together against the wall.

It was slow, so fucking slow and so good. Every time Drew thrust deeper, Justin breathed out.

This was what he'd needed. Drew was what he needed.

Drew kissed his neck, whispered in his ear from behind. Told him how good he felt. How tight he was. How he'd never get enough. That Justin was so fucking hot, hugging his raw dick. That he couldn't wait to fill Justin with his come.

Damned if he didn't want the same thing.

When Drew slammed in again, hot spurts jerked in Justin's ass, and he let loose himself. His balls tightened as he came all over Drew's hand while Drew did the same in his ass.

And then he fucking cried. The pain was there, waiting to crash into him, to turn him into a pile of rubble.

He couldn't hold it back anymore. He'd lost his father. He still felt insecure of his place with his family. He lived in fucking North Carolina and Drew lived here. It didn't matter that it wasn't far, it wasn't here and when in the hell did long distance relationships ever work?

"Shh, baby. It's okay. I got you." Drew's cock still filled him. It started to soften before he eventually fell out. He didn't let go of Justin—kept hugging him, kept kissing his neck.

And Justin continued to cry. Tears poured out of his eyes. Mixed with his come on the floor. And then Drew was holding him again. They were lying down in Drew's bed, and he didn't even remember how they'd gotten up the stairs.

They were facing each other, on their sides. His whole body was squeezed between Drew's legs. His face in Drew's neck. One of Drew's hands on the back of his head as he comforted Justin. As he told him he loved him. As he told him it would be okay.

When Drew said it, Justin believed him.

CHAPTER TWENTY-NINE

H IS WISHES HAD been to be cremated, so that's what they'd done. Today was the intimate celebration of life at Shanen's home.

Justin's mom came from North Carolina to be with him. Drew was there, always there supporting him. Joy, Rod, Landon, Shanen, and Jacob were there, of course, but Drew's parents had come too. It made sense, Justin thought, considering Shanen was their daughter-in-law. Obviously they would want to be there to support her.

"You okay?" Drew asked.

"Yeah. Just thinking about how sexy you look in a suit," he winked at Drew, who rolled his eyes, before wrapping his arm around Justin's shoulders, pulling him close, and kissing the top of his head.

This was the first time they'd been in the same room with Drew's parents since his dad's birthday party, which felt like an eternity ago. He hadn't been sure how Drew would react, but he found himself closing his eyes, relieved that he wouldn't pull away.

When he opened his eyes again, he saw Drew's parents heading their way. They held their heads high, backs straight, confident. His mom wore a lot of make-up and excessive jewelry. You could tell they were used to things of a certain standard, which couldn't feel further from who Drew was.

Justin stiffened slightly. Drew had told him they were okay with his revelation, but it was an instinct to be on edge.

Drew's father's eyes darted to Drew's arm around him, and then at Drew.

"Hello," his mom said. "We wanted to take a moment to properly introduce ourselves. I know we met briefly at the party, but…well…things are a little different now."

Justin straightened himself up and held his hand out, first to Drew's mom, then his father.

"We're very sorry for your loss," his mom said.

Justin's chest got tight. Yeah, he was sorry about it too. "Thank you. I appreciate that, and it was nice of you to come and support Shanen."

Her brows pulled together, but it was Drew's father who spoke. "We're here to support you too since…um…you and Drew are…" His cheeks darkened and Justin saw that he flushed the same way Drew did. But he couldn't focus on that for very long. They were here for him too, because he was important to Drew. *How was he supposed to do this? How could he leave Drew?*

"Dating. They're dating, dear," his mom smiled. "My husband is never at a loss for words. We should document this!"

Drew laughed beside him, before he stepped away from Justin to hug both of his parents. "Thank you," he whispered softly.

When they parted, it was his dad who spoke. "Drew said you worked in construction, but you were enrolled in school. Will you continue both here?"

A cold front swept through Justin's insides, but Drew didn't falter. He replied, "Justin has to go back to North Carolina. It's his home. He has a life there."

Both of his parents looked confused. "Oh. I just assumed…I'm sorry." His dad looked uncomfortable again.

"We'll figure it out," Drew replied, as Justin watched him. Would they? How? Would they try a long distance relationship? Fear spiked inside him. Did they have any chance of making this work? But then…could he just drop his life at home and move here when the past few months had been such an emotional rollercoaster?

Before Justin had the chance to think about it further, his own mother approached them. "You must be Drew's parents. I'm Emily. It's very nice to meet you."

The conversation went on from there. Then the group got together and told stories about Larry. There was laughter and tears, but most of all, there was life because life went on. No matter what happened, you had to keep living.

IT WAS EARLY the next morning that Drew and Justin stood outside Drew's house. It was still dark, the air chilly, but it was peaceful. Drew liked this time of day. He always had. The world seemed so much quieter before dawn.

"Sure was a fun test drive. Lasted a little longer than both of us expected." He was trying to lighten the mood, to show Justin it was okay and that he understood, but the other man didn't smile. He just stared at Drew, who leaned against Justin's car.

"It's more than a test drive. You and I both know that. It's not that I want to leave. Christ, my insides feel like they're torn to shreds at the thought of leaving you...I just...that's home. I belong there. My head and my heart are a mess right now. I need to sort things through. I need some downtime to make sense of it all. In less than a year I found out my dad was dying, that he'd lied to me most of my life. That I had siblings I didn't know. I dropped everything to go to a new state, and tried to find my place in a new family, while leaving my other one behind. I lost my father, fell in love—"

"About time you said it," Drew cut him off, then hooked his finger through Justin's belt loop and pulled him close. His arms immediately went around Justin's shoulders. Justin's fingers dug into his hips as they held each other. "You don't need to explain anything to me. I get it. Like I said yesterday, we'll figure it out. I'll come visit you and you can show me North Carolina in more detail than I showed you Scotland and Ireland."

This time, he got one of Justin's chuckles.

"You gonna keep working out when you get home?" Drew asked.

"Don't know. Not sure it'll be as fun without you. I just did it for the post-workout sex."

"That's because I'm good." They were quiet, stalling. Drew knew it. Justin had said his goodbyes to Joy, Landon, and Shanen yesterday. He'd promised to call and to visit. He'd spent his night with Drew and now they just had to do it. Nothing was going to change.

"You should go...you're supposed to pick your mom up at the hotel in five minutes."

"Do we have time for a quickie?" Justin kissed Drew's neck, nipped his earlobe.

He wanted that, wanted it so fucking badly but they couldn't keep dragging this out. "No. It'll give us something to look forward to when I come and visit you. I'm looking forward to having your dick in my ass again. Maybe I should hit up Rods-N-Ends and buy a toy to tide me over."

"No," Justin squeezed Drew's ass. "It's mine. I want to be the only dick that's ever inside you."

Then don't fucking go. Drew closed down those thoughts immediately. Justin had to do this. He understood it, no matter how much he wanted him to stay.

"Can I at least get a kiss?" Justin asked.

"Yes, sir. That you can have." Their mouths fit together in a slow, languid kiss. Justin's tongue stroked the inside of his mouth, and then Drew's did the same to Justin's. When they parted, they didn't say another word to each other. He moved away from the car. Justin got in. They shared one more look, and then Justin drove away, and Drew fought like hell not to run after him and tell him to come back.

CHAPTER THIRTY

JUSTIN HUNG UP from his phone call with Drew. It had felt good talking to him. The last time had been a few days before, and this was the third call they'd shared in the two weeks Justin had been home.

He'd gotten a dog, which was fucking ridiculous. It wasn't that he hadn't always liked animals, because he had. Still, he'd never really thought about getting a dog before. He hadn't thought much about getting one before bringing Ireland home either. The local shelter had been running a dog adoption drive. He'd driven by and seen the sign. The next thing he knew, he was filling out the paperwork to bring home the stray, mixed-breed.

His house felt too quiet, which made no sense. He'd lived on his own since he was eighteen years old. He had no problems with a quiet house, but suddenly, it felt lonely as hell.

"How you doing, Ireland?" he asked when she jumped on his lap, wagging her tail. "Are you bored?" He rubbed behind her ear. "Yes, you are, aren't you? I'm bored too. What are we going to do, huh?"

When he was greeted by nothing but silence Justin rolled his eyes. "I'm losing my fucking mind." He pushed to his feet. Ireland followed him, wagging her tail like crazy. He opened the door to let her out just as his mom pulled into his driveway.

A few minutes later, Ireland jumped all over her as she made her way to the house. "I got off work early so I thought I'd stop by and say hi," his mom told him before she pulled him in for a brief hug.

"How are you?" he asked before they walked back into the

house. Ireland plopped on her dog bed by the fireplace and they sat at the table.

"Happy to have you home. It's nice to be able to stop by and see you when I want to."

He smiled at her, genuinely. He enjoyed that as well. He'd always had a close relationship with her, but for some reason, the word home made his stomach sour. "It's good to be back," Justin told her. It *should* feel good to be home. He'd always loved it here. Granted, he hadn't known anything else, but that had always been okay with him. He guessed it made sense for him to feel a little unsteady still. He'd been through a lot and now he was stepping back into his life. It had been a hard few months.

"Did you figure things out with school and at Paul's?"

He nodded. "Yeah. I'm picking back up spring semester. I'll go to work with Paul full time until then, and then I'll go to part time." He'd known Paul most of his life. Justin was lucky to be able to come right back to a job.

Justin glanced his mom's way and saw a wrinkle between her brows. "Are you sure you're okay? Something's been off with you. I know you miss your father. I would do anything to make it so that he was still here with you." She reached over and squeezed his hand. "You had a special few months with him. He loved you so much, Justin."

"I know he did." Justin looked down at his small kitchen table, traced patterns on the wood with his finger. "I've made peace with everything as best as I could. There's no changing any of it, and I like Shanen and Landon a lot. Joy's a good woman, too."

She gave him a sad smile, and damned if Justin didn't feel guilty for liking Joy.

"I know she is. They were all nothing but kind to me when I was there. There's a part of me that wanted to hate her. Even before I knew about Landon and Shanen, I wanted to hate her because I'd always known your father loved her. Do I believe he loved me too? I do, but I've always known it was different than the love he felt for her."

"Really?" Justin asked, locking eyes with her. "Even when the two of you were together?" They'd never had this conversation before. How did you bring something like this up?

She sighed. "Yeah. At first I think I wanted to try and save him. Never think you can save a man, Justin. It doesn't work that way, but he was depressed, lonely, and I wanted to fix that. He loved you so damn much from the second he met you, that I told myself it would work. Eventually he'd love me that much too."

He felt like someone sat on his chest, pressing all their weight down on him.

"Of course it didn't work…and that's okay. The two of you were close, and regardless of the fact that I've never married, it's not as if I've spent my life waiting for him."

She had dated a few men through the years, some longer than others. He'd always respected her strength and will to keep going. She didn't need anyone. She'd raised Justin fine on her own before he came back and she would have continued to do so without his father.

"You're in love with Drew, aren't you?" she asked after a few moments of silence.

"Yeah…yeah, I am," he answered honestly. There was no question in his mind that he loved him. "I'm not quite sure how it happened but it did."

"We're never quite sure how love happens. Love isn't something you plan, love is something that happens slowly, in small doses—something someone says once, something they do, the way they treat you, the way they make you feel—all those little moments and then…boom, you're just there. You've fallen."

He liked that. Love was in the small things that sometimes went unnoticed. Some of what she said sounded similar to what his father had told him. He liked that thought. "Jesus, Ma. You should write romance novels or something. People would eat that shit up," he teased her.

She rolled her eyes and chuckled. "Maybe in my next life. I'm pretty settled in this one." They were both quiet. Ireland snored in the corner, and Justin waited, knowing she had more to say.

"Why are you here?" she finally asked.

I don't know was the first thought that popped into his head, but he answered with, "Because I live here?"

She scoffed. "That's bullshit and you know it." That was his mom. She didn't walk on eggshells for anyone. She was always straight to the point. "I'll be okay, Justin."

His eyes snapped up toward her, his throat suddenly tight.

"I'm your mother. No one will ever know you as well as I do. I know you're as loyal as they come, especially to your family. You'd do anything for family. I'm a grown woman. I have a career, a home. I might not be in a relationship with anyone, but I'm even capable of going out and having sex if I want it."

He shook his head and chuckled. Only his mother would say something like that. "I don't think I want to talk about your sex life."

"Me either. I'm just saying, I know how to live. I knew how before I met your father, when we were together, and when we separated. I'll be okay. You won't be leaving me behind. There isn't a part of me who will ever feel like you've chosen them over me."

That was the crux of it, wasn't it? His mother had been a one-night-stand for his dad. They'd gone their separate ways. He'd gone back to Joy and she'd discovered she was pregnant. She'd done a damn good job raising Justin by herself. When things with Joy hadn't worked, his dad had made a home here, and they'd found each other again. When he realized he would die, it wasn't his mom that Larry needed. He'd gone back to his family, and yes, part of that was because of Shanen and Landon, but that didn't change the fact that he'd needed them and Justin had dropped everything to go with him.

He never wanted her to feel as though he'd replaced her—as though he'd replaced one family with another the way his father had done.

"It's not just that," he began. "What would I do? Go there, get a shitty job, move in with him? My life is here. This is my home."

"I'm calling bullshit again. None of that matters. You're throwing excuses at me. I raised you better than that. You look around this place, really look and if you can tell me you're happy here, that it's home, I'll shut my mouth and mind my own business—never mind, who am I kidding? I'm your mama. I'll never mind my own business."

Jesus, he loved this woman. There had never been a time in his life that she didn't support him. That she hadn't been there for him. He wasn't sure there'd ever been a time in his life that she'd been wrong, either.

"Thanks, Mom." This time it was Justin who reached over and squeezed her hand.

She winked at him, "That's what I'm here for. So, how did the two of you meet, anyway?"

He couldn't stop the laugh from jumping out of his mouth. There was no way in hell he could share *that* story with her.

CHAPTER THIRTY-ONE

"NO ONE'S STUMBLED onto my hat yet, have they, Robyn?" he asked her for the hundredth time.

"Nope. You know I'd let you know if they did."

He ran a hand through his hair. He felt naked without the damn thing. He had no idea where it could have gone, but it had been missing for weeks. He should just buy a new one but he liked his old hat. It was worn, it fit his head just right.

"You know they carry those things at the store, right? It's a pretty amazing concept. You go in, pick out a hat, and buy it."

He wrapped an arm around her shoulders and pulled her close. "Ha, ha. When did you become such a comedian?"

"I'm just giving you shit," she teased him. "So...how's your guy? Are you really trying the long distance thing?"

Well, there went his good mood. Drew pulled away and leaned against the counter. The gym was pretty slow right now. He didn't have any more appointments lined up so he was about to head out. "I don't know," he shrugged. "We haven't really said for sure what we're doing. It was mentioned. We've talked a few times. I still want him. If long distance is the only option, I guess we try it. I'm giving him some time to get his bearings."

Sympathy played in her eyes as she looked at him. "You tell him I said to treat you right or I'm going to steal you away from him. You're quite the catch."

He knew she was only giving him a hard time, probably trying to make him feel better. "I'll be sure to tell him you said that. And you're quite the catch too."

They said their goodbyes and Drew headed out for the day. He considered calling Justin, but hell, he didn't want to push the man.

Actually, that was a fucking lie. He wanted to drive his ass to North Carolina, kidnap Justin and bring him back home. He'd just pulled into his driveway when his cell rang. Drew grabbed it from the seat beside him and saw Jacob's name on the screen. Things still weren't perfect between them, but they were better than they had been. They were working on things and that's all you could really do.

"Hello?" Drew killed his truck's engine.

"Hey, do you have plans tomorrow night? Shanen wants you to come over for dinner. Joy, Landon, and Rod will be here as well. She's still struggling with the loss of Larry. She wants her family close."

Drew's heart broke for her. He understood that desire and he felt damned honored to be included in the people she wanted close. "Yeah, I think I can make that work. Thanks for calling."

"Sure...so, have you talked to him?" Jacob asked. It was strange as hell having conversations like this with his brother. This had never been who they were...but he was glad it was who they were becoming.

"I talked to him a few days ago. He's getting things in order. He'll be heading back to school soon. He's...living his life." Which was exactly what he was supposed to do. "Listen, I'm going to run. I—"

"What are you doing, Drew?"

"What do you mean?"

"If there's one thing I've always respected about you—even if it was also the thing that made me jealous of you—it's your fire, your determination to go for what you want, no matter what the risk is. You are who you are and you have never made apologies for that. It's a damn admirable quality and you're losing it now when it's the most important."

Drew sighed, reached for his hat before he remembered he'd lost the damn thing, and dropped his head back against the seat. "What are you talking about?"

"You want him, you fight for him. You fucking go to him if you have to. Don't just roll over and accept whatever happens. If you do, you deserve to lose him. If things don't go your way, at least you know you fought." Jacob sighed. "I've never had to fight for something before. I've always just done what's expected and honestly, it's come easy for me. That's not you. You're a fighter. Prove it."

Drew stared at the phone for minutes after Jacob hung up on him. At first he was in shock—who the fuck was that who'd just told him to go after Justin? Then he was pissed—who did Jacob think he was? Drew was doing the right thing. He was giving Justin the time he needed.

Then he was angry at himself, because Jacob was right. He was giving up, letting whatever happened, happen. He was accepting the status quo and not going for what he wanted, which was Justin. He wanted Justin more than he'd ever wanted anything in his life.

He jumped out of the truck, fire burning in his veins. He fumbled the keys like only Justin made him do, before he got into his house. He took the stairs two at a time as he made his way to his room. Less than ten minutes later, he had a bag packed.

Fuck this. Fuck waiting. Justin was his and Drew would make damn sure the other man knew it.

Drew got down the stairs even quicker than he got up them. He jerked open the door and... "You stole my fucking hat."

Justin smiled and it nearly stopped his damn heart.

"You sure this is yours? It comes with a lot of responsibility. You see, I fell in love with the man who wears this hat. If it fits, that means you're stuck with me. It means you're mine."

Jesus, it felt good to see the man. He was here. He'd come back. He'd... "Fuck you for stealing my damn thunder. I was on my way to you. And are you sure you want to play this game? I won't let you go this time. In the beginning, you said I sounded like I was looking for my happy ending. I wasn't but the damn thing seemed to find me anyway."

Justin took a step closer, stepped into the house. He took the baseball cap off his head, and put it backward on Drew's. "This is home…you're home. I kept saying I needed to go home and it took going back there to realize home isn't a place. It's you."

They were being ridiculous again. Ridiculous and sappy and cheesy and Drew fucking loved it. He reached out, cupped Justin's face in his hands. "I can't believe you're here."

"I have nowhere to stay. I don't have a job. I have a fucking house payment in North Carolina until I can sell the damn thing. Remember all this excitement when you realize how much baggage I've come with."

He didn't give a shit about that. They'd figure it out later. He stepped closer, went to kiss Justin and then… *bark, bark!*

What the—?

"Oh, and I have a dog, too. Drew meet Ireland, Ireland this is Drew."

The dog ran right past him into the house and jumped on the couch. "I've always wanted a dog." Drew smiled.

"You have one now. And can you hurry up and kiss me? I drove nonstop to get here. I want a kiss, then a wall-fuck. That would be fantastic. Then we should get into the hot tub before we fuck again in your bed. I really missed your bed."

Jesus, he loved this man. "Shut up," Drew told him, and then he kissed him. Wanted to devour him. Never wanted to take his mouth off of him.

Justin moaned and leaned into their kiss. Drew swallowed it, kissed deeper. Wanted more. When their mouths parted, they didn't pull away. Their foreheads touched and Drew closed his eyes.

"I love you. My head was a mess when I left, but there's never been a doubt in my mind that I love you."

"I love you too."

That was life wasn't it? People didn't always do the right thing. Sometimes they made mistakes or had to take a different route to get to the same place than someone else did. They detoured, or test drove a hundred different cars before finding the one they fell in love with.

People got hurt, people hurt others, people died, but the living part? Living and laughing and loving? That made everything else worth it. He couldn't wait to start doing that part with Justin.

EPILOGUE

"NICK. I'M GOING to gnaw my fucking arm off. When is the food going to be done?" Bryce whined, making Justin chuckle.

"Would you relax? You're so damn impatient. If you don't relax, I'm letting everyone eat except for you!" Nick replied as he stood at the stove mixing the sauce in the large pot. "If I take it off too soon, the sausage won't be right. There's a science to cooking that you don't understand."

"Oh, I don't need sausage," Rod cut in. "Landon gave me his before we left home. I don't have to wait for his. I just have to touch it and it's ready."

The whole room erupted in loud laughter.

"Holy shit, that was good. I wish I would've thought of that. You have one on me," Bryce told Rod. It seemed they were always trying to one-up each other. It was fun to watch.

"Your partner is crazy," Justin teased his brother.

"I know he is. I can't keep up with him half the time, but that's exactly why I love him so damn much."

Justin nodded before looking across the room at Drew, who played with the dick cards with his brother, Jacob.

As though he felt Justin's eyes on him, Drew looked up and winked. Jesus, he was happy. Happier than he'd ever been because of the man looking at him with dick cards in his hand and because of the people around him.

It had been a few months since their father had passed away. Justin was settled into Drew's home, enrolled in school to start next term, and he'd found a job remodeling houses, which was more the kind of work he was used to than working at the restaurant with Nick.

This was one of the many get-togethers the group had had since Justin moved here. He'd gotten to know his siblings well, felt comfortable around them. They were his family…as was Joy. He smiled thinking of his dad. He would love to see them all now.

"You know I knew something was going on with you and Drew the whole time, don't you?" Landon asked.

Justin rolled his yes. "No you didn't. We were good at the incognito thing."

"Yeah, Mister *I think I jerked off with that guy, oh nevermind. It's not him!*"

Justin laughed at that. Okay, so maybe that had been a little obvious. "It wasn't supposed to be anything important."

"Neither was Rod," Landon replied.

"Or Nick," Bryce added stepping up to them. Justin hadn't realized he'd been close enough to hear.

"But now they're everything," Justin said, knowing the two men were on the same page as he was.

"Yeah," Landon replied.

"Yeah, they are," Bryce added. "Did I tell you guys Nick's sister is letting us spend time with the kids? Both of us."

Nick had told Justin that his sister's husband hadn't accepted his relationship with Bryce, and she was keeping her kids away from their uncle. There'd been one time when she'd gone against her husband's wishes, but then she'd pulled back. It looked like things were changing.

"No shit? That's great," Landon told Bryce.

"How did that happen?" Justin asked.

"She just woke up, I guess. A lot of things have changed for her. She's not living under her husband's thumb any longer. I wanted it so fucking badly for Nick. I'm glad it's happening." Bryce's eyes found Nick and as soon as they did, Nick turned back and looked at him. It was the same thing Drew had done to Justin minutes before. The same thing Landon and Rod did to one another as well.

He remembered when he first met Nick and Bryce at Shanen's for his dad's party, how they looked at each other, the love there. It was the same love Rod and Landon had. The same love he and Drew had.

"When do you guys leave for your trip?" Landon asked, pulling Justin from his thoughts.

"Not for about six weeks." He was ready now. They were going to Scotland and Ireland. They planned to do everything Drew had told him about.

"Dinner's done!" Nick called from the kitchen.

"Finally!" Bryce replied. Everyone made their way toward the kitchen, letting Shanen go first. Justin waited where he was in the living room, and Drew found his way to him.

"Mm...let's skip dinner. I'd rather have my mouth on you instead." Drew wrapped his arms around Justin and buried his face in his neck.

"I like that idea, though I have to admit, I'm a little hungry too." And there was the fact that the sauce smelled incredible. Nick was a great chef.

"Me too. I just always want my mouth on you."

"We can hide out in the—"

"Don't even think about it!" Rod told them. "We're hanging out. No disappearing for sex during family time."

It was important to Rod—spending time together. It was important to all of them, but Rod didn't have family other than the people in this room. Justin was glad to be a part of it.

"I swear, the things I hear. I wish your friend Christi could have come, Bryce. It's hard being the only woman," Shanen teased, earning a round of chuckles from everyone.

They all sat at the table together, and ate. There was laughter and jokes. Conversation and stories and more laughter. Things had changed for all of them. That's what losing someone did to you sometimes, it changed you, made you realize what you had, and made you hold on tight to that. Drew and Jacob were getting along better than ever, and Justin couldn't be happier for his guy.

"I love you," Drew told him as though he could read Justin's thoughts.

"I love you too," Justin replied. He wanted nothing more than to spend the rest of his life with this man, and he knew without a doubt that would happen.

They were cleaning up the dinner mess, when Landon's phone rang. His brother frowned at his cell before picking it up. "Hey, buddy. How's it going?" Landon said.

There was a silence and then, "Yeah, of course. Is everything okay?"

Another pause. "Okay, no problem. Sounds good." He hung up and Rod frowned at him.

"Who was that? Is something wrong?" he asked.

"Yes. No. Actually, I'm not sure. I think it's okay. That was Beckett. He asked if he could come and see me. Said he needs to get away."

"Who's Beckett?" Drew asked, right before Bryce said, "Beckett fucking Monroe?" Well, obviously Bryce knew who he was. "Last year's Supercross champion, Beckett Monroe?"

"I think Bryce just came," Rod said and Justin let out a laugh.

It looked like they had a Supercross rider coming to town.

THE END

JUMP START a Crossroads novella coming Fall 2016.

TOUCH THE SKY—Riley Hart writing as Nyrae Dawn with Christina Lee

CHAPTER ONE
Gabriel

Five years earlier...

Lucas,

Dude, are we really doing this? I can't believe we're going to come out to our families. I mean, I'm glad. I really am. No matter what. No matter how my dad responds—and he will respond—hopefully not with his fist. But fuck, I can take it because it's eating me alive, being locked inside myself like this. I've been going stir crazy, man.

I wish we lived closer and we could meet up someplace afterward, especially if it doesn't go so well. You know my dad; he can be a bastard. But from what you've told me about your mom... I think she'll be great. And my mom, she might just do what she normally does, which is ignore me. But at least it'll be out there and they'll know.

Because shit, it's so lonely... I sound like such a wuss when I say things like that. I'm alone, because no one knows me. Not like you do. I don't feel as empty inside when I message you. It's like you get me. I know you do. But this time next week our families will know who we are too.

And maybe... I don't know, I've got to have hope. I've got

to believe it'll be okay. If not, it's not too much longer until we're eighteen. We'll go to West Hollywood and really live. I can't wait to do everything we talked about! I can't wait to meet you in person one day. I'm so damn glad we found each other on that message board.

We got this,
Gabriel

I STARE AT the five-year-old email with a lump in my throat. I saved them all, even the photos he sent me of himself with that wavy black hair, green eyes, and lips that I pictured kissing on more than one occasion. Mostly, I imagined having a friend. Somebody I could trust through the emotional wreckage that had been consuming my life.

But that message was the final one I'd written to him. The last time I remember being so fucking scared of what would happen. If you didn't count when the steel door locked behind me with my parents on the other side. That was the night some stranger saw me teetering on the ledge of a bridge. I wasn't going to jump, for fuck's sake—I was only chasing a high. Trying to quiet the buzzing noise inside my brain. It was better than feeling numb. Way the hell better.

Moving here wasn't nearly as frightening as all of that. It was a relief to leave San Diego and come to West Hollywood. To drop my general courses at SDU and figure out my own path. This is the city I thought I'd be meeting Lucas in someday, and somehow being here, even though I haven't spoken to him in years, makes me feel like I'm working toward some goal. The same goal I had confided to him so long ago.

I also came because I was itching to get the hell away, to finally be on my own. I was too much of a chickenshit the year after my hospitalization to message Lucas and admit that they'd slapped a bipolar label on me. That I'd been given powerful meds because apparently you can also become delusional or some shit while manic.

My dad's face, though, that was the worst. And when I came out to him in that inpatient therapy session—fuck. Worse than his fist against my stomach. But we never talked about his threatening words, his punishing glares. My mom catering to him and never to me. I was the dirty secret, me and my messed-up head, not him.

My back slides against the wall until I'm sitting on the floor in my room with my laptop on my knees. The cold plaster feels good against my skin. I should delete that email. But I don't. I can't. I think of Lucas often, wonder what he's up to. If he found somebody else who got him. A good guy, a beautiful guy. *Love.* My chest seizes up.

I want that for him, wonder if we could have had it together. Or maybe he would've continued to just be my friend. Hell, I'm not sure I'll be able to have that with anybody. Not with the way the wires are crossed in my brain.

My foot connects with my forgotten glass of soda, spilling it in a small river over the hardwood floor. "Damn it!" My thoughts are all over the place lately, thinking about those old emails, and starting to feel like shit for no reason that makes any type of sense.

I toss aside my computer on the bed and grab for the tissue box to clean up the mess.

"Everything cool in there?" My roommate calls to me through the locked door.

"Fine," I grumble. Gotta keep this place clean or Ezra might find a good excuse to kick me out. Dude smokes his share of weed but he knows when even one thing is out of place in this apartment.

"You call off sick today?" he asks in a muffled voice. The problem with renting a room on the outskirts of West Hollywood from a dude who paints in his home studio is that he knows my schedule too well, including how early or late I get home. But years ago, Lucas and I didn't bank on how pricey the area would be, only that it was liberal and thriving enough for two kids who had wanderlust.

"Nah, the supplies didn't come in on time, so the foreman let us go early." At least I'm being honest. Besides, I don't want to be on that scaffold today. Not yesterday either. Not with these scary hopeless thoughts running through my scrambled brain. Man, I normally love being up there with a birds-eye view of the entire city. And right now we're reconstructing a building in a rundown neighborhood in North Hollywood, which still has a clear shot of the Pacific from the highest level.

I even turned down going out with the construction crew for a liquid lunch. I can hold my own and be the life of the party if you catch me on the right day. Those same dudes would probably rip me a new asshole if they saw me sniveling in my room like this. Lou would understand though; he's been cool to me. He always talks to me about his teen boy's problems, probably because I'm closest to his age.

A knock at my door. "I'm heading across the street to get some food. Want to come?" Ezra asks. There's a small diner we order from on a regular basis.

I'm tired, so fucking tired that my limbs feel like dead weight. I should drag myself up, though. I only do this weeping shit when I'm crashing. Which is why I pulled up those messages from Lucas again. I needed some type of quiet comfort because this part always scares the shit out of me. How I can't control it. I can only just roll with it.

But my body is fighting me, only wants to sleep. Add in my jumbled thoughts and I wouldn't be good company to anybody. I know this pattern. You start to understand your body after a while. If I hold on another day or so, my energy level will return and I'll be on top of my game again.

"Go ahead without me." I shouldn't be anti-social but it's hard enough pretending at work this week. I don't want to pretend with him too.

His feet scuff the floor, and I can hear him hesitating, deliberating. Like he knows. Knows something is wrong with me again. "How about I bring you back something? Have you even eaten today?"

Damn, he feels sorry for me. I glare at my top drawer where my two empty pill bottles have remained unfilled for well over a year. I know I should start the meds again, now that I finally have insurance. They might even help me pack on some extra weight. But then that veil will go up, the one that keeps me at arm's length from the world, and I fucking hate that feeling.

I force myself to stand up and glance in the dresser mirror. My blond hair is all disheveled and I've got shadows beneath my eyes, even though I've been sleeping a ton. I need to get my ass in gear, especially since I have a paper due for my on-line class tomorrow.

Another knock. *Shit.* I had left him hanging. "Gabriel?"

"Uh, sure man," I say, in the cheeriest voice I can muster. "Any kind of sandwich will do."

CHAPTER TWO
Lucas

MUSIC PLAYS IN the background, a guitar riff and a guy with a loud, high-pitched voice who sounds like he's trying to scream over the music.

It's totally not my gig, but for the six to eight hours that I'm at the bar, I don't have much choice other than to listen to whatever they have playing.

It's a straight bar, a shabby, rundown place in an alley in Hollywood that's often filled with the kind of people my mom would have partied with if she were still around. Working here serves its purpose so I stick around.

My shift ended a few minutes ago. I'm chillin' at a small, two-person table at the end of the bar that we use sometimes for breaks and things like that. Leaning over the back of the chair, I continue sketching long lines and perfect squares in my sketchbook. It's a simple building, this one, with a plane flying overhead.

There's a bump against my chair making it move about two inches. "Why do you always turn your chair backward to sit in it?"

Glancing over my shoulder, I roll my eyes at Conner. His short, dark hair is kind of spiky, and he has this happy fucking grin that Conner always has.

We're the only two people who work here that are under the age of thirty, so we talk to each other more than we talk to everyone else. Not that I talk to anyone much. "Why you always so worried about what I'm doing? Something you wanna tell me?" I tease him, but Conner doesn't take the bait. He's straight, but knows I'm gay.

Everyone I work with does, because if there's one thing I won't do anymore, it's lie about who I am.

Conner grabs the other chair and turns it around the wrong way. Cocking a brow at him I nod toward it, but he ignores me. "Why are you always drawing buildings? Never a fucking tree, or a bird, or shit like that. Always buildings."

I flip the books closed. I hate it when people look at my shit. "A tree or a bird? You want me to draw you a tree or a bird? I will." Really, I won't. That's not my thing. For me it's not about drawing as much as it's about buildings. I love them—thinking about how they're put together. There's something about big-ass buildings of different shapes and designs that calls to me. That's none of his business, though.

"No, but you can draw me a naked chick with big old titties."

Conner laughs and I roll my eyes at him. "Crazy motherfucker."

"You got naked dudes in there? You play it off like you're drawing the fucking Wells Fargo building or something, but I bet it's really full of dick and ass."

And, that's about enough of him. Conner's an all right guy but he's overwhelming as hell sometimes. I'm definitely not talking to him about dick and ass, even though I'm quite fond of both. That conversation needs to be saved for someone who wants my dick in their ass or the other way around.

I stand up. "On that note, I'm out of here. Was waiting for the bus, but it should be there soon." After picking up my beanie, I slide it on my head and then reach for my sketchbook.

"Don't run off. I'm giving you shit. What are you doing tonight? Want to go out and have a beer or something?"

There's not a chance of the drinking thing happening for me. My stomach rolls at the thought. My throat burns like I swallowed acid. "Why would you go somewhere to have a beer when we work at a bar?"

"Because we both know this isn't the kind of bar we'd want to hang out in."

Little does he know, I don't hang out in bars at all. It's not that I *won't* be around alcohol, obviously since I work here, but I don't drink. Not at all. Seen what it can do, and don't plan on that being something Mom passes down to me. Working here, seeing the regulars with their everyday drinks, reminds me of what I won't let myself become. "Nah, I'm good," I finally say, answering Conner's question.

"You're such a fucking bastard, Lucas. You never hang out. You think you're too good?" His question is said with a playful tone, but I know he's partially serious. Not that he believes I think I'm too good, but this isn't the first time he's asked me to do something, yet I haven't said yes once. "Dude, come out and get drunk with me," he adds.

There are a lot of things I should be doing with my life that I'm not. My mom had simple wishes for me—stay sober, go to college, make something of my life, don't be like her, and be happy.

I'm still waiting for most of those wishes to come true. Staying sober is the only one I've always known I would make happen. "No. I don't think I'm too good and I'm not going to go get drunk with you. I have shit to do. I come in at noon tomorrow. Do you work?"

Conner frowns, but doesn't argue with my decision to head home. "Yeah, I come in at two. I'll see you later, man." He holds out his fist and I bump it with my own, even though that's always felt like such a lame thing to do.

"Cat'cha later," I tell him before sticking my sketchbook under my arm and making my way to the door. It's mid-seventies out, and blue skies like it always is in Southern California. I like it when I work early and get off at a decent time. The sunshine and perfect weather is what made Mom move to California in the first place, only we were in a shithole in Riverside County. I think Mom and I thought being anywhere in Southern California would be like fucking Disneyland or something. California was going to be this magical land where all the problems we had in Michigan disappeared.

It was a fucking joke. Nothing changed. Nothing ever changes.

People fuck up. People hurt. People let you down. It's like the domino effect—one choice from someone else knocks the next person down, and then they slam into the one after them, and so on. After all the pieces crumble, all you can do is pick yourself back up and try to make up for pummeling the person behind you.

Even though she's gone, I'm still trying to make up for my screw-ups, though probably not as hard as I should.

"Got any change?" a guy asks when I get to the bus stop. I reach my hand in my pocket and give him two quarters, a nickel and three pennies. It's the only change I have, but I don't need it as much as he does. I know what it feels like not to have anything.

He says thanks and walks away. As people move around me, going about their day, I wonder if any of them are *him*. It's fucking ridiculous, and a waste of time to still think about Gabriel all these years later, to picture him in other guys I see strolling down the street.

He was my domino. He knocked me down and disappeared.

I owe him for that. If I ever do see him, it'll be me doing the slamming—my fist against his face.

Acknowledgment

As always, I need to thank my family. My kids deal with a mom who is always writing, or always thinking about writing. It can't be easy. To my husband...thank you for being sarcastic, funny, sweet, sexy, loyal and loving. I try hard to write men who are at least half as special as you.

I owe a big thanks to Maria Fox, Valerie Wentz, and Dawn Bleakley for letting me chat with you about Scotland and Ireland.

Riley's Rebels. You are my crew. My tribe. Thank you for being a part of my daily life.

The M/M Daily Grind. I have so much fun in our group. I feel so honored to be a part of it.

Big thanks to Hope and Jess of Flat Earth Editing and Vanessa and Manda from Prema editing for helping me make Drew and Justin's story shine.

And of course, my readers. Thank you, thank you, thank you. You've made my dreams come true.

About the Author

Riley Hart is the girl who wears her heart on her sleeve. She's a hopeless romantic. A lover of sexy stories, passionate men, and writing about all the trouble they can get into together. If she's not writing, you'll probably find her reading.

Riley lives in California with her awesome family, who she is thankful for every day.

Other books by Riley Hart

Crossroads Series:
Crossroads
Shifting Gears

Rock Solid Construction series:
Rock Solid

Broken Pieces series:
Broken Pieces
Full Circle
Losing Control

Blackcreek series:
Collide
Stay
Pretend

Made in the USA
Middletown, DE
01 July 2022